KERI ARTHUR

Sorrow's Song

A LIZZIE GRACE NOVEL

ISBN: 978-0-6453031-2-4

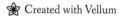 Created with Vellum

With thanks to:

The Lulus
Indigo Chick Designs
Hot Tree Editing
Debbie from DP+
Robyn E.
The lovely ladies from Central Vic Writers
Lori Grundy / Cover Reveal Designs for the amazing cover

Chapter One

They say breaking up is hard to do.

They're wrong.

Breaking up is easy. Living with the consequences of your decision in the long days after is the hard part.

I took a sip of hot chocolate and studied the street below the balcony on which I stood. It was close to two in the morning, so it was no surprise that the street was empty, given this portion of Castle Rock was basically a retail area. The nearby businesses had closed hours ago—even the late-night pizza shop on the corner was shut.

Had it been open, I might have been tempted to wander down and grab something. It would have made a nice change from the copious amounts of cake I'd been consuming over the last week.

I sighed and raised my gaze. Though the night was icy, the storms that had swept the reservation over the last few days had finally moved on, and the sky was clear and full of stars. The moon was in its waning gibbous stage, but her power still sang through me, as crisp and clear as the night

1

itself. I wished it had the power to burn away the ache in my heart and the hurt in my soul, but I wasn't even sure time would be able to work *that* particular miracle.

Not that I regretted my decision to walk away from Aiden.

It had become blindingly obvious even to me that no matter how much he loved me—and he *did* love me, I was certain of that—it was never going to be enough. I wasn't a werewolf, I would never be given approval to become part of his pack, and he would never leave them for me.

Nor would I want him to.

Of course, we have gone on as we were, but sharing a house and a bed and all the good things that came with a caring, loving relationship had become more and more difficult for me. I wanted the whole box and dice—marriage, kids, and to grow old together—and that was never going to happen with him. I couldn't continue to pretend everything was okay when it wasn't. Sooner or later, his duties as alpha in waiting would demand he take a werewolf mate and force him away from everything we had. The fear of that happening was like a cancer in my soul, growing ever darker.

Better to walk away now and hold on to the hope of remaining friends than let that cancer destroy everything that had been good about us.

Of course, none of this would have been a problem if my stupid heart hadn't decided to fall in love with the man.

I sighed and closed my eyes. That was when I heard the song.

It was faint but compelling, haunting but ethereal. It held no real words and drifted on the breeze as joyfully as blossom petals in spring, yet it stirred something deep inside that was as far from joy as you could get.

Fear.

My gaze snapped open, and I looked around, trying to pinpoint the song's origin. Trying to understand why such a beautiful sound caused so much inner turmoil.

It seemed to be coming from the hills that surrounded the eastern edge of Castle Rock, but more than that I couldn't define. Which was inconvenient, given just how big an area that was.

But something was happening out there—something bad—and it needed to be investigated. *Now.* Before it was too late.

I hesitated and then reached out lightly to Belle. She wasn't only my best friend and co-owner of the café we both ran, but also my familiar, and that gave us the ability to converse telepathically even though it wasn't one of my growing array of psychic skills. She, however, was not only one of the strongest telepaths out there but also a powerful spirit talker. It was a talent that had been invaluable on numerous occasions when we'd been hunting down the latest supernatural nasty to invade the reservation.

Whether it would be helpful tonight was a moot point— at least until we got out there and uncovered what was happening.

You okay? came her immediate if sleepy response.

Guilt twinged through me. She and Monty—who was not only my cousin, but also the designated reservation witch, a position that made him the High Witch Council's mouthpiece here, even if the reality meant he did little more than provide magical assistance to the reservation's rangers —had been doing most of the heavy lifting when it came to emotionally supporting me. It hadn't been an easy task, given how much of a mess I'd been the first couple of days after the breakup. Belle deserved her rest and some alone time with her man, but I couldn't escape the notion that the hauntingly beautiful sound was an indication that darkness once again hunted in the reservation.

Of course, I could have investigated without her or Monty's help, but too many of the demons and dark spirits who invaded this place came from the higher end of the power scale for that to be advisable.

A lesson I'd learned the hard way.

I'm fine, I said. *I'm just out on the balcony and heard a strange song riding the breeze and…*

And your inner trouble radar went off.

Yes. It may be nothing but…

Since when has it ever been nothing? Hang on while I grab a coat and head outside. The mental line fell briefly silent. *Not hearing anything specific out here. What sort of music is it?*

Almost unworldly. I leaned on the balustrade, my gaze on the shadow-wrapped hills to the east. *If I didn't know better, I'd say it was coming from near the O'Connor compound.*

Maybe Aiden's mother is still celebrating your breakup.

A smile twitched my lips even as sadness stabbed through me. *I doubt if even she would be that overt.*

Given he's apparently not staying at the O'Connor compound, or even at his own place, but with a friend in the Marin compound, he wouldn't know, so she wouldn't care.

That bit of gossip surprised me. We hadn't been sharing his house in Argyle all that long, and none of my stuff was there anymore. Sure, we'd had plenty of good times there, but from the very start of our relationship he'd been pretty determined life would go on as normal when we *did* break up.

Of course, that had been said before we *had*. The reality

was very different, and something he was obviously strug-gling with as much as me.

Knowing that didn't make me feel any better.

What wouldn't surprise me, however, was his mother celebrating our breakup. The woman absolutely hated me, though I now suspected it wasn't so much me personally as some traumatic event in her past that had involved a witch. For that same reason, I doubted my breaking up with Aiden would in any way change her attitude toward me and Belle.

She *did* at least treat Monty civilly, but then, the last thing she'd want was to upset the apple cart as far as the High Witch Council went. Witches and werewolves had a long and turbulent history, and though that wasn't so much a problem these days, it wouldn't take all that much to devolve again. Especially when the high council were aware there was a wellspring here that was possibly gaining sentience. I had no doubt they'd grab the smallest opportu-nity to take the reservation over in order to examine the wellspring more thoroughly.

What the high council *didn't* know was the fact it was my growing link to that wellspring causing the "sentience."

Of course, said connection was something everyone had thought to be impossible, and it was one that had only come about thanks to my mother. Or rather, from the fact that she'd unknowingly been pregnant when she'd been sent to restrain an emerging wellspring. The unbridled, magical energy of the earth that had almost killed her should certainly have destroyed me. Instead, it had somehow fused to my DNA, giving me a deep connection to the wilder forces of this world—though it was a connection no one, least of all me, had been aware of until I'd come into this reservation a year ago.

I'm still not hearing anything out here, Belle continued,

and that suggests the song's coverage is finite. Maybe if you deepened our connection...

I did so and, a heartbeat later, her being flowed into mine, fusing us as one but not so deeply that I lost physical control or that her soul left her body and became a part of mine. It not only meant she could see and hear everything I was but could also use her talents through me if necessary, and vice versa.

Wow, she said, after a couple of seconds. *That really is an evocative sound, isn't it?*

Yes, and whatever the hell it is, it's building to a crescendo. We need to investigate.

Agreed. I'll wake Monty and see you out the front of the café in a couple of minutes.

Thanks.

Her being left mine, and the link between us once again deactivated. I spun and stepped back inside. The living accommodation above the café was small but, as the old saying went, perfectly formed. There were two decent-sized bedrooms, a bathroom big enough to hold all the junk two women accumulated, an admittedly tiny kitchenette, and a living area just large enough to hold a three-seater sofa, a coffee table, and a big-screen TV. Belle still spent two or three days a week sleeping here at the café, even though Monty had asked her a couple of times now to move in with him. I could completely understand her refusal to. Hell, look what had happened to Aiden and me when I'd finally taken that damn step.

Of course, the situation with Monty and Belle was very different, simply because there was nothing stopping their relationship from progressing to marriage and kids except her own reluctance to accept that his determination to marry her was real and serious.

I quickly got dressed, then grabbed my phone and headed downstairs to the reading room. It was the area we used when I needed to employ psychometry to find lost items or people, or when customers wanted Belle to contact the spirits of loved ones. It also happened to be one of the safest places in the reservation. Not only was the café surrounded by multiple layers of spells that guarded us against all manner of things—from preventing anyone intending us harm entering the café, to protecting us against a wide variety of supernatural nasties—but there was a whole range of additional measures within the reading room itself. No spirit or demon was getting in here uninvited, even if it somehow broke through the main spells.

I grabbed a backpack and threw in everything I thought we'd need, including my silver knife and a few additional charms designed to ward against demons. While the one around my neck would protect me from all manner of evil, I had no idea what we were dealing with, and it was always better to be overprepared than under.

Something else I'd learned the hard way.

I pulled on my coat, then slung the pack over my shoulder, grabbed my keys, and headed out the front door. Monty's old station wagon roared around the corner a few seconds later and came to a sliding stop in front of the café. As tire smoke filled the air, I opened the door and climbed inside. "Is there any reason for the dramatic nature of that stop?"

His grin flashed. He was a typical royal witch in looks, with short crimson hair that gleamed like dark fire and bright silver eyes. "The beast has occasional problems with the brakes locking, but it's nothing to be all that worried about."

"Oh, that's a statement I do *not* find comforting." I

7

grabbed the seat belt and hauled it on. "Head toward Barker Street and turn right."

As he took off, Belle turned to look at me. Her long black hair was swept up into a messy bun, and her eyes were as bright as polished silver in the shadows of the night. At just over six feet tall, she was something of an Amazon, and almost the polar opposite of me. I was five inches shorter with a body that tended to curviness rather than muscle—although surprisingly, the recent influx of cake had not added to those curves. I also had pale skin rather than dark, freckles across my nose, and the crimson hair of a royal witch. Though my eyes had once been green, they were now silver. The wild magic might be making a whole lot of both physical and magical changes to me, but that was the only visible one.

"Have your psi senses come up with any further input on the song?" she asked.

I gripped the panic bar as Monty slid sideways into Barker Street and roared down the empty street. "Nothing more than the unhelpful 'death this way comes' stuff."

"And the song is still coming through strong?"

Suggesting she couldn't hear it—not without deepening the connection between us, anyway. "Yes, which is a surprise given the noise this rattletrap is making."

Monty leaned forward and lightly patted the dash. "Now, now, beastie, just you ignore her."

"You've named this old rust bucket and not the Mustang?" I said, in mock surprise.

"Oh, she has a name," Belle said in a resigned tone. "It's Red, and he croons to her in his sleep. I've concluded he cares for that damn car more than me."

"Not more," Monty said, grin flashing. "As much."

"Be still my beating heart."

Her voice was dry, and he laughed. "I've known her a lot longer—"

"No, you haven't," Belle retorted. "The three of us grew up together."

"I meant on an *intimate* level."

"If you're suggesting you're intimate with your car, I'm getting out of this relationship right *now*."

He laughed again. "I meant I helped to rebuild her. I know every part, and every wire. I know exactly how to make her purr. That's very much still a work in progress with you."

"That doesn't say a lot about your sexual initiative, given you've been together for weeks now," I said, amused. "Take the next right."

"I meant on an emotional level rather than physical." He didn't bother flicking on the indicator; he just hauled the old car into the street, no doubt leaving more rubber on the road as he accelerated away. "Belle's still refusing to give in to the inevitable."

"I am not marrying someone I haven't seen since childhood and who I've only been officially dating for weeks," Belle said dryly. "Jumping in feet first is fine and dandy for a casual relationship, but never works for anything long-lasting."

That she was no longer denying the possibility of a long-term permanent relationship was definitely a giant step forward.

"My grandparents would refute that statement. They got married after knowing each other for two weeks."

"Your grandparents are crazy. Lovely, but crazy."

He grinned again. "A truth I cannot deny."

Their banter continued, but I tuned it out and concentrated on the song instead. Partly because the closer we got to it, the fainter it seemed to be getting, even though it still seemed to be scaling up to its crescendo, and partly because their teasing manner reminded me of what I no longer had.

"There's a sharp left coming up," I said, blinking back unwanted tears. "And the first section of the road is dirt, from memory."

"Meaning slow down," he said, amused.

"Yes, but not so much because of the road's condition but rather the roos. We'll be running close to the boundary of the O'Connor compound, and the roos are in plague proportions around there."

"That surprises me," he said. "I always thought kangaroos would have enough sense to avoid wolf territory."

"They don't hunt roos," I said. "Not in wolf form, anyway. It'd be bad for the tourist industry if it ever got out."

As Monty slid sideways onto the dirt road and slowed a fraction, the song in the air sharpened abruptly and then fell silent.

Death stepped into that silence; it was a brief caress of darkness filled with so much pain and unending sorrow, it echoed through time itself.

Then it, too, faded away.

Leaving me with absolutely nothing to track and no idea where, exactly, that death had happened.

I swore softly. "I just lost the signal, and someone was just killed."

"Well, fuck," Monty said. "Do we continue on? Or just ring the rangers and let them worry about it?"

"It won't hurt to continue on," Belle said. "You never know, Liz might pick up the trail again, or I might sense a soul rising."

I doubted we would. There'd been something very final

in that wash of death. Something that suggested there'd been no soul to rise or move on.

I shivered and hoped like hell intuition was wrong. We'd battled a soul stealer once before; it was not an experience I ever wanted to repeat.

"Worth a shot, I guess," Monty agreed.

He continued until we reached a crossroad, then braked, sending the car into a slight slide before he got it back under control. "Which way?"

I hesitated, looking right and left. "The road to our right skims the O'Connor compound, and my initial impressions suggested our singer was close to their boundaries. Also, get the fucking brakes fixed."

He laughed and turned onto the narrow dirt road. "I've got it booked in tomorrow. The only reason I'm risking it is because Red's tires aren't designed for dirt roads, and we had no idea where this song of yours would lead us."

"Then we should have taken the SUV."

"It would have taken too much time to swap over. Besides, the council have already replaced two—or is it three?—of your vehicles," he said, amusement in his tone. "I can't see them being pleased at having another replacement wrecked."

"Meaning," Belle said, "he's more than happy to get this one wrecked and replaced."

Monty flashed her a smile and didn't deny it.

The headlights speared the darkness ahead, highlighting the soldier straight lines of grapevines in the vineyard to the left. To the right, there was nothing but wilderness. Though this road wasn't the designated boundary for the O'Connor compound, it was only a further ten or so meters in.

We came to another offshoot road, but this one led into

the compound and would be heavily guarded. It wasn't worth attempting to enter when we had no real excuse now. It would only give Aiden's mother more ammunition against me.

We drove on. After a while, the trees thinned out and, up ahead, the moonlight caressed dark water. Instinct immediately twitched.

"Stop here."

Monty immediately did so. "You saw something?"

"No."

I undid the seat belt and climbed out of the car. The breeze stirred around me, crisp and cold and clear of any scent of death or darkness. The trepidation didn't ease any.

I shoved my hands into my coat pockets and walked over to the wire fence that separated the grassy verge from the water. It was only a small dam, and in the bright night its banks were fully visible. There was nothing but the occasional cow pat to suggest anything had visited this place recently.

And yet... My gaze swept over the water. It probably wasn't all that deep, but that didn't really mean anything, as many of the dams around this area were spring fed.

Was it possible we were dealing with some sort of water demon? They generally preferred lakes over tiny watering holes like this, but the underground springs that fed them would provide a water demon or spirit an easy way to move around.

Only trouble was, they all tended to feed on flesh rather than souls.

I shivered and rubbed my arms.

Belle stopped beside me. "Anything?"

"No. But I've got a feeling water played a part in the death I sensed."

"That isn't entirely helpful, given the number of dams and reservoirs in this reservation." Monty stopped on the other side of me and motioned to the water. "Shall we go closer?"

I wrinkled my nose. "I don't think it'll help."

"But it can't hurt, right?" He lifted the wire so Belle and I could climb through. "You might get more of an insight if you're closer."

"I doubt it."

But I nevertheless climbed through the wire, and we picked our way through the low-running gorse and cow pats. As we neared the water, luminous threads of power became visible. The main wellspring—the one that had been unprotected for so long—was situated within the O'Connor compound and wasn't that far away from where we stood.

There was a second, much newer wellspring in the reservation, of course, but very few people knew about that one. It was very well guarded, not only by the soul of Katie O'Connor—Aiden's sister—but also by the ghost of Katie's witch husband, Gabe.

I lifted a hand, and the closest couple of threads curled around my fingers and wrists. They were fragile moonbeams that pulsed with power and came with not only a sense of kinship but lit the inner wild magic so fiercely that it momentarily felt as if I was being consumed by fire.

One day, instinct whispered, I would be.

One day, my soul would merge with the force of the reservation's larger wellspring, and I would become its voice in a way Katie never could.

Goose bumps ran across my skin, and I shivered. The moonbeams pulsed, as if in response. It only increased the trepidation; the filaments were responding to what I was feeling, and that was scary.

I sucked in a deeper breath, pushed the fear away. The dam wasn't particularly large, and the banks sweeping down to the water showed a good amount of erosion—from both the weather and the cattle who obviously used it—but there was nothing here that tweaked my instincts any further.

"The trouble radar getting anything new?" Monty asked.

"No."

"Then we should get back into the car and keep going."

I nodded and followed him and Belle back across the paddock and through the wire fence. There were no more dams along this section of the road—at least none that were visible—and we eventually reached a main road.

"Left or right?" Monty asked.

I hesitated, glancing both ways, and then said, "Left." Going right would mean we'd end up at a T-intersection and the Sutton Grange Winery, and my psi instincts said whatever we were hunting would not be found there. Which was a shame, as I did rather like their wines. *Not* that I'd had much in the way of alcohol of late. In fact, aside from that first terrible night when I walked out of Aiden's house, I'd been avoiding it altogether. It was far better to stick to cake and chocolate than go down a path that might lead to using alcohol as a crutch to numb the hurt.

No man was worth that. Nor wolf, for that matter.

After a few more minutes, we came to another T-intersection. We went left again.

"If memory serves me right, there's a reservoir up ahead," Belle said. "It'd be closed for the night, but we can magic our way in."

"A reservoir is definitely more likely to attract a water spirit or demon," Monty said. "It's worth checking it out while we're here."

"Agree," I said. "Though it could take us a while to walk around the perimeter, and the night is getting old."

"Tomorrow's Monday." Monty flashed a grin over his shoulder. "We can all go back to bed if we don't find anything."

"Or in my case, go back to drinking hot chocolate and eating cake."

"That works too," he said. "Though do please leave some for the cake-deprived amongst us."

I smiled, as he no doubt intended. "You're sleeping with one of the café's main cake makers. I think you get more than your fair share."

"There's no such thing as too much of a good thing, though." The wicked glance he cast Belle's way suggested he wasn't talking about cake anymore.

She rolled her eyes, something I felt through our link rather than saw.

"Insatiable?" I commented.

"Depends on whether we're talking about cake or sex. And to be honest, it's a close-run thing in either case."

"Because both are necessary to life," he said, voice dry. "You know this."

I chuckled softly as he pulled into a dirt driveway and stopped at the simple farm gate that barred entry into the reservoir. He jumped out, magicked the padlock, and swung the gate open. As we drove through, the headlights picked out two small buildings to the right, and several picnic tables and a larger cream building that was probably the toilet block to the left. The embankment wall in this section was quite low but rose quickly as it swept away to the right.

The grass covering the embankment was short and green, and there was a water pipe that ran from its crest to the first of the two buildings to our right. Some sort of pump house, obviously.

Monty stopped off to one side of the graveled drive, and we all climbed out. Without all the buildings and trees to block it, the wind was stronger and colder out here in the open, but it wasn't the reason for the shiver that ran through my soul.

It was the scent of death.

Of agony.

I lightly rubbed my arms but didn't feel any warmer. "Whatever I sensed, it happened here."

Monty flicked on his flashlight and swept the bright beam around. "There're no bodies in the immediate area."

"Because it's still in the water." I hesitated. "Why don't you call the rangers while Belle and I head up to the crest and see if we can spot it?"

I didn't wait for an answer. I simply strode away, not needing a flashlight to see where I was going. Between the moon and the stars, the night was as clear to me as day. It hadn't always been that way, of course. While the changes to my sense of smell and sight were in part due to the wild magic, we suspected it was also a result of my connection to Katie. The theory was that the multiple times we'd become one—either to track down supernatural entities or so she could speak directly to her mother—had somehow incentivized the wild magic into making an ultimate version of me. Katie didn't believe it would ever result in me being able to fully shift shape into a wolf, but in truth, none of us could really say for sure where it would all end, as nothing like this had happened before.

Or so we currently believed.

That might well change once Eli—who was a retired investigative witch for the Regional Witch Council and one of the two men I'd basically adopted as my grandfathers—had finished translating a very ancient tome Monty had borrowed from the high council's archives. It was an account of earth magic, its uses, and its dangers, and earth magic was what ancient witches had once called the wild magic.

We reached the wall's crest and stopped. The water spread out before us, a dark and mysterious blanket that could have concealed dozens of demons.

Belle swept her light across the water. "I'm not seeing a body."

"No." I hesitated, listening to the wind and the secrets she held. "The death I'm sensing is located past the spillway somewhere."

"Lead on, then."

I turned and followed the narrow gravel path toward the spillway. Thankfully, we didn't have to climb down into it, as the water had obviously been low enough for long enough that the gravel path could loop around the spillway's lip. But when this path joined back up with the main one, I stopped and studied the muddy slope that swept down to the current shoreline. It was barren of both life and death, but that didn't make me feel any easier.

Footsteps vibrated lightly through the ground, and then Monty said, "They'll have someone here in twenty minutes."

Meaning whoever was on call was staying out of Castle Rock. I hesitated, and then asked, "Who answered?"

"Jaz."

Relief swirled through me. While I'd probably have to

confront Aiden sooner rather than later, I wasn't quite ready to do so yet. Not when everything was still so raw.

And having put that thought out there, it practically guaranteed the man would show up. I knew for a fact he regularly monitored calls, even when he wasn't on after-hours duty.

Monty stopped beside Belle. "Anything twitching the sensory lines, Liz?"

"Nothing visible, but there *is* something here. I can smell it on the wind."

He glanced at me sharply. "Yet more changes?"

I hesitated. "It's more of an ongoing sharpening rather than additional changes."

Which wasn't a lie. My olfactory senses had been gaining strength for a while now; I just didn't normally 'smell' emotions in the way that I now seemed to be, even if I'd always been able to sense them via my psi talents if I was close enough.

But werewolves *could* smell emotions.

I headed down the rocky slope, watching where I placed each step to ensure I didn't end up on my butt or breaking something. That was the last thing I needed right now.

It didn't take us all that long to walk across the muddy ground that had once been under the water line and climb the next ridge. The bones of an old gum stood in solitary watch over the small cove.

In the shadow of its roots lay a man.

A man who was naked and who had pale blond hair that gleamed silver in the moonlight.

A man every instinct said was an O'Connor werewolf.

Chapter Two

Despite the fearful leap of my heart, I knew straight away it wasn't Aiden. The build on this man was too fine, and even from this distance he looked a lot shorter.

Monty pulled out his phone and took some photos of the area before we headed down the slope and made our way across to the water and the body. There were no footprints along the shoreline, which suggested our victim hadn't entered the water from this area.

After a few more photos of the body and its location in relation to the tree, Monty handed Belle the phone to record what he was doing, then waded out and gently turned the victim over.

He was an older man, and his face was heavily weathered by time and the sun. Though I'd been expecting a look of horror, his expression was serene and at peace, and it was totally at odds with the deep sense of violation and utter agony that rode the air.

"Oh, fuck," Belle said, her voice filled with the horror that pulsed through me. "He's been soul stripped."

Monty looked up sharply. "Are you sure?"

"Utterly." She crossed her arms and looked at me. "Can you tell if the spirit or demon remains in the area, even if it's not singing?"

"Most spirits tend to leave the area after feeding—unless, of course, they're after a buffet," Monty said, obviously trying to inject a bit of humor into an otherwise grim situation.

I rolled my eyes at him, and he raised an eyebrow. "Hey, that's a half-serious statement. Just because we haven't yet come across a demon or dark spirit who does that doesn't mean they're not out there."

"Then let's hope they're something we never *do* come across."

I squatted on my heels and ran my fingers through the still, cold water. Though I had no sense of the soul eater, the aftereffects of its presence lingered; it was an oily stain of darkness that fouled the center of the lake.

But *only* the center.

I looked up. "It's not here, but our victim was killed in the middle of the lake. It's more than possible he swam out to it."

"Which means the song you heard was definitely a lure," Belle said.

"And a powerful one at that, if it had this poor man stripping off and diving into icy water." Monty wrinkled his nose. "Do you think it's some sort of siren?"

I hesitated. "Aren't sirens generally found in the sea?"

"We could be dealing with some sort of river-based offshoot," Belle said. "There's certainly plenty of water-based demons mentioned in Gran's books."

Those books were in fact an extensive library of supernatural entities and spells Belle had inherited well before

20

we'd left Canberra as sixteen-year-olds. We'd spent the last few months creating a full electronic record of each book, and while it was a time-consuming process, it was also a necessary one. Not only as a means of protecting her grandmother's life's work against loss in a bushfire—and this area was certainly prone to those in the summer months—but it also gave us a backup in case the High Witch Council ever discovered we had the majority of Nell's library, which for all intents and purposes should have been gifted to the National Library in Canberra when she'd died.

"If we *are* dealing with a siren, then it's likely a female. Most of them are." Monty glanced at me. "Could you tell from the song?"

"It did have a feminine feel."

"Do you think she's just putting her song out there to see who she can ensnare?" Belle asked. "Or is it more likely she's targeting her victims?"

"Sirens don't tend to target," Monty said. "The one fly in the ointment is the fact they're known flesh eaters, not soul."

I rose and dried my fingers on my coat. "Yes, but this reservation does like throwing the weird ones at us."

The wind stirred around me, once again whispering secrets as various scents teased my nostrils. The heady scent of musk and man, along with the softer scent of jasmine and femininity.

Aiden and Jaz.

I took a breath that came back out quivery. "The rangers are almost here."

Monty glanced at me sharply. "Aiden?"

"And Jaz."

The concern in his expression flared brighter. "Are you going to be okay?"

My smile felt tight. Fake. "I guess we'll soon find out."

"Then why don't you and Belle leave right now? You can scoot around the shoreline and take my car. I'm more than happy to handle the situation here, and I can grab a lift back home with one of them."

I was shaking my head even before he finished. "I'm going to have to face this situation sooner or later, Monty. I might as well do it now and get it over with."

"Are you sure?"

"No." I forced another smile. "But thanks."

He nodded, but his expression remained uneasy. My gaze drifted back to the incline, my heart going a million miles a minute and my breathing somewhat erratic. Belle twined her fingers around mine, a physical touch accompanied by a wash of mental strength. I gripped on tight to both.

He appeared on the crest of the hill, and my gaze swept his length, drinking in the sight of him as fiercely as a dehydrated person would water.

The moonlight played amongst the silver in his dark blond hair and highlighted the somewhat sharp planes of his face. Like the majority of werewolves, he was tall and rangy, but his shoulders were lovely and wide, his arms lean but muscular, and he moved with a predator's grace.

The urge to run to him, to throw myself into his arms, to drink in his smoky, musky scent and feel the press of his muscular body against mine one more time was so damn strong, I took a half step forward before I could stop myself.

I tightened my grip on Belle's fingers and breathed deep. I could do this. I *had* to do this. It wasn't like permanently moving to another town or state was an option for me now—not with my growing connection to the older wellspring—so I needed to get used to crossing his path on a regular basis.

His expression held little in the way of emotion, but his aura practically crackled with it. Love and hurt, frustration and joy, relief and pain; it was a vibrant, turbulent mix, with no one emotion stronger than the other.

It was stark evidence that he was hurting every bit as badly as me, but that was little consolation, given a thread of acceptance seemed to run underneath the brightness of the storm. He might not have liked me ending things so abruptly, but there was at least a part of him that seemed to have accepted it was probably for the best.

And that just made me want to cry all over again.

I somehow dragged my gaze past him and could suddenly breathe again. Jaz was a brown-haired wolf with lightly tanned skin and golden eyes who'd become—along with her husband, Levi—good friends of ours. She was also one of the few werewolves openly critical of Aiden's adherence to pack rules when it came to romantic "entanglements," as she'd put it. I'd been worried it might affect her working relationship with him, but it hadn't so far. Which really shouldn't have surprised me, because as obtuse and as stubborn as the man could be, Aiden was also very fair minded.

She gave me a thumbs-up from behind him, though I wasn't entirely sure whether it was meant as a "keep your chin up" encouragement or a "he's in an okay mood" sign.

Maybe it was both.

He stopped several feet away, his expression impassive and his hands thrust deep into his coat pockets. I couldn't help but wonder if the urge to reach out—to once again feel skin on familiar skin—was just as fierce for him as it was for me, then smacked the thought aside. It didn't matter, because it wouldn't change anything.

"What have we got?" he asked, his tone as neutral as his expression.

"Body in the water, obviously," Monty said in a sharp manner designed to drag Aiden's attention away from me. "No signs of physical trauma, and we don't believe he drowned."

"I did presume—seeing the whole gang is here—that we're dealing with something *other* than a natural death." Aiden's voice remained neutral and at total odds with the continuing turmoil in his aura. Despite the professional front, there was a part of him wanting to wrap his arms around me and hold on to me. "Any idea what might have caused it?"

"A soul stealer of some kind," I replied, a little surprised by the evenness of my tone. "She lured her victim here with a song, but more than that we can't say."

"Meaning we're dealing with a siren?" Jaz said, surprised. "They really do exist?"

"Unfortunately, yes," Belle said. "The tales of sailors being lured to their deaths by their bewitching song is based on truth, even if fiction has fudged many of the other facts about them."

"And you heard the song, Liz?" Aiden's gaze briefly found mine again. Everything he couldn't say—*wouldn't* say—was right there in his blue eyes.

A thick fist of grief and desolation rose. I swallowed heavily and said, "Yes, although it faded well before we reached the reservoir."

"How did you find the body, then?"

"Luck," Monty said.

"Alongside a little psi intuition," I added.

His gaze held mine a fraction longer than necessary, then he nodded and moved into the water. "Damn, it's Jerod O'Connor."

"Friend or family?" Monty asked.

"The latter," Aiden said, "But he's an omega, so I've not had that much to do with him."

Omegas in werewolf packs held much the same position as they did in actual wolf packs. They were the most subordinate, usually because they were the smallest or the weakest in the pack and were generally tasked with the more menial duties that came with running a large wolf compound.

And it comes as no surprise that he hasn't had much to do with the poor man, Belle said. *His bitch of a mother would hardly want a bottom-rung wolf darkening her halls.*

Not to defend her in any way, but the O'Connors have five different family lines living within the compound. He might be from one of those other lines.

Belle mentally sniffed. *I prefer to think the worst of the woman.*

So do I, to be honest. I squeezed Belle's hand and then untangled my fingers. *I'm good.*

Sure?

For the moment, yes. Which didn't mean I wouldn't drop into a sobbing heap once I got home again, but hey, it *had* only been a week. In previous breakups it had taken months for my emotional equilibrium to be restored.

Of course, I hadn't loved those two men quite as deeply as this damn one, even if at the time I'd thought the opposite.

It will *get easier with every meeting you have,* Belle said with comforting assurance.

I know it will.

And if I said that often enough, I might just believe it.

"How likely is it that the siren will come back?" Aiden asked.

"Not very," Monty said, "but I'll hang around, just in case."

"You can't stay here alone," I immediately said. "It's too dangerous if we *are* dealing with a siren."

"He's hardly alone," Aiden said with just the slightest edge of annoyance.

"I meant he can't be the only witch here, especially when sirens target *males*. Her song might snare him or you before either of you can react, and Jaz will be incapable of countering it."

"I can knock them both out," she commented, her sideways glance at Aiden suggesting it was a task she'd enjoy. "That'd work."

Monty laughed. "Yeah, thanks, but no. Besides, it'll take some damn powerful magic to snare me after only a few notes, which should give me time—"

"Overconfidence will be your downfall one day, Monty," I said.

"It's not overconfidence when I—"

"There will be no argument on this," Belle cut in. Her voice was stern but there was a twinkle in her eyes. "I've only just become accustomed to having you in my life, and I really don't want the hassle of breaking in another man just yet."

"If that isn't a declaration of love, I don't know what is."

She merely rolled her eyes at him.

"If our siren has already sung for her dinner," Jaz said, "would she really come back here again tonight?"

"Maybe not," Monty said, "but given this reservation's tendency to toss up the worst versions of the various demons and spirits, it's not beyond the realms of possibility that this one might prefer a buffet over single serve."

"Demons at a buffet," Jaz muttered. "That's an image I did *not* need in my life."

Monty dragged out his car keys and tossed them to me. "Belle and I will stay, then, as we've probably had more sleep over the last few days. Just remember to go easy on the beast's brakes."

I opened my mouth to argue and then closed it again. In truth, between the two of them, they should be able to cope with any supernatural or magical attack. Especially when Belle could also use our link to funnel my strength and abilities if necessary.

"What's wrong with the wagon's brakes?" Aiden asked sharply.

Monty shrugged. "They're slightly dodgy. I'm getting them fixed tomorrow."

Aiden's gaze met mine. The storm of emotions in those rich blue depths had not eased, though determination and concern had stepped briefly to the fore.

"Then Jaz will take you home, Liz. There's no way I'll risk—" He cut off the rest, but the words nevertheless hung heavily in the air—*your safety like that.*

We once again stared at each other for several—seemingly very long—seconds, and then I nodded. There were plenty of things we could—and undoubtedly would—argue about in the future, but it was pretty pointless doing so over something as unimportant as this. Three of us really *didn't* need to be here. Besides, the café might be closed tomorrow, but there was plenty of prep work that had to be done, and Belle had a well-deserved day off. If I didn't manage to get at least a little sleep, I'd probably end up doing myself some damage. A sleep-deprived state and razor-sharp knives were never a good combination.

I tossed Monty's keys back and then glanced at Jaz. "Ready anytime you are."

She nodded and glanced at Aiden. "I'll take her statement in the car."

"Ciara shouldn't be too far off now—can you wait for her to arrive and direct her our way?"

"Will do, boss."

As the two of us walked away, my shoulder blades burned with the heat of Aiden's gaze. He was obviously as determined as me to make this whole separation thing work, and it stirred as much fury as it did sadness. If only the man would put as much effort into making *us* work.... But that was an impossible task, given we were witch and wolf and never the twain shall meet. At least, not on a permanent basis and certainly not in this reservation, unless an impending death was a factor in the situation, as it had been for Katie and Gabe.

I'd *known* all that going in. Seriously, my stupid heart needed to be bitch-slapped.

Once we were over the hill and out of immediate earshot, Jaz said, "How are you coping? Really, I mean?"

I smiled and touched her arm. "Better than I was."

"Hmm," she said, sounding unconvinced. "Aiden said the same thing."

I half smiled, though my heart wasn't entirely in it. "Did you really expect any other answer from the man?"

"Well, no. But in this case, his actions do speak louder than his words, and he's been a little... testy, shall we say." She glanced at me, a smile creasing the corners of her golden eyes. "You have no idea how often I've had to stop myself telling him to grow some balls and marry the woman he obviously loves."

"I'm not a werewolf, Jaz. He'll never take that step, and you know it."

She harrumphed. "What I know is that some things are worth fighting for. I hold on to the hope that he'll realize that."

"I don't."

She harrumphed again. "Well, you can take heart in the fact that a good proportion of wolves are on your side, not his."

"A good proportion of the two non-O'Connor packs, I'm thinking."

"Well, yes, but there are a few in his own pack who have had words with Karleen over her handling of the whole situation."

Whole situation. What a quaint way to describe a relationship that had been a meeting of hearts... even if only acknowledged by one side.

"It won't change anything, Jaz, but I appreciate the support."

She grimaced. "Stating the truth is hardly that."

"Unfortunately for us all, Karleen has her truth too, and she's the alpha."

Jaz sighed. "Yeah. And if Aiden had been anyone else's son but hers, there might have been hope."

I hesitated, but couldn't help asking, "Do you know why she hates witches so badly?"

"Other than the whole thing with Katie, you mean?"

"Gabe didn't kill her, Jaz."

"That's not what the coroner said."

"The coroner didn't have access to all the pertinent information."

She glanced at me. "And you do?"

"Belle can talk to souls, remember."

Though in this particular case, it was me who had the direct line to the souls in question. But Jaz had no idea that both Katie and Gabe's lingered here, and I had no intention of enlightening either her or the other rangers. Aiden knew, as did his mother; it hadn't helped her opinion of us—*me*— in any way.

"Ah, of course." Jaz grimaced. "In truth, I think Katie's death was merely the proverbial icing on the cake. There have been rumors swirling for years that one of Karleen's siblings was killed by a witch, but no one in the O'Connor pack has ever confirmed it."

"And no one was curious enough to go looking?"

"To be honest, no. It's a private matter and not something that has ever affected the rest of us, so there's been no need."

Well, it affected *me*, and I was seriously intending to investigate, even if it was all too late. "Any idea how long ago it happened?"

"When she was a teenager, apparently." She glanced at me, her eyebrows raised. "I take it you're going information hunting?"

"Curiosity generally kills cats, not witches."

She laughed. "Let's hope it remains that way."

Amen to *that*.

Headlights swept across the skyline as we began the long climb up to the crest of the wall. By the time we reached it, Ciara was out of the car and walking toward us, her kit slung over her shoulder. She was just as tall and rangy as her brother, but unlike Aiden, her hair was on the browner side of blonde.

"Liz," she said, her tone a little surprised but otherwise friendly. "Didn't expect you to be out here."

"I'm more attuned to supernatural movements than Monty, I'm afraid."

"I take it he's up there?"

"With Belle, yes."

She nodded and glanced at Jaz. "Am I just following the footprints?"

"Yes. They're just over that small ridge, near the shoreline."

Ciara nodded, gave me a friendly nod, and moved on.

Jaz opened her SUV, and I climbed into the front seat. She hit record on her phone and took my statement as we got underway. With that done, she said, "Can I ask you a favor?"

"Of course you can." I shifted in the seat slightly. "What do you need?"

She hesitated. "There's a woman who works in Levi's café whose mom has gone missing. We've been unable to find her, so I was just wondering if you'd—"

"Use my psychometry to find her," I finished for her.

She nodded and glanced at me. "I know it's a bit cheeky to ask when it's part of your business and you're normally paid, but Lucy—"

"Jaz, stop. You don't need to explain because I'm more than happy to help out." A smile tugged at my lips. "Besides, finding a missing woman might be a nice distraction from thinking about there being a siren in the reservation."

Or, indeed, my broken heart.

She wrinkled her nose. "Do you really think she'll hit us again?"

"When has any supernatural nasty simply killed one person and then moved on?"

She sighed. "Never, but one can always hope."

One could, as long as one didn't expect it to happen. Not when it came to this sort of thing, anyway. "How many days has Lucy's mom been missing?"

"Just on twenty-four hours. Her car, purse, and keys remain in her house, and there's no sign of a break-in or foul play."

"Which suggests she either left of her own accord and got lost, or she knew whoever has taken her."

"The former is a possibility," Jaz said. "Apparently her memory has been deteriorating, and she's been found wandering, lost and confused, three times so far this year."

"Surely if that had happened, though, someone would have spotted her by now." Unless, of course, she was deliberately avoiding being seen for some unknown reason. "Is she a wolf?"

"No, human."

Which made it highly unlikely she'd be able to outwit the sensitive noses of the wolves trying to find her.

"I'll need something personal of hers to use—something she wore close to her skin on a regular basis. Jewelry or a watch are usually pretty good options."

Jaz nodded. "I'll let Lucy know. What time tomorrow—today, given the time—suits?"

"I need to make some cakes and slices, but you should be right anytime after twelve."

She nodded and the conversation moved on. It felt good. Felt like at least a little part of me was getting back to normal.

Once back at the café, I returned the backpack to the reading room and headed upstairs. While I really didn't feel sleepy, I nevertheless stripped off and climbed into bed. Surprisingly, I did fall asleep.

But it was neither deep nor restful. Instead, it was filled with dreams of bloody faces and eyes that had been burned from their sockets.

And that could only mean the siren wasn't the only evil that had stepped into the reservation.

Jaz arrived at the café just as I was finishing the last batch of slices. I stuck the tray in the fridge to set and then, after wiping my hands on a tea towel, opened the front door and let them in.

Lucy was my height but wiry, with short, spiky pink hair and olive skin. Her brown eyes were puffy and red, and she was surrounded by a fierce halo of fear and worry—which was understandable in a situation like this.

"Thank you for doing this," she said, her voice soft but anxious. "She's never gone missing this long before, and I'm not sure what else to try."

I nodded and closed the door. "I hope Jaz explained that's there's no guarantee I'll be able to find your mom. It really depends on the amount of resonance left on the item you've bought with you."

"June. Her name is June," she said. "And it's still worth trying. We've run out of other options."

I led them into the reading room and switched on the lights before motioning Lucy toward a chair on the far side of the table.

"I've brought a watch, a ring, and a necklace." She sat down and dragged out three small plastic bags from her purse. "I haven't touched them, just like Jaz said."

"Good." I sat down opposite and motioned her to place the items on the table. "Once I start the session, you'll need to remain quiet. Questions might disturb the psychic vibes."

They generally didn't, but I'd started telling customers that because it was easier than trying to counter endless questions while I was attempting to locate whatever it was they'd lost.

"Can I observe?" Jaz asked. "I've never actually seen this part of your gifts in action."

"Sure, but there's usually not all that much to see."

Jaz nodded, crossed her arms, and leaned against the doorframe. I took a deep breath to center my energy and then reached for the first plastic bag. It contained the ring, but the minute I opened it, I knew it wasn't going to be of any use. The metal was silent; there was nothing in the way of sensory or emotional vibrations emanating from it.

I put it down and picked up the necklace. This time, there was a flicker. I quickly dropped it into my palm and closed my fingers around it, but the connection was too fragile to follow. It had simply been too long since she'd worn this necklace, and her resonance had all but faded.

Which left the watch.

I crossed all mental things that it would at least provide some sort of answer, then slowly opened the bag and dropped the watch into my hand.

Almost instantly, my psychic senses sprang to life, the stream of inputs hitting so hard and fast I was forced to back off a little. June was definitely alive, but how long she'd remain that way was another matter entirely. The pulse coming from the watch spoke of a faltering heart. Combine that with a wave of pain so fierce it had my breath catching in my throat, one thing became obvious: if we didn't get to her soon, we'd wouldn't be finding her alive.

I carefully deepened the connection, creeping along the psychic line in an effort to get some sense of direction while trying to avoid getting sucked into the vortex of her agony. Belle wasn't here to pull me out if that happened, and I had no desire to become lost in another's mind and face the prospect of their death also becoming mine.

As the connection deepened, the sheer weight of June's pain and terror became overwhelming, wiping out any hope of understanding what was happening. Which left me with the watch's pulse of life; as long as it remained this strong, I could track her.

I opened my eyes and glanced at Jaz. "There's enough of a connection with this watch to find her."

Jaz raised an eyebrow, obviously sensing what I *hadn't* said. "Is she close?"

"Impossible to—"

I cut the rest off as Lucy thrust to her feet so abruptly the chair tumbled backward. "We need to go. *Now.* Before something happens to her."

I dropped the watch back into the bag and sealed it. Though my skin was no longer touching the metal, I could still feel its distant pulse. It was a warning we did indeed need to hurry. "Jaz and I will, but I'm afraid you can't—"

"What I *can't* do is remain behind," Lucy said, desperation in her voice and her expression. "I need to be there when you find her. She's... not good with strangers."

"Which is something we'll take into account," Jaz said softly. "But if Liz says you can't be with us, then you can't."

"But *why?*" Lucy's gaze ran from me to Jaz and back again. "What difference will my presence make? Or are you not telling me something?"

I fought the urge to reach out and squeeze her hand. Her emotions were thick and fierce, and while my mental shields were coping, a touch might just blow a hole through them and leave me overwhelmed.

"I'm afraid my ability to follow a link is dependent on a calm environment. Your emotions in the confined space of a car that has no spell around it to mute emotional output would overwhelm my ability to find her."

Which was only partially the truth but enough to at least mollify her.

"You can find her, though?"

"Yes." Whether she'd still be alive was another matter entirely.

She swept up the two plastic bags and then glanced at Jaz. "You'll ring me the minute you know anything? Even if—"

She stopped and blinked fiercely. She was well aware this might not end well.

"I promise," Jaz said softly.

Lucy nodded. "I'll go home and wait then."

"Jaz, can you show her out while I grab a few things?"

As the two women left, I gathered up the backpack and exchanged some of the stronger charms and potions aimed at the supernatural for those designed for healing and health. Then I headed upstairs, swapped my runners for boots, and grabbed my coat.

Jaz was leaning on the banister when I came back down. "Is June alive?"

"At the moment, yes."

"You don't think she'll remain that way?"

I hesitated. "She's in extreme pain, and I couldn't pinpoint its cause."

"Right then, we'd better move."

She spun and marched out. Once I'd locked the front door, I climbed into her SUV, did up my belt, and then dropped the watch back into my hand. The pulse of life was even more erratic, an indication of severe stress. But the link remained strong, giving me clear directional indications.

"Turn around and head for Louton."

Tires squealed as she obeyed. I kept my fingers around the watch and did my best to ignore the growing wave of terror and confusion as I probed lightly around the perimeter, trying to get some feel for what was happening to her.

It didn't help. Nothing did. It was almost as if June was locked inside her mind, unable to see or speak. Which, if she had some form of dementia, was possible. But I couldn't help remembering the dreams that had assailed me last night and shivered.

I did *not* want to be dealing with anything or anyone who would burn out a person's eyes....

I pushed the distressing images away and tried to concentrate on only the location data coming through. As we reached the outskirts of Louton, I said, "Right at Memorial Park."

She nodded, tugged the SUV into the side road, and accelerated away. "How far are we, do you think?"

I glanced briefly at the watch. The thread tying it to June was stronger, which meant we were close. "Five minutes, if that."

"And June's state?"

"Alive."

She glanced at me. "It sounds like there's a 'at this second' missing from that."

"Because there is."

Jaz swore and pushed the SUV even harder. Between the scream of the engine and the scream of the siren, it was impossible to talk, but I was okay with that. It wasn't as if there was all that much to be said right now anyway.

We quickly left Louton behind, and the scrub and trees closed in. I knew from experience just how dangerous it was to be wandering around on foot in this area, thanks to the multiple number of abandoned mines and shafts the gold rush of the late 1800s had left behind. It June *had* been up here alone, then it was more than possible she'd fallen into one. It would certainly explain the extreme pain and the lack of sensory input, as many of the shafts were deep enough that daylight only penetrated a few meters.

The road slowly began to climb. As we topped the ridge and passed a telecommunications tower, I said, "Slow down and turn off the siren. I think we're close."

She obeyed. As we cruised down the other side of the hill, I spotted a sign saying Percy's Reef Gold Diggings.

"There," I said, pointing, "Left there."

She turned in and slowed down. The gravel road was narrow and rough, with the scrubby trees hugging its edges casting long shadows. As we reached the beginnings of a loop-around that would take us back to the road, I spotted what looked to be a metal roof barely visible through the trees.

"Stop," I said. "She's in that building, whatever it is."

Dust puffed around the front of the SUV as Jaz braked. "It's an old miner's hut that's sometimes used by hikers to escape the rain."

"June isn't a hiker, is she?"

"She's definitely a wanderer, but it's doubtful she'd ever come out this far."

She climbed out and moved to the back of the vehicle. I grabbed my pack and slung it over my shoulder as I got out. There was no sign of another car and no indication that one had even been here recently. For all intents and purposes, the place looked abandoned. Only the scent that ran on the air—one that spoke of man, sweat, and ammonia—suggested otherwise.

I glanced around at the sound of steps. Jaz had a pack slung over her shoulder and was belting on her gun, and that made me feel a whole lot safer. Between the two of us, we had both human and supernatural attackers covered.

Theoretically, anyway.

She motioned me to take the lead. I did so cautiously, every sense—psychic and physical—on alert. The pulse in the watch continued its unsteady, unhealthy beat, but as much as instinct urged me to hurry, I didn't dare, because I had no idea what we were walking into. Besides, this entire area was pitted with old mine remnants. While some were visible, it was the ones we couldn't see that worried me.

A stone building appeared ahead. It was a small hut, probably only one room, with a big old stone chimney at one end and part of a door sitting on the ground beside it. The old tin roof looked solid even if rusty, which I guessed was why it was used as a shelter for hikers.

Someone *had* been using it recently, as smoke still drifted from the chimney. I hope like hell June had lit it, even if every instinct said she hadn't.

I ignored the rising tide of trepidation and flexed my fingers as I looked for anything in the way of protecting magic. There was nothing. The only other scent in the air aside from sweaty man and ammonia was agony.

I paused briefly in front of the door, but there were no windows, and the daylight didn't reach far past the doorway. There was no sign of June, but an odd mewling sound was coming from the right. I stepped over the remnants of the door into the building, tiny flicks of energy dancing across my fingertips in readiness ... and stopped so abruptly that Jaz had to do a quick step around me to avoid me.

June sat on a wooden chair a few feet away from the still-burning fire. She was slender, with short pale hair and skin, and wearing a pretty pink dressing gown and slippers. Blood stained the front of the gown, but I couldn't immediately see the cause, as her head was dropped so that her chin was resting on her chest. Her hands and feet were lashed so tightly to the chair that her skin was raw, and the rope bloodied.

I drew in a deep breath that didn't in any way ease the creeping sense of horror, and said, "June? Lucy sent us here to find you. You're safe. We'll get you out of—"

Her head snapped around at the sound of my voice, and horror became full-blown.

It was my dream come to life, except for one detail.

Not only had her eyes been burned out, but her mouth sewn shut.

Chapter Three

Bile surged up my throat, and I clapped a hand against my mouth in a useless attempt to stop it. Then I pushed past Jaz and ran into the bush at the side of the hut, where I was completely and violently ill.

When there was nothing left in my stomach and the dry heaves had eased, I wiped my mouth and straightened. I'd seen far worse in my time here in the reservation than a woman with her eyes burned out and her mouth sewn shut, so it was a little surprising that my stomach had reacted so fast. But maybe it was the intent behind it. Like someone didn't really want to kill her, just stop her from seeing and speaking.

To him, instinct whispered. *It's about him more than her. About his inadequacies and need for revenge.*

I frowned. If that were true, why had he dragged her all the way out here and then left her alive? He'd definitely mutilated her here rather than elsewhere—the waves of horrific pain that still weighed heavily on the air were testimony to that—and even if he'd initially attacked her from behind and placed a hood over her head, he would have had

41

to remove it at some point. She'd be able to describe him, even if she could no longer see. Besides, covering her eyes meant he would have had to lead her through the scrub, and surely if he *had*, she'd have fallen. Pink slippers weren't exactly the best footwear when it came to hiking through the bush, even if the ones she was wearing had a rubber sole. But there were no scrapes or cuts on her bare legs, and her hands weren't scraped. It just didn't make any sense.

As I sucked in a deeper breath to fortify myself and go back in, Jaz stepped out.

"You okay?" she asked softly.

"Yeah. I just wasn't expecting—" I stopped and waved a hand toward the hut.

Jaz grimaced. "There are certainly less horrific ways to stop someone screaming."

"I'm thinking he wasn't worried about her screaming. Not out here. This was personal to him."

"Retribution for something she's said or done?"

"This is definitely about revenge, but I don't believe it's specifically aimed at June." I hesitated and then shrugged. "That's all I'm getting along the psychic lines at the moment."

"Your psi senses can be annoyingly capricious at times."

"Tell me about it." I took another deep breath, then added, "Okay, let's get back in there and do what we can to help her."

Jaz led the way. She'd cut the ropes from June's hands and feet and eased her down to the floor, but the older woman continued to shake, her aura a turmoil of confusion, horror, and agony.

As June made another distressed sound, Jaz wrinkled her nose. "Have you anything in that pack that can help ease her pain? The ambulance will be here in ten minutes, but her pulse rate and breathing suggest she might not last that long without relief."

I swung off my pack and knelt on the opposite side of June. "I have, but I think removing those stitches will go a long way to helping her condition."

I tucked the watch into my sock so I could keep it close to my skin and still feel its pulse. It would tell me what June's aura couldn't—whether her heart was faltering, thereby sending her sliding toward death.

"Is that wise? It's not exactly a sanitary—" Jaz stopped and grimaced. "I guess the bastard who did this wasn't exactly concerned about a sterile environment, was he?"

"No." I pulled a small pot from the backpack and unscrewed the lid. "June? I'm going to numb your mouth so I can cut away the threads. It may briefly hurt, and I'm sorry, but it shouldn't last more than a minute or two, okay?"

June responded with a desperate sound. I swallowed heavily and glanced at Jaz. "You'll have to hold her head still. No matter how careful I am, it will be painful."

She shifted and gently placed her hands on either side of June's head. I briefly closed my eyes to gather mental strength, then leaned closer and carefully spread the sweet-smelling lotion across the older woman's swollen and bloody lips. She immediately bucked but didn't lash out, and her scream was a muted sound of desperate agony that remained buried in her throat.

Tears sprang to my eyes, but I blinked rapidly and resolutely continued. After a few more seconds, the effects of the lotion obviously started to kick in, because she stopped screaming. She still had to be in distress, given what had been done to her eyes, but this lotion was designed for external use, and I really didn't know how it would react if I rubbed it into her eye sockets.

I waited a little longer to ensure the lotion had time to do its stuff, then drew a small pair of scissors from the traditional medical kit—something we'd started carrying just in case the lotions and potions weren't enough. I carefully picked up the thread's knotted end near one corner of her mouth and gently cut it away. I repeated the process on the other side but didn't pull the entire thread free. I couldn't. Her lips had swollen so dramatically that, even with the numbing salve, doing so would have caused her severe discomfort. Instead, I carefully cut each loop of the thread and then gently tugged these smaller bits from her flesh.

When it was finally done, I replaced the scissors and pulled two bottles of holy water from the backpack. One of the many interesting things we'd discovered since coming here was the fact that holy water was not only a good deterrent against vampires, demons, and the like, but it also had amazing healing properties. It wouldn't bring back June's sight, but it would at least heal the worst of the scarring.

I carefully trickled it over June's lips then, as she started licking her them with some desperation, dribbled some into her mouth.

"Not too much," Jaz said. "We have no idea if she has internal injuries."

I nodded and poured the remainder over her eyes, washing out the wounds and hoping it helped, then unstopped the second bottle and poured it over the rope burn marks on her wrists and ankles. The tumultuous storm in her aura eased a little, but the watch still spoke of a heart that was struggling.

"The ambulance should be here any second," Jaz said. "Do want to head out and make sure they don't miss the entrance?"

I pulled the watch from my sock and handed it to Jaz, then grabbed my pack and walked out. The afternoon air remained cold, and that strange scent was now so faint that only a deeper intake of breath found it. Instinct was saying I needed to track it before I lost it, but instinct in this case was crazy. I wasn't about to do it alone, and Jaz needed to keep an eye on June. If the older woman's heart *did* fail, Jaz was better equipped to give first aid, as all rangers had to undergo training on a regular basis.

I walked up to the road and stopped next to the sign. After a few minutes, an ambulance crested the hill, lights and siren on. I stepped out and waved them down, then spotted an all-too-familiar truck not far behind them. It seemed that fate had decided a week of grieving was more than enough and was now determined to keep throwing Aiden and me together.

The ambulance's sirens fell silent as it drew closer, and then a paramedic wound down the window, getting further directions before moving on. I jogged after it without bothering to wait for Aiden. He'd been close enough to see where he had to turn, so he didn't need any further instructions from me. I was hoping he'd roll on past, but I should have known that was never going to happen. He slowed next to me, and the passenger-side window slid down. "You want a lift?"

And be in a confined space with him? No way in hell was I ready for *that* sort of closeness. Not just yet.

"It's not far," I said. "I'll meet you down there. They're in the old hut."

He hesitated, then nodded and continued. By the time I got back, he'd parked close to Jaz's SUV and was leading the medics down the track to the hut. I thrust my hands into my sweater pockets and followed but didn't go in. Aside from the fact space inside the hut was tight, it was still too filled with the vibrations of horror.

Not to mention the deliciously warm aroma of musky, smoky wood emanating from the man I could no longer have.... I blinked and then scrubbed a hand across my eyes. I really needed to stop the pity party.

The weird scent I'd noticed earlier was now little more than a tickle of unpleasantness that danced on the breeze. The urge to follow hit so hard that I was halfway around the hut before I could stop myself.

Aiden obviously heard my movement, because he came back out. "Problem?"

I hesitated. "Can you smell a scent that's a mix of sweat and ammonia?"

He raised his eyebrows. "Only just, and I'm a wolf. How are you smelling it?"

It was a question that surprised me, given he was aware the inner wild magic was busy reshaping what I was to... well, who really knew. "My olfactory senses have been sharpening for a while now, remember."

"Yes, but to be wolf sharp? That's... unexpected."

"And probably the least of the changes, if current suspicions are true." I raised a hand to stop the questions I could see in his eyes. "That smell is connected to whoever did this to June, and we need to track it before it fades completely."

He hesitated. "Give me a minute to tell Jaz and grab the ropes."

I nodded. He'd started taking climbing gear whenever we entered areas filled with old mine shafts, simply because I had a bad habit of finding them. That was something I'd really prefer to avoid this afternoon—right along with being alone with him. Fate definitely wasn't on my side when it came to the latter, so I hoped she was more favorably inclined when it came to the former.

He returned a few minutes later, the rope and harnesses slung neatly over his broad shoulders. "Jaz will seal off the immediate area and do a search once June is transported. I've asked Ric to meet the ambulance at the hospital."

Ricardo Pérez was a recent addition to the team and a replacement for the ranger we'd lost so brutally a few months ago. He'd come to Australia as part of the international exchange program—which was designed to stop both local and overseas packs from becoming inbred—and had initially taken up ranger duties in Queensland's only werewolf reservation. He'd transferred down here last week to be closer to his sister, who'd apparently arrived as an exchange a few months ago. Both were now staying with the Sinclair Pack, though I had no idea if that meant they'd found mates or not. I hadn't met either and only knew as much as I did because Jaz liked to gossip.

"Given the state she's in, it's not likely he'll be able to take her statement for some time," I said.

"No, but he can keep guard outside her door, just in case this bastard has another go at her. Shall I lead?"

I nodded. Better me following him than the other way around. I'd be too damn conscious of his gaze on me and would probably fall right into another damn mineshaft.

We followed the rough old track up the long hill and, rather surprisingly, it didn't tax my strength or trouble my legs as much as it once would have. I *had* taken up jogging recently, but as with most exercise programs I'd started over the years, it was a half-assed effort. I suspected the increase in fitness wasn't due to exercise but another example of changes being made.

The view from the top of the hill was basically more of

the same—acres of scrub, weedy trees, and random piles of tailings. How the hell had he dragged June through this? Had he carried her? Her frame was tiny, so I guessed it was possible, but it would still take some compliance on her part and strength on his—unless, of course, he'd simply drugged her first. She *had* been missing for twenty-four hours, after all, and her horrific injuries were much fresher than that.

"Our felon isn't a wolf, so why the hell would he be heading out this way?" I said. "There's nothing here."

Aiden started down the slope. "What makes you think he's not a wolf?"

I hesitated. "His smell, mainly. There's something off about it, and I'm thinking a werewolf's ability to heal all manner of injuries during a shift would have fixed whatever is causing it."

"Not all ailments or wounds can be healed by a shift."

The dark edge in his reply made me want to kick myself. His brother had been caught under a falling tree a couple of weeks ago, and it had all but destroyed his leg. Belle, Katie, and I had formed a connection to force Dillon's unconscious body to shift shape and save his life, but the last I'd heard, he was still in hospital. Which should *not* have been the case, given he was a werewolf and the leg had been repaired, even if it had left him with a permanent limp.

"How's Dillon, Aiden?" I asked softly.

"He's not good."

The vivid wash of lemon-yellow through his aura spoke of his fear for his youngest brother. I wanted to reach out, to hold and comfort him, but resisted. I wasn't yet strong enough for that sort of intimacy. But I would be, one day. I had to be, because it wasn't like I had any other choice, given I had to live in this reservation and keep doing this job, at least until the waves of power that had washed from the once-unguarded main wellspring stopped striking the distant shores of darkness.

"Mentally?" I asked. "Or physically?"

"Both."

"What are the doctors saying?"

"That its natural for him to be struggling right now given everything he's gone through, and that we need to give him time."

I hesitated and then said, in an attempt to lighten his mood, "At least he has what many patients haven't—a fabulous support network to help get him through this. Plus, he's an O'Connor. You lot are stubborn bastards at the best of times."

He briefly glanced over his shoulder, amusement lurking around his lovely lips. "I resemble that remark."

I laughed and, just for a moment, it felt like old times. Like we were one again.

He must have felt it too, because his amusement quickly faded. "Liz, we really need to talk."

I steeled my heart against the underlying plea in his voice. "No, we don't, because there's nothing that can be said that hasn't been said a dozen times."

"I refuse to believe this situation is impossible. There has to be a solution that works for us both."

It was said with an edge that suggested I'd been wrong before—he *hadn't* accepted the finality of the situation, and he had no intention of giving up on us. There was a part of me that danced in giddy delight at the thought, a part that wanted to be chased and won all over again... but to what end? The things that had torn us apart hadn't gone away. They would never go away, no matter what changes the wild magic made. To step back into a relationship with him would only prolong the inevitable agony.

"A solution?" My laugh held a somewhat bitter edge. "Haven't you heard anything I've said?"

"Of course I have, but I want—"

"It *all*. Your nice cozy life with me and your werewolf mate whenever she pops along. That's fucking selfish, and you know it." I drew in a breath and did my best to rein in my anger. "I don't want to keep doing this, Aiden. I want to remain friends, but if you're going to bring this shit up every time we work on a case together, you'll have to delegate a liaison."

"*That* is impractical."

"So is forcing me to relive the hurt every time we meet."

"That's not—" He stopped and scrubbed a hand through his short hair. Frustration vibrated through every part of him, but he knew the truth of what I was saying. That was evident in the brief—if annoyed—swirl through his aura. "Fine. Friends it is."

It was grudgingly said, and I couldn't help smiling. He hadn't accepted *anything*. It was more likely he was simply planning to play a longer game.

It wouldn't help. He had to know that.

We continued in silence for a while, but as we picked our way up another rock-strewn slope, I said, "This is a hell of a long way to be dragging or even carrying an old woman. Why wouldn't he have used the road like we did?"

"Until we know our attacker's motives, that's a question that can't be answered." He glanced at me over his shoulder. "Any more insights on that?"

"Not really." Jaz had obviously made her report and told him what I'd said on his arrival. "What's out this way, besides more scrub?"

"There's a couple of remote farms, but the scent is leading us back toward the main road. There's a parking area on the other side of the next hill."

"It makes no logical sense to use that one rather than the one closer to the hut."

"I think it's pretty obvious we're not dealing with a fully rational mind. Not given what he's done to June."

As we crested the next hill, the scent completely faded. I swore in frustration even though, given how faint it had been for a while now, it was not unexpected. The parking area—which was little more than a cleared patch of ground to the left of a dirt road—was empty.

But I could see tire tracks from where we stood, and they appeared fresh.

We walked down, and Aiden knelt next to them. "These belong to a truck rather than a car."

I crossed my arms and looked around. There were a couple of plastic bags and take-away drink cups dumped behind one of the trees closer to the road, but they'd been there for some time, if the state they were in was anything to go by.

"Is this parking area used very much?"

"Mainly in summer by tourists on day hikes."

He pulled out his phone to take a couple of photos, then walked to the right of the parking area. I trailed after him. Close to the edge of a muddy puddle was a solitary shoe print.

"Any idea what type of shoe has a tread like that?" I asked, as he took more photos.

"Some sort of hiking shoe from the look of it." He shrugged. "I'll get Maggie to come up here and do a casting of both tracks. In the meantime, we should head back. We can take the road from here—it'll be easier."

Said road was definitely easier, but the lack of a treacherous terrain only managed to concentrate the tension still hovering between us.

I knew it *would* get easier, but that didn't make the here and now any less challenging.

By the time we arrived back, all I wanted to do was run from the man and the memories his closeness evoked. Jaz had taped off a large area around the hut and was in the middle of a line search.

"Anything?" Aiden asked once we were close enough. His voice was clipped, suggesting he was no more comfortable than me.

"There's a partial print on the iron poker he used to burn her eyes out. He was using gloves for the most part, though, as there's a bit of silicone stuck to the metal."

"Nothing else?"

She shook her head. "He's been very careful."

"I'll finish up here, then, while you drive Liz back." He glanced at me and half reached out, then caught the movement and stepped back, out of touching range. His hands, I noticed, were clenched, the knuckles white. "If you uncover any information about our siren, let me know."

There was a very faint emphasis on *me*. The man did *not* want me going through Jaz or anyone else unless absolutely necessary. Which was fine. I'd tell Monty, and he could pass it all on.

Coward, thy name is Lizzie.

I nodded, then turned and walked across to the SUV to wait for Jaz. His gaze burned into my spine and did all sorts of things to my heart.

And I wasn't sure even time could stop that from happening.

"So," Jaz said as we drove out, "were there words said?"

I half smiled. It was pretty obvious she meant on a personal level rather than the case. "There was nothing more than has already been said."

"Yes, but did he listen?"

"He always listens. Believing is another matter entirely."

She laughed. "That is the trouble with alphas. So glad Levi isn't one—it would definitely lead to trouble in paradise."

I echoed her laugh and the conversation moved on. But as we reached the café and I opened the passenger door, she leaned over and caught my hand. "You do know we're here if you ever want to talk or rant or just get drunk one night if things get overwhelming, don't you?"

"I know." I squeezed her hand. "Thank you."

I got out, slammed the SUV's door shut, and then headed inside. Once I'd returned the backpack to the reading room, I went into the kitchen to look for something to eat. It was close to five, I'd missed lunch, and my stomach was rumbling unhappily. Obviously, there weren't any lingering aftereffects from the vomiting episode this afternoon.

I settled on steak and a pile of fries, then headed upstairs to search through our online archives for any information about freshwater sirens.

There were, I discovered, at least a dozen of them, and three that were possible candidates.

The first was a Lorelei, which was basically a freshwater siren who lured fishermen to their deaths with their song in much the same manner as their seagoing kin. The second was a river nymph, though there was no mention of them using their voice to lure prey closer. The third was a rusalka. They were the souls of women—young or old—

who'd passed before their time and were destined to haunt the river or waterway in which they'd died. While Nell's notes said not all of them were malignant, those whose deaths had come about through betrayal of some kind were doomed to forever seek vengeance. She also noted that they lured men, either by their looks or their song, into the water then entangled their victim's feet with their long hair and submerged them until they drowned. None of the three mentioned soul stripping, but as good as Nell's notes were, even she wouldn't have been able to document all the variations of evil.

If we *were* dealing with a rusalka, however, Aiden and his crew would need to search through their records to see if there'd been any drownings or murders near that reservoir.

I picked up the phone to send him a text and then saw it was well after midnight. I'd been on the computer longer than I'd thought. I scheduled the message to send at nine and then bookmarked all three pages, shut down the computer, and went to bed. And once again dreamed, though at least this time it was about the golden-haired little girl with eyes the color of summer skies who would one day bless my life.

It filled me with hope that no matter crappy by love life currently was, it wouldn't remain this way forever.

* * *

Belle came in a few minutes after seven the following morning, just as I was putting the last tray of veg prep into the fridge.

"Want a coffee?" she asked. "Or perhaps a pot of tea?"

"Tea would be good," I said. "You want toast?"

"No. Monty spoiled me with bacon and eggs this morning."

I raised my eyebrows. "What the hell was he doing up early enough to do *that*?"

"Ciara's doing the autopsy on Jerod O'Connor this morning, and he wanted to be there." She crossed her arms and leaned on the doorframe. "I think he's gained a morbid fascination for them."

I cut two thick slices of the sourdough and popped them into the toaster. "Or maybe it's simply a matter of caution. We don't know how Jerod died, and it's always possible there's a trap on the corpse none of us saw."

"I guess it wouldn't be the first time."

No, although the one occasion it *had* happened didn't involve magic but rather a grenade in a dying victim's gut. I'd barely survived that one.

"So, what happened yesterday afternoon?" she asked. "I kept getting these vague wisps of horror, but you were shut down pretty tight."

"With good reason. Two of us did *not* need to go through that shit."

She raised her eyebrows. "Explanations, woman, not statements that only arouse further curiosity."

I smiled and gave her a quick update. "Whoever did this to June is human rather than supernatural, I'm certain of that much."

"No *human* could do that to an old woman," Belle countered, anger in her voice and expression.

"No *sane* human," I agreed. The toast popped, so I placed it on a plate and slathered walnut toffee butter over both pieces. I'd gained a craving for the stuff and now had it for breakfast most mornings. "I think it's fair to say whoever did this is psychologically impaired."

"You didn't get any vibes about him?"

"Only that it's about revenge. June is merely a symbol of his rage rather than the cause."

Belle blinked. "Given what he did to her, is it possible his mother is abusive, and this is his way of dealing with it?"

"Why attack a random stranger though? Why not his mom, if she's the problem?"

"It's possible to hate someone yet not be able to confront either them or your emotions. You know that."

Yes, I did. Though punching my father's smug and superior face had in the end given me a *whole* lot of satisfaction. "Why now, though? What on earth could have set him off?"

The kettle began to whistle. Belle pushed away from the doorframe and walked around the counter to make the drinks. "Could be anything—the breakdown of his own relationship or even his mother dying, which would have left him with no avenue of ever confronting the situation or her."

I followed her out and walked over to an unset table. She joined me a few minutes later with a tray holding my teapot and cup, and her mug of instant coffee. Once she'd placed everything down, she propped the tray against the table leg and then sat opposite me.

I picked up a slice of toast and bit into the walnutty goodness. "If this is the result of a relationship breakdown, surely he would have gone after someone the same age as his partner rather than a woman who could be his mom."

"Unless his mother was the reason for the relationship breakup." She took a drink of coffee. "Until we know more about him, anything is possible. Hell, it might even be a one-off."

I gave her "the look." "In this reservation?"

"Hey, miracles do happen. The fact that I'm in a relationship with Monty is evidence enough of that."

I laughed. "If we're not too busy this afternoon, I might head up to the second wellspring to see Katie."

"Sure, but why, when you don't need to go up there to chat to her anymore?"

I hesitated. "I need to talk to her about the changes that are happening and what it might mean, and the second wellspring is the only place her spirit can appear without it draining my strength."

She eyed me for a minute. "You think she's lying about what she does and doesn't know?"

"No, but Gabe certainly could be. Remember, he knew enough about the wild magic to bind Katie's soul to it."

"He knew a spell. That's hardly the same thing."

"He wouldn't have done it without knowing and understanding the consequences."

"Except he *didn't* understand the consequences. The power he invoked blew him apart."

"I know but—"

"You're feeling restless and need to do something about understanding these changes rather than just waiting for Eli to transcribe that book."

A smile tugged at my lips. "Anyone would think you could read my mind."

Though amusement glimmered in her silver eyes, concern shone deeper. "I understand the restlessness, but you need to be cautious. There's something off about that lake attack."

I raised an eyebrow. "Why would you think that? Did you find something else after I'd left? Or has Monty said something?"

"No, but—" She hesitated. "I had a dream."

Precognition wasn't one of Belle's gifts but the day we'd merged souls to oust the white lady who'd taken up residence in her body had seen her not only gain it but a strengthening of her own psychic talents *and* a jump in her spell-casting power. While neither of us had been tested since we'd left Canberra, I had no doubt Belle now had the casting strength of a royal witch, even if neither of us had the knowledge.

"That's unfortunate."

"Yeah. And as that old TV ad goes, *not happy, Jan.*"

I smiled. "What did the dream say?"

"That it wasn't a coincidence the victim was an O'Connor."

"Why would a siren be targeting the O'Connors?"

"Asks the woman who has spent years bitching about the lack of information her precognitive dreams give."

My smile grew. "There was always a chance yours would play nicer than mine."

She snorted softly. "Considering mine's a wash over from yours, that was never likely."

I laughed and poured myself a cup of tea. The delicious scent of pear and jasmine filled the air and made me smile. As did the cup—it was smaller than the ones I usually used and was a simple pale blue in color with a gold handle. Like many of the items we used in the café, we'd salvaged it from a secondhand store, though not just to be thrifty. They all had a history and a presence the sensitive could feel. While most would scoff at the thought of something as simple as a cup making any sort of difference to a person's mood, I knew from experience the *wrong* choice could have an unsettling effect on the user.

This cup spoke of happiness and hope. Of dreams that had shattered and been made whole again.

A deliberate choice on Belle's part, no doubt.

I took a sip and then said, "I take it you mentioned the vision to Monty?"

She nodded. "He's going to question Ciara this morning."

"At least she's a little more open to talking about family stuff than Aiden."

"Not by much." Belle's tone was wry. "But it could be worth asking Katie. She is one half of the reservation's protection ring, after all."

I picked up the other bit of toast and bit into it. "That makes it sound like something involving organized crime."

"Well, the two of you *are* something of a crime-fighting duo these days, so it's kinda appropriate." She drained her cup and pushed to her feet. "I'll finish setting up, if you want to take your time with your breakfast."

"Thanks, I will."

We opened at eight and had a steady run of customers. Even lunch was busy, which considering the sky had opened up and it was absolutely pelting down, was a good sign that my breakup with Aiden hadn't affected our business. Unless, of course, they were all coming here in the hope of watching the continuing drama if Aiden *did* happen to make an appearance. I doubted he would, given he disliked public displays of emotion and, even from the beginning of our relationship, had a thing about feeding the gossip brigade.

By two, things had started to ease off, and the need to get out of here was growing, as was the suspicion that Aiden would make an appearance once the café closed for the day. Leaving was only delaying the inevitable, of course, but I just wanted twenty-four hours of breathing space before I saw him again.

I slid a coffee and cake order for the sole remaining couple in the café across the counter and then said, "I might head out to see Katie, if you don't mind."

"Running before he even makes an appearance is a new level of cowardice, you know." It was lightly said, but the gentle wash of her thoughts told me she understood. "You need me to tell him anything?"

"That he's never going to get me back unless he's playing for keeps?"

She laughed. "Oh, he's well aware of *that*. To say the man is seriously confused would be an understatement."

"Except there's nothing to be confused about. Nothing can change the situation—it is what it is."

"*He* can change the situation. He will one day be alpha, remember."

"Not with me as his wife, he won't be. Besides, his mom isn't going anywhere, and she'll ensure that even if he brings the possibility up, the pack rejects it."

"His mom won't live forever."

"And neither will I. Besides, we both know she'd do anything in her power to thwart me, even if that means finding a way to outlive me."

Belle laughed. "Flee with my blessing. I doubt we'll get anyone else in here now other than Monty."

Monty came in at two-thirty every day for afternoon tea. He of course swore it was to see Belle, and while that *was* true, we all knew it was because he had an insatiable sweet tooth and adored our cakes and slices. "We're out of carrot cake, and it's not scone day—he will not be pleased."

"He'll cope just fine with the black forest cake." Her voice was wry, and with good reason. Monty hadn't yet met a cake or a slice he didn't appreciate. "Just be careful in this weather. I don't think the council will appreciate you wiping out another SUV on that damn road."

"That rollover wasn't my fault."

"No, but until we're sure what we're dealing with now, being careful is only sensible."

"Shame that I'm not," I said.

She tossed a tea towel after me, eliciting a laugh. I scooped it up, threw it into the laundry bag, and then headed upstairs to swap my sneakers for waterproof hiking boots. In this weather, I was going to need them.

I grabbed the backpack from the reading room just in case I hit trouble, dumped my purse into it, and then pulled on my coat and dashed out to the SUV. Even through there was little more than two meters between the back door and our allotted parking space, the bottom half of my jeans got soaked.

Visibility was low, and the madly swishing wipers weren't doing a whole lot to fix that, so I pulled out onto the main road cautiously before accelerating away.

It probably wasn't the best sort of day to be tracking up the narrow and muddy track that led to the newer well-spring, but I needed answers, and the sooner the better.

I finally reached the turnoff a few kilometers away from Maldoon and did my best to avoid the dirt road's many potholes while keeping well away from the soft edges and the long drop into the heavily treed valley below. Eventually, I spotted the turn that led to the walking track and navigated the increasingly dangerous and narrow dirt road carefully. It was a damned relief when I finally reached the small parking area.

I slipped my phone and keys into my coat pockets, then tucked the backpack behind the back seat where it'd be hidden from a casual glance. While it was unlikely anyone other than a werewolf would be wandering past, given this morning's storm, there'd apparently been a spate of thefts from remote houses and cars around this area recently.

I climbed out, locked up, then pulled up my hood and began the long climb up the muddy, slippery track. Thankfully, it was no longer raining, although the occasional rumble of thunder suggested it hadn't gone entirely away. Despite the weather, however, animals still moved about, though if the scent lingering on the cold air was anything to go by, they were mostly rabbits.

The path eventually began to level off, but the day's gloom increased, leaving huge swaths of the forest blanketed by a wet fog.

It didn't matter, though, because the wild magic was now here. The luminous threads danced through the shadows like fragile moonbeams, lighting the way and filling the air with a song that was alien and yet not, and one I'd heard intermittently if distantly over the years. I hadn't known what it was then, but I did now—it was the wild magic, calling me, seeking me.

Or rather, seeking what lay locked inside.

But this particular song was washed with worry.

Life and death type of worry.

Chapter Four

I ran up the hill as fast as I could, all but flying over rough ground.

The number of luminous threads multiplied as I drew closer to the wellspring, but I had no sense of immediate danger despite the continuing wave of concern in their song. Whatever troubled Katie, its source wasn't a threat against the wellspring itself.

Which was a relief, even if it didn't ease my inner tension.

I reached the edge of the wellspring's clearing and stopped. It wasn't a very large area, and it was strewn with rocks and other debris from the landslip that had taken out a good portion of the cliff directly opposite. At the base of this was an ankle-deep rock well. Water bubbled up from a seam near the cliff's base, lapped over the edge of the basin, and then wound down the gentle slope, eventually joining the larger streams farther down the mountain.

That tiny well was the source of the wild magic, and the air above it shimmered with its force. Its output had ramped up since the last time I'd been here, and I couldn't help but wonder if that had anything to do with not only Katie's presence here but my growing link with the main wellspring. While they might be separate entities, all wellsprings had the same source—the deep heart of the earth's outer core. No one alive today understood why it had developed into a collective force or how it found its way to the surface through the springs, but the ancients certainly had. Why we'd lost that knowledge when they could be so dangerous was one of the great unanswerable mysteries.

The gentle moonbeams clustered around me, and it was through them that I could see Katie. Here in the clearing her form was solid rather than that of a ghost, though if you looked closely enough you could see the shimmer of the wellspring's force behind her. She was a typical O'Connor—tall and rangy, with blonde-brown hair and a sharp but pretty face. In fact, she was basically a younger version of Ciara.

Standing behind her was a wispy male figure with scarlet hair. Gabe, whose soul was destined to haunt this place forever.

"What's wrong?" I said. "Why are you worried?"

"Something attacks my pack." Her melodious voice ran with fear. "I cannot see it, but I know it's there."

I released a somewhat relieved breath and approached the wellspring. Its energy flowed around me, warm and welcoming. "We think it's some kind of siren."

"Sirens don't usually travel from their own waterways unless summoned," Gabe commented. "It would be rare for one to come here willingly."

"If this were a normal reservation, I'd agree." This close to the wellspring, the multitude of colors that pulsed through it was rainbow bright. Its power caressed my skin, my soul, and filled me with a deep sense of kinship.

"Why are you so certain that your pack is being targeted? The death didn't occur on pack grounds."

I sat down on a rock on the right side of the wellspring and held out my hands in much the same manner I would if it were a fire. The gossamer threads played in and out of my fingertips, and heat rippled through the rest of me. Once it had scared me, but that was before I really understood why it was happening.

Of course, I was still scared of where it would eventually lead, but hopefully that wouldn't happen until a long —*long*—time in the future.

Katie didn't answer my question, instead noting, in obvious amusement, "You're glowing."

"It's not me but rather the inner wild magic responding to the wellspring."

"The wild magic is a part of your DNA, not a separate entity," Gabe said dryly. "You have to stop thinking of it that way."

I wrinkled my nose. "Separating it out makes it easier for me to control it."

"Only for the time being."

My gaze narrowed. "Meaning what? What do you know about the wild magic that you haven't actually told me?"

He grimaced and sat on the rock on the other side of the well. The wild magic buzzed through and around him, tiny fireflies that made his outline shift and waver. Katie sat next to him and twined her fingers through his. It was a potent reminder of the closeness I'd walked away from, and the ache stirred anew.

"When I was researching the binding spell," he said, "I came across some references to a people called the Fenna.

From what I could ascertain, they were a race of enhanced witches who guarded the wellsprings."

"Then why is there no record of them anywhere?" I asked. "And why aren't they guarding them now?"

"I don't know. As I said, the information was vague and scattered. There was one reference that said the Fenna were created, not born, and that conception binding more often than not resulted in a loss of all lives."

My eyebrows rose. "Conception *binding*? That suggests they were having sex at the wellspring itself."

"Only at unbound emerging ones," he said.

One piece of the puzzle that Katie's binding represented fell into place. "Which is why you chose to test the spell here rather than at the older wellspring."

He nodded. "It was mentioned that a newly emerging wellspring offered the greater chance of survival."

And Katie was dying anyway, so she really didn't have all that much to lose. Gabe, on the other hand, had paid a far higher price, but I had a feeling it was one he didn't regret. After all, he was here, with the woman he loved, for all eternity.

"So, if the child the binding created survived, it was subsequently bound to that wellspring?"

"If the information is to be believed, yes."

"Then why do I seem to be merging with the older wellspring here and not the one that's fused to my DNA?"

Gabe shrugged. "That might forever remain a mystery, given how little we truly understand about the wellsprings these days."

"But if you had to guess?"

"Then I'd suggest it's because your mother protected the emerging wellspring rather than performing the binding, so while the merging happened, it was incomplete."

"That still doesn't explain why the binding seems to be happening with the older wellspring here."

Gabe shrugged again. "Perhaps the book Eli transcribes will provide the answers."

"Did I mention patience is not one of my virtues?"

They laughed, a merry sound that ran cheerfully around the clearing.

"Once he has the Fenna as a search term, I'm sure he'll be able to find all the answers you could ever want," Katie said.

Maybe. Maybe not. "Was there anything you found that would explain why I seem to be gaining some wolf attributes?"

"No, but there was a reference to werewolves being the preferred seed givers. There would have been a reason for that."

"Maybe wolf genes gave the child a greater chance of surviving the wild magic's power," I said.

"Or maybe their DNA was vital not only for the embryo's survival but also the Fenna's ability to protect," Katie said. "They were *enhanced* witches, remember."

"Which is good news for any kid Aiden and I might have if by some miracle we got back together, but where does it leave me? I'm witch born, not mixed race."

"I don't know, which is why I haven't mentioned it before now," Gabe said. "But if the wild magic *is* capable of enhancing genetic material, it would certainly explain the increasing power of your magic."

Katie glanced up at him. "Is it possible my presence in this wellspring is causing a genetic reaction in Liz every time she interacts with our wild magic?"

Gabe pursed his lips. "I wouldn't have thought so. From

the little I gleaned, it only enhanced what was already present."

"And yet I'm gaining wolf-like senses, my wounds are now healing faster than they should, and I've gained a sudden aversion to silver."

Katie's gaze sharpened. "When did that happen?"

"Discovered it during our hunt for the hone-anna and still have the goddamn scar."

"Wounds created by silver always scar." She pursed her lips and studied me thoughtfully. "You're not pregnant, are you?"

"No, I'm not."

"Are you certain of that?"

"I've been on birth control and haven't skipped a period, so yes. Why?"

"Because if you were, it might explain the reaction."

"How? Even if I was by some miracle pregnant, it would be smaller than a grain of rice and wouldn't have even developed a neural tube yet. How could a speck without a central nervous system or brain be the cause of such a reaction?"

"Because the fertilized egg would contain wolf DNA, and with the wild magic embedded into your DNA, that might just be enough."

"That doesn't explain the other changes though, and we really haven't melded that often for it to be a cause."

"Which once again brings us back to the book Eli's transcribing and the answers it hopefully contains," Gabe said.

A smile tugged at my lips. "As I've already said, I'm impatient, and it's taking a goddamn eternity."

"Transcribing archaic Latin is no easy task, especially for someone who isn't a scholar." He held his free hand out to the shimmering waves rising from the wellspring, and both their forms solidified to the point that I could hear the twin beats of their hearts. Which was impossible, of course, and yet I couldn't help but wonder... if the wellspring could do that, perhaps it could also allow further intimacies. I really hoped so, for their sakes.

"In the meantime," Katie said, "what makes you think we're dealing with a siren?"

"I heard her song."

"That *is* interesting, given their song is usually only heard by men," Gabe said.

"How can we be sure? None of the texts I've read actually say that."

"No doubt because it's never been deemed necessary, given they all mention fisher*men*." Amusement crinkled his pleasant features. "They've always been the prey of choice for sirens."

I glanced at Katie. "Have you any idea why one would be targeting the O'Connor pack?"

Katie made a "I don't know" gesture with her hand, and I frowned. "Was there ever a murder—recent or historical— of a woman near a riverbank or dam?"

"Not that I'm aware of." She eyed me speculatively for a second. "Why aren't you asking Aiden these questions?"

"Because I'm avoiding the man."

She laughed. "You can't do that forever. Not in a reservation this size."

"I know."

"He has to play the long game in this matter," she said. "He has no other choice. You must hold to hope."

"Says the woman who declared not so long ago that the choice to walk away was his to make."

"Yes, but he didn't choose to break up. You did."

"Same thing."

69

"No, it's not. I also think you're forgetting how stubborn my brother is."

"Stubborn doesn't mean squat when he values his pack more than me, Katie. And you haven't answered my question about your pack."

She smiled, though the amusement failed to touch the corners of her eyes. "Remember what I said to my mom when we confronted her at Aiden's party?"

"That she would regret forcing us apart? You surely can't think *that* has anything to do with this."

"It was more than regret—I said she'd pay dearly on a *personal* level." Katie took a deep breath and released it slowly. "And now we have what appears to be a siren in the reservation targeting my pack. I do not think it is a coincidence."

"Both wellsprings are well protected," I said. "The waves that still wash through the deeper reaches of darkness are old and could not have made such a specific call."

"I know that, and yet I still believe this is no coincidence."

My gaze flicked to Gabe. "And you agree?"

"I think it's possible given emotions such as anger are a huge draw to demons and many other mythical creatures. The wellspring's power might be shielded, but her threads are not, and they have the ability to roam wide."

"But they haven't gone beyond the reservation... have they?"

"As far as I'm aware, no. But Katie doesn't yet fully control this wellspring and may never control the other one. It's possible the wall of emotions that have risen over the last few months have echoed elsewhere, either via the threads or even through the deeper depths of one or both wellsprings, into other springs."

I frowned. "I know wellsprings are all connected deep in the earth, but how could something like that even be possible?"

"Who can say, given how little we really know about either them or even the connection you have with them?"

My frown deepened. "If anger *did* draw the siren here, why then target the O'Connor pack?"

"We're presuming it's Mom's anger," Katie said. "But what if it's yours? What if the combination of your anger and your grief were the chief catalyst for drawing attention here?"

A chill ran through me. "I don't want your mom dead, Katie. I simply want her to give Aiden the same choice she gave you."

"I'm well aware of that, but it's a possibility, however unlikely, we cannot discount. Especially given your connection to the wild magic."

I shoved a hand through my tangled hair. "I hope you're wrong. I really do."

And yet she probably wasn't, given that only yesterday I'd seen evidence of the threads faintly echoing my emotions.

"As do I," she said. "But whatever the reason this siren creature is here, I fear she has not finished with my pack."

And I feared Katie was right. "Speaking of your mom, what do you know of her past? Why does she hate witches so much?"

"You mean aside from the fact she blames Gabe for my death, despite the fact I was already dying from leukemia?"

I smiled. "Aside from."

She wrinkled her nose. "Not much has ever been said, but I presume it had something to do with the attack on her sister when Mom was fourteen."

"Her sister's name?"

"Bryanna. I believe she'd just turned sixteen when the attack happened."

Any attack on a family member would be horrendous to deal with when you were only fourteen, but Karleen's hatred ran so deep that there had to be more behind it than that. "I take it a witch was involved?"

"I believe so, but Mom was never very specific about it."

Which didn't exactly help me any. "I don't suppose you know what year it occurred?"

"Mom's eighty-eight now, if you want to do the math." She grinned. "It was never my strong suit."

Eighty-eight in werewolf terms was probably the human equivalent of mid-to-late fifties. While a werewolf's capacity to heal all wounds did fade as age set in, they generally lived almost twice as long as humans.

"Did it happen here, or in another reservation?"

"She was born in the Axton pack, in Flintshire, which I believe is a county in North East Wales. Her dad's first name was James."

Which should at least give me a starting point, given most National Libraries and Archives—both here and overseas—kept records of not only birth and death notices, but also copies of newspapers, be it in paper, microfiche, or online.

Movement through the scrubby grass that ringed the clearing caught my attention, and I glanced quickly around. It was a bush mouse looking for some seeds to eat, but it was at that point I realized just how late it was. I glanced at my watch and saw it was close to six; I'd been up here a whole lot longer than it seemed.

I pushed to my feet. "I'd better go. I forgot to bring a

flashlight and don't want to be tackling that track in complete darkness."

Gabe raised an eyebrow. "Why not just create a light spell or even call in a will-of-the-wisp? You have before."

"With the possibility of a siren swimming through our lakes and rivers," I said, voice wry, "I'm feeling the need not to attract attention to myself."

"Wouldn't matter if you did," he said, amused. "You lack an attribute they prefer."

I grinned. "In this reservation, with my luck, there's every possibility we've attracted a bisexual siren."

Katie laughed. "Then the wild magic will accompany you down. No need for spells of any kind."

"Thanks." I hesitated. "One more question—I don't suppose you can tell me anything about Jerod O'Connor? Can you think of any reason why he might have been targeted?"

Katie shook her head. "As Aiden said, he was an omega. While they're a vital cog in keeping things running smoothly, they have no voice in the pack. It makes no sense for him to be called above others."

"Then let's hope we're all wrong and his death isn't the start of a murderous run on your pack."

"I'd rather hope she just moves on," Katie said.

So did I, but it was hardly likely a siren would journey all the way here just to kill one wolf.

I said my goodbyes and left. The luminous threads spun ahead of me, forming a longish net of fireflies that provided enough light to traverse the treacherous slope. Night had fully closed in by the time I reached the SUV, and the air had gained an icy touch. I shivered and quickly climbed into the SUV... and then noticed the smashed side window and the glass all over the passenger seat and floor.

My heart skipped several beats and I quickly turned around, energy pulsing across my fingertips, a wildfire of magic ready to unleash.

There was no one there, but the backpack was gone.

I swore and drew in a deeper breath to calm the annoyance that surged.

And smelled it... smelled *him*.

The man who'd butchered June had been here.

Chapter Five

The first thing I did was lock all the doors. I might be able to protect myself far better than most, but I'd learned the hard way not to take too many chances.

Up to a point, anyway.

I scanned the area, but no one appeared to be hiding in the trees that hugged the parking area's boundary. Of course, that didn't mean he wasn't waiting deeper in the forest.

There was a part of me that wanted to start the SUV and get the hell out of here, but I wouldn't be able to live with myself if, in doing that, another woman was put through the same torture as June. His scent said he was close enough to track. We had to at least try.

I tugged my phone out of my pocket and called Aiden. He was working the late shift this week, if I remembered the schedule correctly, so any call to the station would have been shunted through to him anyway.

"Lizzie," he said, voice sharp. "What's wrong?"

"I'm up at the parking area near Katie's wellspring. June's attacker broke into my SUV and stole my backpack."

He swore. "You okay?"

"Yes, but his scent is fresh, and if you can get someone here fast enough, we might be able to track him."

"I'm ten minutes away. Hold tight, and I'll see you soon." He paused. "Do not go after him alone. Not up there."

"I won't."

Mainly because while the Marin pack might have given me permission to park here and use the track up to the well-spring, I was forbidden to go anywhere else within their compound unless accompanied by a pack member or one of the rangers. The last thing I wanted was to do anything that would jeopardize my access to Katie and Gabe.

I studied the area again, then used the banking app to report the theft of my credit and ATM cards. At least most of the shops in Maldoon—aside from supermarkets and pubs—would now be closed, and even if he used the card's tap facility to grab food or alcohol, he wouldn't yet have had time to drain my accounts.

I crossed my arms and leaned back in the seat. I was briefly tempted to turn on the radio and listen to some music but resisted. If he came back, I wanted to be able to hear him.

Fortunately—or perhaps unfortunately, given I could have bound him with magic unless he was spell protected—he didn't reappear. Owls hooted from the trees, possums scrambled around searching for their next meal, and one rather chubby-looking wombat trundled past, looking thoroughly disgruntled over the fact he was forced to detour around the SUV.

Twin lights finally appeared in my rear view, pinning

the vehicle in brightness. A few seconds later, Aiden's truck pulled up beside mine. I climbed out, then hurriedly zipped my coat all the way up. The night's temperature had taken a nosedive toward freezing.

The wind hadn't picked up, though, so the ammonia scent lingered, even if it was much fainter than it had been. Aiden walked around to the back of his truck, pulled a couple of flashlights from one of the storage lockers, and handed one to me. "In case we need them."

I nodded, my fingers brushing his ever so slightly. Warmth flitted through my soul and flared briefly in his bright eyes.

But all he said was, "This way."

He didn't turn on the flashlight, and neither did I. The blanket of night was absolute as we moved deeper into the scrub and trees, but wolves could see several times better than humans in the darkness, and my sight now echoed that.

We initially headed across the hill rather than up or down, making good speed despite the thickness of the undergrowth, but soon began to climb. All the rain over the last few days had made the narrow trail treacherous, and though I slipped a couple of times, I always managed to catch my balance. Aiden offered help up a few rougher patches, then quickly released me, but that only succeeded in ramping up the tension growing between us.

Eventually I said, as much to break said tension as needing to know, "How come you were so close?"

"I was on the way back from investigating a break-in at a farmhouse not far from here."

His voice was even and friendly despite the tension that crackled between us, and I wasn't sure whether to be relieved or annoyed. Contrary, thy name is Lizzie.

"Did it happen tonight?"

"It was discovered tonight. I suspect it happened a day or so ago."

"Could it have been June's attacker?"

"The only thing taken was food, so if he's hiding out in the scrub rather than laying low in town, it's possible."

"I don't think he's in town, but I don't think he's camping out, either." I carefully navigated a particularly rough section of path—though calling it a path was something of a misnomer given it was little more than a faint roo track. "I think he's living in a remote house or farm."

He glanced briefly over his shoulder, his eyes blue diamonds in the darkness. "What makes you think that?"

I hesitated. "Gut feeling, nothing more."

He grunted, and we continued for a few minutes in silence. The terrain grew rougher and steeper, which to me suggested that if our felon was human, he was extremely fit. Either that, or he was part mountain goat.

"Did you get my text about drownings?" I asked.

"There are drownings in the reservation every summer," he said. "But there's been nothing at or close to that reservoir."

"And murders?"

"Again, nothing near that reservoir."

"Well, damn," I muttered. "That all but erases one possibility."

"One? You have others?"

I gave him a quick update and then said, "It's extremely rare for sirens to move location, though, which is what made me think it might have been the rusalka."

"There have to be other supernatural entities who use song to entice."

"You'd think so, but the database search didn't bring

anything else up. I've yet to check the books we haven't transcribed, though."

The hillside up ahead had collapsed, leaving a three-foot-high embankment that stretched a good way either side. Aiden leapt up, then turned and once again offered me a hand.

Though I didn't really need his help, I nevertheless clasped his fingers and let him haul me up. This time, he didn't immediately release me, and for several seconds, we just stood there, staring into each other's eyes, saying so much without saying a word.

Then a bittersweet smile twisted his lips, and he let me go and continued up the path. I followed, once again cursing fate for showing me what could be before forcing me to walk away in order to preserve what was left of my heart.

As we walked around another collapsed section, he said, "Did your research pull up a means of killing a siren?"

"Well, if you believe Greek mythology, they'll die if someone hears their call but wanders on by without answering. Apparently, it causes them to become so bereft they fling themselves into the water and perish."

"I'd have thought a creature capable of living in water would find it difficult to drown," he said, amusement edging his voice.

It was nice to hear that amusement. Nice to see it replace the tension that remained, however briefly. It gave me hope that we could make this situation work once the pain and hurt had faded.

"*That* is the fly in this particular ointment. There was a mention of a bronze knife dipped in a victim's blood, but I'm not entirely sure that's even practical."

"Blood is removed from bodies during the autopsy, so that in itself would not be a problem."

"Maybe, but the bronze knife might be." I pursed my lips. "I might ask Ashworth about it. He's been in the ghoulie-hunting business for a long time—it's possible he's got one tucked away somewhere."

"Bronze knives aren't rare, though. You can buy them on eBay and in most places where you can buy kitchen knives."

"Yes, but most bronze knives made these days have a steel core."

He grunted. "Let me know if Ashworth or Eli haven't got anything suitable. There're a few smiths in town who might be able to make something."

"Will do." I leapt over a small stream and then glanced around at the faint caress of energy. A tiny thread of wild magic was now tracking us through the trees to the right. Katie, not so inconspicuously seeing what we were up to. I smiled and added, "Are we still in Marin grounds?"

"Yes."

"Then how is it possible for him to be trekking through here without attracting attention?"

Aiden shrugged. "We're on the outskirts of their boundary, in an area that sees little human traffic. They don't do daily patrols in the winter months."

"Is that common knowledge?"

"Only amongst the packs."

While I might not believe our boy was a wolf, the fact he was moving through pack grounds without challenge seemed to suggest otherwise. "Is there anything up here? A hut or an old mine that he could be using?"

Just because instinct said he was living in a remote

farmhouse didn't mean we should totally ignore other options.

"There's a fire watch tower nearby. The Marin use it in summer on extreme fire days."

"I can't imagine a tower would be the best place to camp out."

"There's a hut on top."

I still doubted he'd be camping out. If this *was* about exacting a perverse sort of revenge on his mother, it's entirely possible he was still living with her. Or, at the very least, still living in their family home. "So why would he break into my SUV? It was a bit of a risk given he couldn't know it didn't belong to a pack—"

I cut the rest as the throaty roar of an engine shattered the silence.

Aiden swore and leapt forward, his form flowing from human to wolf in the blink of an eye.

I quickly created a tracking spell and cast it after him. It caught the tip of his disappearing tail and a golden thread of magic spooled out behind him, giving me a visible trail to follow. I raced after him, going dangerously fast over the rough ground, and yet I didn't fall or even slip once. It was as if speed somehow made my footing surer.

We came out of the bush onto a wide, barren summit. The fire tower dominated the space, the structure so tall that the hut on top looked minute. Aiden had already run through the middle of its wide metal legs and was chasing the car down the other side of the hill.

I stopped and leaned over, my hands pressed against my knees as I sucked air into my burning lungs.

That's when I smelled it.

Death.

I swore and looked around. The scent wasn't coming

from the scrub that lined the edges of the summit but rather from above. From the tower itself.

I raised my gaze. It had three platforms in all, with the first two being open structures and the top consisting of a metal fence behind which sat the hut. On top of its roof were a few antennas and a small satellite dish. Sturdy-looking metal stairs to the right of the structure led up to the first platform, then zig-zagged up through the middle to the next one. I couldn't see the final ladder from where I stood.

Other than the scent of death, there was no immediate evidence of foul play. Was it possible the smell wasn't human-based at all, but rather a roo—or perhaps even a deer —that had been killed and skinned somewhere nearby?

Possible, but unlikely, given we were in Marin grounds and it would have been simpler for them to take their prey back home.

I walked over to the stairs, but as I reached the base, Aiden reappeared and quickly shifted back to human form. His face was smeared with mud, and he was panting hard.

"Got close enough to get his number plate then shifted shape and sent it to Tara for a trace," he said, and then stopped abruptly. "Death and blood ride the air."

I nodded. "Coming from the hut area, I think."

"Any magic?"

"Not that I can sense."

"Then I'll lead."

I nodded and motioned him to proceed. He brushed past me, an altogether too brief moment of closeness, and then bounded up the steps. I quickly followed, keeping close on the off chance I'd missed something. The braided charm he was wearing should protect him from most magical and even demonic attacks, but it wasn't a hundred percent perfect. I might have broken up with the man but that didn't mean I wanted to see him hurt.

Though I supposed as far as hurting goes, I'd done a damn good job of that myself.

I pushed the random sliver of guilt away and concentrated on not falling over as we raced up. The first platform was empty, and there was nothing to see on the horizon except for the distant glow of lights coming from the various farmhouses dotted through the hills and scrub. We moved on, the metal stairs vibrating slightly under our weight. The second platform was half the size of the one below, with the stair up to the last platform dominating a good portion of its area.

Again, it was empty.

We climbed the last section more cautiously; aside from the fact we had no idea what waited above, this last bit was a straight ladder rather than zig-zag stairs. The scent of blood and death grew stronger as we neared the top, and every psychic bit of me said that, as much as I might wish it, we weren't dealing with a slaughtered animal.

Aiden paused a couple of steps below the platform and glanced down. "I can't hear or smell anyone on the platform, but wait while I do a quick check."

He leapt up the remaining two steps in one smooth motion and disappeared to the right. Though his steps were light, I could not only feel their vibration through the metal but "see" him through the thread of wild magic that trailed after him.

He did a complete circuit and reappeared above me. "Whatever we're smelling, it's coming from inside the hut. I take it you're intent on coming in?"

I raised an eyebrow. "How long have you known me?"

A smile briefly teased his lips. "I know, but one of these days you'll surprise me by doing the sensible thing."

"Your life would be boring if I did."

"If there's one thing no one could ever accuse you of being, it's boring."

I snorted and climbed the remaining steps. He caught my elbow to steady me, and the heat of him washed over me, warming the chill from my bones and pushing my pulse into a ragged dance. It would have been easy, so easy, to step closer, to brush my lips against his, to claim the kiss I'd been wanting since yesterday.

But that was a slippery slope from which there might be no coming back.

"Thanks," I said, and motioned him forward.

Frustration flared in his eyes but all he said was, "The door is this way."

I followed him around to the back of the structure, then stopped as he pulled on some gloves then gripped the handle, quickly thrusting it open.

The stench of blood and decay that washed out had my stomach threatening to rise again. I drew in several deep breaths to fill my lungs with fresh air and resolutely followed him in.

The darkness that briefly wrapped around us was filled with a violent mix of death and agony, and it was so damn strong that I briefly struggled to breathe. The urge to leave was so fierce that I took a step back before I could stop myself. This was ridiculous. I'd felt worse, *seen* worse, than what more than likely waited here. I could cope. I *could*.

Thankfully, there was no hint of a soul lingering in the darkness, confused and uncertain. This death, no matter how violent, had been ordained.

Aiden pulled the flashlight from his pocket and turned

it on. The sudden flare of bright light chased away the shadows and showed the death in all its bloody glory.

It was another older woman with short, silver-gray hair. Like June, this woman's mouth had been sewn shut, but her eyes had been cut out rather than burned.

Unlike June, he'd taken it one step further and slit her throat from ear to ear.

Her blood covered almost every surface of the hut's small interior except the back wall, which to me suggested that's where she'd been standing when he murdered her.

He would have been covered in her blood when he'd left this place, but maybe he didn't care. Or maybe it gave him a macabre sense of pleasure. Although, if he *had* been covered, surely we'd have seen some evidence of it on the stairs, and that suggested that maybe he'd waited for the dripping to stop.

"Fuck," Aiden said, that one word filled with the horror that echoed through me.

"Yeah." It came out little more than a croak, and I rubbed my arms in a vague attempt to ward off the horror that continued to run through me.

He glanced at me sharply. "You okay?"

I nodded, even though I wasn't. Even though I wanted to do nothing more than run from this death and from the man who could do this to defenseless old women.

Aiden looked unconvinced by my reply, but then, the man knew me well enough to know when I was lying. He returned his gaze to the victim. "This isn't a fresh kill. The color of the blood suggests it's at least a few days old."

I'd been so consumed by the amount that I hadn't even noticed it was a darker brownish color rather than the almost glossy red of fresh blood. "Which means she was killed *before* June, and that makes no sense. Why kill one and not the other?"

"It makes all the sense in the world if your arrival interrupted his plans."

I thrust a hand through my hair. "It would certainly explain why his scent had initially been so fresh in that hut. If I'd gone after him then—"

"June might well have died." Aiden put his flashlight down and pulled out his phone. "Besides, you didn't know the area, and it's possible he was armed with more than just a knife."

"I know but—"

"You did the right thing, so stop with the what-ifs. They never help." He glanced up at me. "While I make a record of everything, can you head out and ring the station? Tala should still be there."

I nodded, knowing full well he was giving me a reason to leave. I stepped out, made the call, then leaned against the metal barrier and breathed deep in an effort to remove the lingering wash of death from my lungs. It was then that I noticed the distant lights of Maldoon. If you could see them from this tower, it was more than possible our killer had spotted me arriving this afternoon and decided to investigate. My timing, it seemed, sucked. But at least it resulted in finding this poor woman's body.

I turned back. "If she was murdered several days ago, why would he have come back here this afternoon?"

"Possibly for no other reason than wanting to sit here and gloat."

I raised an eyebrow. "What makes you think that?"

"Smudges in the blood suggest he was sitting on the floor just in front of her."

I shivered. We definitely weren't dealing with a sound

mind. "If he was doing that, why would he then risk breaking into my car? Aside from the fact it's a fair old hike down there, his clothes would have reeked of her death."

"Most humans aren't aware how strong the death scent is, or how keenly a werewolf can smell it."

"What if he's a wolf?"

"Then maybe he doesn't care. Maybe he gets off on the scent of death as much as he does providing it."

How our killer got his jollies wasn't something I needed to think about. "It was still a big risk to take."

"If he *is* responsible for the break-ins around the area, he could be desperate, especially if his mother *is* dead. He might have been left without access to her accounts or money and has none of his own."

"We're dealing with a grown man rather than a teenager, so that surely can't be the case."

"Depends how dominating his mom was and how broken he was."

True. "I take it you're running a search through the death records to see if there's anything that matches what we're dealing with here?"

"I am indeed." He glanced at me. "We'll make a ranger out of you yet."

I smiled. "Thanks, but my current two jobs are more than enough."

Lights swept across the darkness, then a car appeared below. "That'll probably be Ciara," he said. "You want to head down and direct her up here?"

I nodded. "I'll contact Belle and ask if she can come pick me up. I take it you'll want to run the SUV for prints and evidence?"

"Yes. I'll drop it around to the café once we're done." He paused. "Am I still welcome to come in for coffee?"

87

"Of course you are." It might well be a test of our emotional endurance the first couple of times it happened, but we'd at least survived the last couple of days, and things between us would surely get better in the long run. They had to, because I really didn't want to lose him as a friend even if I could no longer have him as a lover. "And it'll give the gossip brigade something new to talk about."

He snorted. "As if they ever need more fuel for their fires. In fact, I wouldn't be surprised if they already knew about these murders and had multiple theories as to who is behind them."

I raised my eyebrows. "Have you actually asked them?"

"And risk the news of a possible granny killer spreading far and wide? No way."

I laughed, took the SUV's key off the ring, and tossed it to him. "I'll ask Belle to monitor their conversations. You never know, we might come across a nugget of information."

"Unlikely, but worth a shot."

"Aiden?" Ciara called from down below. "You up the top? Please say you're not. I'm not up to hauling my ass all the way up there tonight."

I turned and peered over the metal wall. "Sorry, we are."

"Of course," she grumbled. "Why would the murder be in a nicely accessible place like the ground?"

I grinned and glanced back to Aiden. "Sounds like she's having a bad day."

"More likely man trouble," Aiden said. "She's been dating several for a while now, and one of them has asked for her hand."

I raised an eyebrow, surprised more by the fact he was telling me that than Ciara having several boyfriends. Wolves really didn't do monogamy until their hearts had been taken —which, in many respects, made Aiden's forsaking other lovers and setting up house with me even more unusual. Maybe if he hadn't, I wouldn't have foolishly hoped for more.

"And this is a problem because...?"

"It wasn't the one she's keen on."

I laughed again and pushed away from the wall. "Let me know when you're dropping by with the SUV. I'll make sure we've got some brownies left."

"I will." His aura was bright with a dozen conflicting emotions. "Thank you."

I nodded and left before I did something stupid. Like tell him I was sorry, that I missed him, that I needed him in my life as more than just a friend.

All of which was utterly true but didn't change my determination to see this through and come out the other side whole and happy.

I clattered down the stairs, giving Ciara a nod in greeting as we crossed paths at the midway point, then reached out for Belle.

You called? came the somewhat breathless mental response.

I'm sorry, I said, *did I interrupt something?*

Yeah, interval training.

Is that the new code word for sex these days?

She mentally slapped me. *No, idiot, I'm at the gym.*

Have you finished?

Just about—why?

I need a lift, but I can ring Ashworth and Eli if it's easier. I need to talk to them anyway.

It's not a problem, but why do you need a lift? What has happened to the SUV?

It got broken into by June's attacker, and Aiden needs to check it for evidence.

Was it a targeted attack or just random, do you think?

Random. And yet, now that Belle had mentioned the possibility that it *wasn't*, I couldn't discount it. If he'd seen my arrival from the tower and somehow also managed to catch a glimpse of me yesterday, then maybe he broke into my car simply to see who I was. It was, in fact, a more likely scenario than just randomly deciding to track through rough bush for several kilometers on the off chance he might find something useful.

If he did break in to see who you were, Belle said, obviously following my thoughts, *then maybe you can use it to your advantage. Was your phone in the backpack?*

No, but my knife was. I've handled it enough that I could try tracing it via psychometry.

While I hadn't tried to trace anything of mine before, I couldn't see how it would differ all that much to tracing a customer's lost item. And it had the benefit of me not having to touch either the customer or their items and risk being overrun—however briefly—by their emotions.

It's worth a go. She paused. *You going to tell Aiden about the attempt or are we flying solo on this?*

I'll tell him if it amounts to anything. Right now, he and his team have their hands full.

That's an excuse, and you know it, she said. *How bad was it this time?*

Surprise flitted through me. *You didn't feel the wash of horror?*

No, but that doesn't surprise me. Your ability to shield has ramped up since you broke up with Aiden. I suspect it's an inner wild magic enhancement caused by your fear of overwhelming me with your emotions.

I doubt the changes would work that fast, but I do think it's a good development rather than a bad.

It's also fucking annoying. I mean, how can I help you if I can't even reach you?

I grinned. *I will always reach out if I need help.*

Only when necessary, and only if doing so doesn't risk me.

Which is a necessary step for when you and Monty get married and start having babies.

She did the mental equivalent of an eyeroll. *That is years off yet—*

Ha! So you concede you and he have a future together!

I concede nothing. Where are you?

At some old fire watch tower on the edge of Marin grounds. I'll send the coordinates to your phone. I paused. *I'm not sure what the road up here is like, so it might be wise to use the Suzuki rather than Monty's rattletrap.* Especially if its brakes still weren't fixed. The Suzi was also all-wheel drive, which meant it would cope better than the Ford if the road was particularly bad.

We'll do a change-over at the café, then, and head up.

We? You've convinced Monty to do intervals with you?

No, because it's his weights night. The man did not get his physique sitting on his butt eating cake, no matter what he tells you. See you soon, and keep dry if you can!

I sent her the coordinates, then walked over to one of the picnic tables sitting under the tower's legs and spent the time cruising all the social networks to see what was happening in the wider world. Interestingly, there was plenty of buzz coming from the various Canberra news sites about not only the upcoming court case against my father—who'd forced me to marry the now dead Clayton Marlowe when I was barely sixteen—but also the mediation case dealing with Clayton's will. The fact I'd inherited a good chunk of his estate had surprised the hell out of me, but according to my brother, it had been my "bride price." No one had told me about it, of course, and that was no doubt intentional. My father would probably have had the whole lot transferred into his name once I'd produced the heir Clayton had required. Clayton's family were naturally fighting that inheritance, but I had no doubt the prenup was watertight. My father did *not* muck about when it came to increasing the family's portfolio and prestige—and that's what the marriage had been all about.

That, and getting rid of the underpowered daughter he still held partially responsible for the death of the family's shining light and the woman who'd been slated to take over his position on the high council—my sister, Catherine. That she might still be alive if they'd only listened to me—believed my visions—didn't ever stir the faintest wisp of guilt through their collective consciences.

Of course, Clayton's heirs—and no doubt my family—believed I would give up that inheritance for what was basically a pittance in comparison to the estate's worth, but they were in for a rude awakening. I'd earned that money, not only in all the years we lived on the run, in fear of being found by him, but also for the terror and pain he'd inflicted on Belle.

In some respects, I was looking forward to going up there in a few days and showing them all they could no longer push me around. But I also feared it. Feared what my father or brother might do to Belle in an effort to control me. They knew about the wild magic, even if they didn't fully understand its implications, and that made me a valuable family asset for probably the first time in my life.

But I could worry about it once we were boarding the

plane rather than now; doing so would only lead to sleepless nights and indigestion.

I just hoped we solved these murders before we all had to leave.

I flicked over to Instagram and scrolled through the various cooking pages I followed to get some new cake ideas for the café.

Belle arrived twenty minutes later. The headlights briefly pinned me as she drove around the base of the tower and stopped closer to the table. I ran over and jumped in.

Neither of them had taken a shower, and the smell of their sweat was strong enough to have my nose wrinkling. I didn't mention it though, as them taking time to shower would have meant more time for me waiting in the bitter cold.

I tugged on my seat belt as Belle headed back down the dirt road and then said, "Can we grab something to eat on the way home? I haven't had dinner yet, and I'm starved."

"We can detour to Maldoon if you like," Monty said. "I've heard there's a new burger place open that has the best loaded fries in the reservation."

"While that is a pretty big claim, and one I'm happy to test out at a later date, right now, I've a hankering for a thick, juicy burger with the lot," I said. "How did the autopsy go this morning?"

"Burgers to autopsies... not what some would call a good segue." His voice was dry. "The results were, as expected, that he drowned."

"No sign of magic, I take it?"

"You were at the lake. If there had been, we would have spotted it then."

Maybe. And maybe I'd been too distracted by Aiden's

imminent arrival. "Was there any indication that he'd struggled?"

"No."

Frustration stirred. "I take it drowning will be the official cause of death?"

"Yes, because it was. And if you'd hadn't heard the siren's call, we'd be none the wiser." He shifted around in the seat to look at me. "Why is that, do you think?"

I hesitated. "It could have something to do with my growing link to the main wellspring. The threads of her power are not being contained by our magic these days, even if they're not venturing *beyond* the reservation's boundary."

Why I was so certain of that, I couldn't say. It wasn't like I'd done a boundary check lately to check the possibility. It was just a feeling....

"Main wellspring?" Monty raised an eyebrow, his expression annoyed even if his voice was mild. "That suggests this reservation has more than one; you've been keeping a big old secret from me, just as I suspected."

I swore softly and scrubbed a hand across my eyes. "It's not my secret to tell, and it's very well protected—as evidenced by the fact that neither you, Ashworth, nor Eli have had any sense of it."

"Would it have anything to do with Katie and her ghostly husband?"

"Yes, it does." I grimaced. "I'm sorry, Monty, but we couldn't risk telling you or anyone else about it. And you've got to promise not to say anything to Canberra. They can't ever know what's happened there."

"What *has* happened?" He glanced at Belle and then back to me. Realization stirred through his expression. "It's

Katie, isn't it? Gabe has somehow bound her soul to the wellspring, hasn't he?"

I sighed. There was little point in denying anything now. "Yes, and while she can use the wild magic to monitor the reservation, she can't do anything more at this point. She needs me to be her mouthpiece."

"Then the growing sentience we're seeing in the wild magic is due to her presence?"

"Actually, no, it's due more to *my* connection with the main wellspring."

He was silent for a moment, then said, "How was she infused? If such a spell existed, the council surely would have used it by now."

"Gabe cobbled it together from fragments of ancient spells he'd found," I said. "Can you imagine what the High Witch Council would do if they ever realized such an infusion was possible? I can, and it wouldn't be pretty."

He grunted. "I understand the need for secrecy—I'm just a little pissed that you both kept it from *me*. I mean seriously, I'm related to one of you and will eventually marry the other."

"And have you mentioned your marital intentions to your family yet?" Belle asked, rather pointedly. "Or are you keeping us a secret from them? Because hey, if you're against secrets being kept for good reasons then..."

She trailed off, and he grimaced. "Until you say yes, there's little point."

"Until you ask, one can't say yes. And no, that is *not* an invitation to ask." She pursed her lips. "I will inform you, however, that I do want the whole romantic, on one knee declaration before I'd even consider the question."

"Good to know," he said, then glanced back to me. There

was a glint in his eyes that suggested Belle might well regret making the "big, romantic declaration" thing a requirement. "When are you going to attempt to find your knife?"

"When I get back to the café—why?"

"Because I'd really prefer to grab a shower before we head out again."

My lips twitched. "I'd really prefer you did, too."

He laughed. "Is your nose *that* sensitive these days?"

"I'm afraid so."

"Then I shall deodorize Suzi before we hand her back."

I grinned. "Appreciate it. But nothing too strong."

"God, the two women in my life are such bossy bitches."

I laughed, and the conversation moved on. We grabbed our burgers and Monty's loaded fries in Maldoon, eating the former in the shop before sharing the latter on the way home. And I have to say, they did live up to the hype.

Once I'd made myself a cup of hot chocolate and shoveled a handful of mini marshmallows into it, I headed into the reading room. I thrust the table across a couple of feet to make room on the floor and sat cross-legged on the old carpet that covered the various runes we'd inked into the boards.

I took a sip of chocolate, then closed my eyes, breathing deep for several seconds to center my energy. Once calm had descended, I pictured the knife. Imagined its weight in my hand, the gleam of light off its silver blade. Felt the warmth of the stained brown leather that covered its handle. Once its image was fixed and real in my mind, I unleashed my psychometry ability.

For a second, nothing happened. Then the image briefly wavered, and a translucent, shimmering piece of string no thicker than a hair began to spool out from the butt of the imaginary knife. It snaked through the café and out the front door into the darkness and the rain.

For a second, the string paused, then it turned up the street and went across the road. On the other side, a dark-colored four-wheel drive was parked sideways across a couple of parking bays. There was a man in the driver's seat, and though his features were shadowed, he was large enough that his bulk dominated the space. Beside him, on the seat, was my backpack.

The bastard who'd attacked June and killed the woman in the tower was now sitting down the road from the café, watching me.

Chapter Six

I sucked in a breath and tried to calm the irrational rush of fear. He'd never get in here, not with all the magical protections around the place. He also wasn't a witch, but even if he were, if Clayton—who'd been one of the most powerful witches in Canberra—hadn't been able to unravel my spells, he surely wouldn't.

June's attacker couldn't harm me. Not unless I went outside. But that didn't make his presence any less unnerving.

I tugged my phone out of my pocket and rang the ranger station. There was a pause as the call was transferred, and then Aiden came on the line. "Ranger Aiden O'Connor speaking. How may I help you?"

"Aiden, it's me. Have you finished up at the tower yet?"

"For tonight, yes. It was just getting too dangerous up there with the thunderstorms coming in. I take it there's a problem?"

"You could say that." My voice was dry. "June's attacker is sitting in a Toyota four-wheel drive near the corner of Mostyn and Urquhart Streets."

Aiden swore. Violently. "You're all right?"

"I'm in the café and perfectly fine. I did a psi-search for my knife, and that's how I found him. My backpack is sitting on the front seat."

"He must have seen you yesterday. It would explain why he risked breaking into your SUV." He paused for a second, and in the background, I heard the blinker going. "I'll call Tala—she's the closest to you right now. Sit tight, and don't approach him. The knife might not be the only weapon he's carrying."

"I'm not silly, Aiden."

"I know you're not, but I'm also well aware that you sometimes leap before you think."

He hung up before I could reply. I picked up my hot chocolate and padded out of the room, then up the stairs. I didn't turn on any lights; aside from the fact I didn't need them, I didn't want my watcher to see me on the balcony. He was far enough away that he shouldn't, but I had no idea if he was using night vision goggles or binoculars or something else along those lines. Given how careful he'd been at both crime scenes when it came to evidence, anything was possible.

I slid open the glass sliding door but didn't step out onto the balcony. Instead, I leaned a shoulder against the doorframe and sipped my chocolate. It gave me just the right angle to see his car without being overly obvious, and if he *did* have some sort of night vision apparatus, it shouldn't raise any suspicions.

The four-wheel drive lay wrapped in shadows and rain, and from where I stood it was impossible to see if anyone sat inside. There was no light, and no obvious movement, and had it not been for my tracking attempt, I wouldn't have worried about the vehicle even if I had noticed it.

I took a sip of my drink, then quickly cast a locating spell around my free hand. According to Monty, who'd taught it to me, this spell differed slightly from a standard tracker in that it had no time restrictions, per se, but the signal could get lost if the subject moved out of range. Which wasn't a real problem, because it certainly wouldn't be the first time we'd driven around the reservation in an effort to find a tracker.

Once the spell was ready, I cast it toward the Toyota. It was a tumbling mess of untidy threads and definitely not my finest work, but as long as it did the job, it really didn't matter. It skimmed under the bumper bar and attached itself to the bottom of the vehicle. I activated it, then cocked my head, listening. The steady beat of the magic's pulse came through loud and clear. At least if he *did* move before the rangers managed to get here, we could find him.

In the distance, thunder rumbled, briefly drawing my attention away. A thick fork of lightning split the darkness, coloring the underside of the heavy clouds a soft pink. The intensity of the rain increased, and would no doubt get worse once that storm fully hit Castle Rock.

As I returned my gaze to the Toyota, it came to life. The headlights came on, its high beams briefly pinning the street below in brightness as the vehicle swung away from the parking bays, turned right, and disappeared up Urquhart Street. I cursed, dragged out my phone, and called Aiden.

"How close is Tala?" I said before he could say anything. "Because our killer is now on the move, heading north up Urquhart."

"She's still five minutes out, and I'm at least ten. I don't suppose you manage to cast some sort of tracker spell on him, did you?"

"I did indeed. Do you want me to grab Monty and go—"

"No," he cut in. "Given we're dealing with a human or a wolf rather than a supernatural being, we should be right without Monty's help once you find him."

"Finding him depends on how fast you get here. The locator has a limited range."

"Unfortunately, there's nothing we can do about that, other than to try and pick it up again tomorrow if we do lose him."

Which no doubt meant lots of tense hours spent driving about in his truck. Joy. "Okay. Tell Tala I'll meet her out the front."

I hung up, slammed the sliding door shut, and then headed downstairs.

So came Belle's comment. *We were right.*

Yeah. At least this means you and Monty can stay home and keep warm.

As you should. You're pushing your limits, Liz, and I really don't think it's wise.

I knew she meant physically rather than emotionally and, to be honest, while I might not have had much sleep of late, tiredness wasn't really a problem right now. Of course, having said that, I'd probably crash tomorrow.

It's not like I have any choice. It's my spell, and I'm the only one that can track it.

She didn't answer immediately, and I had the impression she was explaining the situation to Monty. *Monty says it is possible for one witch to track another's locator spell, but only if they're physically close—which would apply in this case because of the connection I have with you.*

Well, we're unlikely to be physically close any other way, because ew.

She laughed. *He said if you don't have any success tonight, he could tune into your spell's signal through me and take over the hunt. It's not like he has anything else to do at the moment.*

He does know that now he's put that thought out into the world, the shit will hit the fan?

I did say that. He called me a fatalist.

I snorted. If anyone was a fatalist, it would be me. Belle always tended to look on the brighter side of things. *I think it would be better if I go with him—unless the café gets too busy, of course.*

In this weather? Unlikely. But even if it did, Penny and Celia will both be there tomorrow.

Penny was the waitress who'd been with us since the beginning, and Celia was her niece. She'd started off part-time, but when I'd become assistant reservation witch, we moved her to full-time. It meant that even if darkness wasn't giving us grief, either Belle or I could take time out to do the books and the orders rather than doing them after hours.

Sounds like a plan, I said. *See you tomorrow.*

Be careful out there.

Always.

Her amusement shimmered down the line as she broke our connection. I swept my keys off the bench where I'd tossed them earlier, then headed out to wait for Tala. She appeared a few seconds later, pulling up right in front of the café so I didn't have to dash through the pouring rain to reach the SUV.

"Still heading down Urquhart?" she asked in a no-nonsense but not unfriendly tone.

I grabbed the seat belt and pulled it on. "For the moment, yes."

She grunted and did a quick U-turn before speeding back up the street. She was a typical werewolf in build—tall and rangy—and had the dark skin and wiry black hair of the

Sinclair pack, though hers was shot with silver. She was a lot older than Aiden, as she'd become a ranger in her thirties after trying out several other jobs first.

"What's he driving?" she asked.

"A black Toyota four-wheel drive."

She slowed the vehicle to get safely around the corner and then accelerated away again. "Did you get the plate number?"

"No. He was too far away, and I didn't want to do anything that might spook him."

She grunted. "He's obviously switched vehicles, because the registration Aiden gave me belonged to an old Ford sedan."

"That's no real surprise. The speed he was doing driving away from the tower suggests he might have been aware we were following him."

"It also suggests we're dealing with someone who knows a thing or two about evading the cops."

"Meaning he might have a criminal record?"

"Possibly, but until we know a little more about him, searching the database won't help."

"I take it the Ford was stolen?"

"Years ago."

I frowned. "Why would he risk driving a stolen car?"

She shrugged. "He may not know it's stolen. Thousands of cars are taken every year, and many are sold privately to interstate buyers. If the plates are changed, or if the new owner doesn't check the stolen car register or run a VIN check, then no one is any wiser."

The locator tugged us right, onto Barker Street. Before too long, we were on the Midland Highway, speeding away from Castle Rock.

But the locator's pulse was fading. Fast.

"He's on the freeway," I said. "And we're losing him."

Tala swore but was already pushing the SUV to its limits. It had no more speed to give.

We swept onto the freeway. The rain was so fierce that even with the wipers going full pelt it was difficult to really see anything. Even the headlights from the few cars going the other way were fuzzy and insubstantial. The SUV powered around a corner, the emergency lights washing blue and red across the barely visible trees that stood behind the crash barrier. The road remained empty, and the locator's signal was now intermittent.

A few kilometers farther on, I lost it entirely.

I blew out a frustrated breath as Tala slowed down. "Sorry."

She shrugged. "He had a good head start, so it's hardly your fault we lost him. At the very least, we now know he's using a black Toyota. White tends to be the color of choice for those sorts of vehicles here in the reservation, so it gives us a decent starting point."

I nodded. "And at least he won't suspect we know he's driving it."

"He didn't see you watching him or placing the spell?"

"No."

"Excellent. That gives us a better chance of finding him."

"If he hasn't ditched my backpack, I can probably attempt to find him again through psychometry."

She turned the vehicle around and then said, "With everything else that has happened, I think it's probably best if you rest up for the night. We can try it tomorrow if the regular methods get us nowhere."

I nodded, in truth more than a little relieved. Using psychometry to find my own stuff hadn't drained me anywhere near as much as finding other people, but I could nevertheless feel the wash of tiredness.

The rain was torrential by the time we arrived back at the café, the thunder so loud it was pointless even saying goodbye. I dashed inside, made myself another cup of hot chocolate with even more marshmallows than before, and then called Ashworth.

"Lizzie," he said, his Scottish accent a little heavier than usual this evening, "how are you coping, lass?"

I smiled. "I'm doing okay, but you sound as if you've had a few drinks. What's the occasion?"

"We generally don't need an occasion to imbibe fine whiskey, but in this case, it's our anniversary."

"You should have told me! I would have made you a cake."

"Lass, we eat enough of your lovely cakes as it is. Any more, and Eli won't be fitting into his pants."

"And Ashworth already doesn't," Eli said in the background.

I laughed. "Well, happy anniversary to you both, and sorry for interrupting your night."

"Don't be hurrying off, lass," he said. "You rang for a reason, so out with it."

"It's nothing that can't wait—"

"Nonsense. Get on with it."

I grinned. "Okay, it's just that I was talking to Gabe—"

Suddenly realizing I hadn't actually told them about Gabe, I cut the rest of the sentence off. But it was far too late.

"This would be the ghostly Gabe who haunts the second wellspring, I take it," he said blandly.

Surprise held me silent for several seconds, but eventually I croaked, "You know about that?"

He laughed. "You can't keep a secret like that from a canny old bastard like me for very long. But don't worry, it's a secret that's safe with me and Eli."

I puffed out a breath. "How did you find it?"

"Via the differences in the filaments that roam this place. The wild magic from the older wellspring has a very different resonance to that of the newer one."

Huh. I hadn't even thought about that, which was stupid, given it would be obvious to anyone who knew anything about wild magic and who'd been here long enough to study them.

"Why didn't you say anything?"

"We figured you'd tell us eventually," he said. "We did guess that your reluctance has something to do with Katie's death and Gabe's subsequent disappearance."

"It does."

"And she's the reason the wild magic is gaining sentience?"

"Partially. I'm the other reason—the magic within me seems to be merging with that of the older wellspring."

"Then it's even more vital Eli transcribes the book and uncovers what the hell all that means."

"Which is why I'm calling—tell him to look for any mention of the Fenna."

"Hang on while I put you on loudspeaker." He paused for a second. "Okay, what are the Fenna?"

I gave them a quick rundown of everything Gabe had mentioned and then said, "I don't suppose either of you have heard of them?"

"No," Eli said. "Though I did come across an early mention of energy channelers in the *Earth Magic* book, and it sparked a vague memory of an old professor who'd claimed that there'd once been witches who could channel the force of the wellsprings."

"Channeling a wellspring's force is very different to being bound to it via conception, though."

"Not if one is necessary for the other," Eli said. "Unfortunately, the professor died some twenty years ago now, but I believe he did write some papers on it. I've contacted his family, and they're currently going through what remains of his personal effects to see if there's any further information."

"His family?" I asked. "Why not the national witch library? Wouldn't all his research papers have gone there on his death?"

"Only those the high council deemed worthy," Eli said. "He was considered something of a maverick by many, and his theories regarding wellsprings were never given much weight."

"I take it they never bothered even exploring his theories?"

"There was one trial. It didn't go well."

"Given what Gabe said about the binding often resulting in a loss of all lives, that isn't surprising."

"No, but what *is*," Ashworth said, "is that Gabe was even able to find the spell that has bound Katie's spirit."

"He didn't have the complete spell. He recreated it from the various old snippets he'd found about wellsprings."

There was a long silence. "Which is why you were desperate to keep the second wellspring a secret," Ashworth said. "You didn't want Canberra descending on the reservation."

"And we both know they would."

"Indeed," Ashworth agreed. "I would be interested to speak to him at some point—once all the hullaballoo with the main wellspring attracting darkness has died down, of course."

"I'm surprised that you haven't already tried."

"Oh, he has" came Eli's comment. "But he was stopped before he got too far into Marin land and told unless accompanied by a ranger, he had no reason and no right to be there."

"When a Marin marches you off their property," Ashworth added, "they do so decidedly firmly. I had bruises coming out for at least a week."

"Why weren't you using a concealment spell?"

"I was. It was unraveled before I got to the wellspring."

"Gabe *did* raise a whole lot of protections around it before the spell killed him."

"And technically, those protections should have died when he did," Eli said. "That they haven't suggests he's either linked them to his presence or the wellspring itself."

"I never actually asked." In all truth, I hadn't even thought about it.

"It's one of the reasons I'd like to speak to him. I had no awareness of the unraveling spell before I walked into it and no time to examine it before a wolf appeared and I was escorted out."

"The wolf probably heard you." Concealment spells didn't hide sound, and no matter how cautious Ashworth was, the terrain was bad enough that sneaking was impossible.

"I did have a sound-muting spell active—"

"Trust me, that wouldn't have made much of a difference to the wolf if he'd been patrolling nearby." I sipped the hot chocolate. "The other reason I'm ringing is to ask whether you or Eli have a bronze knife."

"I do indeed, but why are you needing it? What has stepped into the reservation this time?"

"Some sort of siren, we believe."

"Really?" Surprise echoed through Eli's voice. "They're not known for moving beyond the sea. Even the few siren-like beings who lurk in fresh water rarely move out of their own territory, so something must have called it here."

"And it wouldn't be the wellspring's echoes of power," Ashworth said. "They're not interested in that sort of thing."

"Could a spell have called her here?"

"It'd have to be a pretty powerful spell. In Victoria, the only true sirens are found along the shipwreck coast portion of the Great Ocean Road," Eli said. "That's a very long way from here."

"And even if someone *had* cast such a spell," Ashworth added, "there's every chance we would have felt it. How many men has she called?"

"Only the one so far."

"And you're sure it's a siren because...?"

"I heard her song."

"Which should *not* have been possible." Eli's voice was grim.

"Katie suggested it's possible that my connection to the wellspring has somehow caused it to echo my grief and draw this entity to us."

"That is possible," Ashworth said heavily. "But it's also mythical law that sirens never call to the sisterhood, only to the men who betray them. Even if you are the reason it's here, you shouldn't be able to hear her."

"Mythical law isn't infallible."

"No, but it gives us a place to start. I'll contact a few

bods I know in Canberra and see if they can shed any light on what might be happening."

"Thanks. In the meantime, I'll let you go. Enjoy the rest of your evening."

"Oh, we most certainly will," Ashworth said, and hung up on Eli's laugh.

I picked up the TV remote and cruised through the various streaming services until I found something that wouldn't tax my brain too much, then grabbed a slab of lemon meringue pie and settled down on the sofa to while away the hours.

It was close to eleven when I heard the hauntingly beautiful song of our siren again.

I swore, grabbed my phone, and rang Aiden. At this rate, the man was going to think I'd brought trouble into the reservation just to have a legitimate reason to keep contacting him.

"Lizzie," he said, the alertness in his voice telling me I hadn't woken him up. "He hasn't returned, has he?"

"No, but I'm hearing the siren again, so we need to get out there and stop her before she kills again."

"Damn it, things just aren't giving us a break, are they? I'll be there in five."

"You're staying at the station?"

"It's easier when I'm on call."

He'd been on call a lot when we'd been together, and he'd always taken the calls from his place in Argyle without a second thought. Perhaps I'd been right in thinking he was staying away to avoid the memories it would evoke.

"I'll be waiting out front," I said and hung up. I tucked my phone into my back pocket, then ran downstairs to the reading room. I might have lost the backpack and my silver knife, but I still had plenty of charms that might be useful, and holy water worked well against almost anything. Thankfully, we'd found a local priest more than happy to bless as much of the stuff as we needed in exchange for a good donation to his church.

I shoved everything into a spare backpack, then grabbed my coat and keys and headed out again. Aiden pulled up a few seconds later and leaned across the seat to open the passenger door for me. I jumped in, belted myself up, and then said, "Swing around. The song is coming from the same general direction as last time."

Aiden did a sharp U-turn, the truck's tires sliding sideways on the wet road surface before they caught and hurtled us forward.

"Have you any idea why the hell this thing is hunting in my pack's grounds?"

I hesitated. "It's possible her proximity is nothing more than chance. That reservoir is one of the larger bodies of water in the reservation."

"Actually no—there are at least three others that are bigger," he said. "I don't think this is happening by chance. It feels targeted."

I thought he was right, but I was loath to admit that until we had some proof. But tonight might just provide that proof if we didn't get there in time.

"As of now, there's no real evidence to back that up."

He cast me a somewhat dark glance. "What, your intuition is silent?"

"Mine is, yes, but that doesn't really matter when others are having visions."

He raised his eyebrows. "What others? Belle? Your second sight has leached over to her, hasn't it?"

I directed him left and then right. We were definitely heading in the same direction. If she'd claimed that reservoir as her home, then maybe we simply needed to find a means of either forcing her on or removing her permanently.

"Yes, but in this case, I'm talking about Katie. She believes the pack is being targeted and that it has something to do with your mother's actions against me and my connection to the wellsprings. She also believes your mom will pay a very personal price."

The glance he cast me was sharp. "Sirens don't attack women, do they?"

"No, but we don't yet know if we're actually dealing with a siren, especially given I'm hearing her song."

"Which means I'll need to talk to Mom." His voice was grim. "And *that's* certainly something I've been avoiding."

"She's your mom and your pack leader. You can't avoid her forever."

"I can if I deal solely with my father. She's really not necessary to my life or my job."

I reached out and placed a hand on his thigh—an automatic gesture I just couldn't control. His muscles leapt under my fingers, then his hand came down on mine and lightly squeezed. "Aiden—"

"I know what you're about to say," he cut in softly. "But after inviting Mia back here without even consulting me, well, I'm done with her."

So, Mia was his last straw. Not me. Not the way she'd treated me.

I guessed that said it all.

I slid my hand from under his and said, "Right into McIvor Street."

He obeyed. His expression was a mix of frustration and anger, and I suspected it was aimed at me as much as his mother.

But he knew how to fix us. He just didn't love me

enough to confront the pack and demand they accept his choice in partner.

And I *did* understand why—I really did. He was an alpha born and couldn't settle for anything less than leadership, even if it cost him his heart.

Understanding didn't make accepting it any easier, however. Not for either of us.

He slowed the truck as we drew closer to the reservoir and then said, "We going in?"

I hesitated, listening, then shook my head. "The song is reaching its peak, but it's not coming from the reservoir."

"Meaning she can move around. Not a good development."

"But also not unexpected. I mean, if we're not dealing with a home-grown rusalka, then she either came here overland or through the waterways."

He frowned. "Sirens can't leave the water, though, can they?"

"That depends on which myth you're reading. Some of the older ones say they have the ability to transform into birds, snakes, or even humans."

"It would be nice if just once this damn reservation could attract a nasty that's simple to find and kill," he grumbled.

I couldn't help smiling. "As the wash of the wellspring's power begins to fade, it *will* stop attracting higher-level demons and dark spirits."

"Something to look forward to, for sure."

His tone was dry, and my smile grew. But it didn't last for long, as the haunting call reached a peak and then cut off abruptly.

The ensuing silence was eerie. Frightening.

"Next left," I said urgently. "She's got someone."

"The next left is a gateway into a vineyard," Aiden said. "Is that the one you mean?"

"Yes." I gripped the front dash as the truck slewed sideways and he accelerated through the open gateway. The dirt road swept along the edge of vine rows that filled the paddock to our right edge but on the left, there was nothing except long green grass. The gravel road began to rise sharply, then a sweeping turn revealed a large dam.

"There," I said, pointing. "She's there."

He braked so hard, mud slammed past the front of the truck, briefly blocking the headlight's glow. While he called in help, I grabbed the backpack, then leapt out and slid down the steep slope, barely keeping my balance on the slick stony ground. Thunder rumbled overhead, and the rain pelted down with renewed force. A thick fork of lightning struck the old gum sitting high on the banks of the dam, splitting it in half. In that brief but fiery explosion, I saw the figure floating facedown in the middle of the water.

Wild magic stirred frantically above him.

Aiden slipped down the slope and joined me on the edge of the water. "Ah, fuck, we're too late."

"No, we're not. There's still a chance we can revive him."

"Is she still in the water?"

"I can't feel her, but hang on." I quickly bent and dipped my fingers into the dam. There was no sense of anything other than emptiness and death. "She's not here now, but that doesn't mean she won't come back. I'll have to go in."

His expression suggested he did not think *that* was a good idea. At all. "It's freezing both in the water and out— you'll get hypothermia before you get back to the shore."

Then you'll just have to warm me up... I shoved the

admittedly delicious thought away and began stripping off. "And if she comes back and attacks you, I'll be going in anyway. It's safer this way."

"Safer for me, not for you."

"I have magic to call on. You don't."

"That does not, in any way, ease the worry."

It didn't ease mine, either, but I wasn't about to admit that. I finished stripping off, rolled all my clothes into a ball, and tucked them into my coat. At least I'd have something warm to get back into, because he wasn't kidding about the night's chill. I hated to think how much colder it might be in the water.

"No matter what happens," I said, stepping into the water and barely holding back my gasp. "Do not come in."

"If you get into trouble, I will not just stand here and do nothing."

It was said with such savagery that I glanced back at him. His eyes were glittering blue spots of anger. "Aiden—"

"Don't bother finishing that," he cut in. "I have no intention of permanently losing you, so don't get into trouble, and everything will be fine."

A myriad of different emotions welled within, and I was suddenly blinking back tears. I continued on. When the water hit my nether regions, I gasped again, this time out loud, and then dove in and swam out. The storm of wild magic above the stranger's body made him glow, but I wasn't getting much in the way of information about who it was, which suggested Katie hadn't gotten here in time to see.

I reached the floating form and, using a mix of physical and magic strength, flipped him over. Katie's emotions surged, smashing through every shield I had protecting me from the sensory input of others and utterly swamping me.

The weight of them was so fierce and heavy it forced me down, under the water.

The wild magic caught me, dragged me back up to air.

Sorry, she said, her tone broken. *I didn't mean...*

It's okay. Just... keep back and let me do this.

"Liz" came Aiden's frantic shout. "You okay?"

"Yes. Fine. Coming back now."

I tucked my hands under the stranger's armpits and pulled him closer, resting his head on my shoulder while allowing his body to float out in front of me, then kicked back to the shore. It seemed to take forever, but the dam wasn't that big, and it probably only took a few minutes.

Aiden waded out into the water once we were close enough, then stopped abruptly, his face twisting with grief.

"Aiden?" I said through chattering teeth. "What's wrong?"

He sucked in a deep breath that didn't in any way ease his grief. It swirled through his aura, fierce and bright, and that, combined with the weight of Katie's reaction, told me it was someone close to home.

"It's my uncle, Josh O'Connor." His gaze met mine, his eyes bleak. "He's Mom's brother."

Chapter Seven

At least it wasn't his dad... But, in reality, his uncle was no better. Especially when said uncle was also Karleen's brother.

It *did* explain the sheer weight of Katie's grief.

Aiden grabbed the man from me and then reached down, gripped my arm, and helped me up.

"Are you all right?" he asked, his gaze sweeping me critically.

I nodded and crossed my arms in a useless attempt to warm my breasts. They hurt. Everything hurt—ached—with the cold.

He didn't look convinced but nevertheless released me and dragged his uncle onto the shore, where he cleared his mouth and nose of water and then began CPR.

I padded across to my coat, cursing the cold and the continuing rain as I hastily pulled on my clothes and shoes. It didn't warm me up any. If anything, it made me feel even worse, thanks to my underclothing soaking up the moisture and clinging wetly to my skin.

But I didn't say anything. I just stood there, shivering, as

Aiden performed CPR and the luminous threads of wild magic circulated above him. Katie, urging him on, praying for a miracle.

I wasn't entirely sure one would be in the offing.

Katie, I said, as much to keep my mind off the numbing cold as needing to know, *did you arrive before or after Josh was killed?*

Before. Her sorrow echoed through me again, and I found myself blinking back tears caused by her pain. *But I was coming up from behind him, and the threads in front were unable to see who it was.*

I frowned. *Why not?*

There was a barrier between us. An invisible forcefield of some kind. No matter what angle I viewed him from, I couldn't see who it was. I couldn't even hear her.

If both were invisible, how did you know someone was even there?

The barrier emitted a slight buzz that pulsed weirdly through the wild magic's particles. It was that wrongness that drew me here in the first place.

Did you see the siren? Did she emerge from the water once he dove into it?

I believe so, but again, she was invisible to my sight.

I frowned. If she'd been visible to her victim, she should have been visible to anyone else who was watching. *Does Gabe know why?*

She hesitated, suggesting she was asking him. *He said given she appears to be targeting specific men, it's possible the magic in her song stops others from seeing or hearing her. It would explain why only one is answering her call rather than many.*

If that were true, then it was even more likely Aiden's pack *was* being deliberately targeted.

And *that* was definitely not a good thing.

The sound of approaching emergency vehicles washed across the darkness and, a few minutes later, an ambulance and an SES truck pulled up. The paramedics scrambled down the hill with their gear and took over CPR while the emergency boys dragged a stretcher from the rear of their truck.

Aiden stepped back to my side and swept a hand through his wet hair, his face grief stricken. There were tears in his eyes, but I couldn't see if they tracked down his cheeks thanks to the rain.

I couldn't just stand here while he was in so much pain....

I turned, wrapped my arms around his neck, and pulled him close. His arms immediately snaked around my waist, and he held on tightly, his breath warm against my neck and his body shaking with grief. We stood there in the rain and the cold, not saying anything, not needing to say anything.

For a few precious minutes, we were one again.

"Ranger?" one of the medics said. "We're going to need your help getting him up the slope."

Aiden dropped a brief but somehow intense kiss on my forehead, then stepped away from our embrace and walked over to the medics. The night felt colder. Lonelier.

Josh was placed onto a stretcher, his breathing now assisted by bag mask ventilation. With the four men on each corner of the stretcher and one of the medics working the bag, they began the long climb back up the hill.

I followed, but my feet were so numb with cold that I slipped numerous times, bruising my knees and scraping my hands. I didn't really feel either, though no doubt I would once I started warming up.

By the time I reached the top of the hill, Aiden was

standing outside the ambulance, watching his uncle being hooked up to various machines.

I stopped beside him. "You need to go to the hospital with him."

He glanced at me. "I need to get you home and warm."

My smile was edged with sadness. "I'm not your priority here, Aiden, and your mom will never forgive you if something happened to your uncle without a family member by his side."

His expression gave little away, but his aura's emotive swirl said plenty. He knew I was right. He just didn't want to accept it.

One of the medics glanced at us. "You coming or not? We need to get moving."

Aiden hesitated, then slipped the truck's key free from the keyring and handed it to me. "Are you sure you'll be okay to drive? I can ask—"

"I'll be fine, Aiden. Go."

He hesitated again, his gaze flickering briefly to my lips, then he climbed into the back of the ambulance and claimed the empty seat. The ambulance driver jumped out, slammed the rear doors shut, and then said, "We'll need you to move the truck—we can't turn around here."

I retreated to the truck, climbed into the driver's seat, and started her up. After turning the heat up to full blast, I continued down the rough old track until I found a wide, flat paddock that made the perfect turn-around point. I drove in, then moved out of the ambulance's way, letting it and the emergency services truck turn around and head to the main road before following.

I was almost home by the time my teeth stopped chattering, but ice seemed to have taken up residence in my bones. I parked the truck behind our building and dashed upstairs, throwing Aiden's key onto the kitchenette's bench before stripping off and jumping into the shower. It took a good ten minutes before I felt less like an ice block and more like my normal self. I half thought about grabbing another hot chocolate, but it was close to two now and I really needed to sleep.

Or at least attempt to.

I dragged on my winter pj's and crawled into bed. Surprisingly, I was asleep almost before my head hit the pillow.

Unsurprisingly, I dreamed, but it was a mess of teeth, torn flesh, and the brutal need for revenge combined with bloody lips and sightless eyes. Which no doubt meant two things.

Our granny killer hadn't finished his bloody work.

And Karleen was coming for me.

* * *

The soft ding of an incoming message woke me. I reached out sleepily and swept my fingers across the bedside table until I found my phone, then pried open an eye to look at the screen.

It was barely five, and the message had come from Aiden. *You awake?*

My heart did what felt like a backflip. I hastily sent back, *Am now. Everything okay?*

Sorry, didn't mean to wake you—

It's fine, I replied. *I have to get up soon anyway. How's your uncle?*

Alive, thanks to you, but he remains unconscious. The doctors are unsure why.

Probably shock.

Though according to a side note in one of Nel's books, siren survivors often risked being "lost forever in the beauty of the song and unable to find their way back."

There were also plenty of older legends that described sirens as beings who consumed flesh, souls, or 'life's energy.' The latter would have aged his uncle dramatically, though, and that obviously hadn't happened, because Aiden would have said something. Josh also hadn't appeared to have chunks taken out of him, and the fact he remained alive perhaps put a question mark on her being a soul sucker. If she'd taken his soul, he wouldn't be alive.

Unless, of course, she simply hadn't had the time to fully feast on it thanks to Katie's arrival. And if that were the case, then it would certainly explain why he wasn't responding to treatment. A body needed a full soul in residence to function.

Do you think Belle will be able to help him? he sent back. *Perhaps she could reach into his mind and help him find a way back to consciousness?*

It's not so much a case of can she, but whether your mother will be willing to let her try.

I flipped off the blankets and padded out to turn on the heating. The storm had finally eased, but the upstairs living area was an icebox.

I'll talk to Dad. He'll make it happen.

I wasn't so sure about that, but I guessed it did depend on just how much she valued her brother's life. *Are you still at the hospital?*

No, walking back to the station.

Then why don't you come by for breakfast... if you'd like to, that is.

You sure?

Wouldn't ask if I wasn't.

122

Be there in ten, then.

I pulled on my work clothes, shoved my feet into my Uggs, and then grabbed his car key and padded downstairs, turning on the lights and the café's heating as I did. After filling the kettle, I went into the kitchen and fried up bacon and eggs. Minutes later, the bell above the door chimed softly, and the delicious aroma of musk and man drifted toward me. I couldn't help smiling happily.

Would I ever get over the sheer joy of seeing him every day?

Probably. One day. In the very distant future.

If I didn't, it was going to be tough to find someone else to fill the hole he'd left.

I fought the desire to throw myself into his arms and kiss him senseless and plated up the bacon and eggs instead. He swept his car key from the counter, then walked into the kitchen, looking worn out, physically and emotionally.

I handed him his breakfast and the plate of toast. "It's not the brownies I offered yesterday, but it's the next best thing."

My voice was perhaps a little too bright. Too forced. There was something in his eyes that said he understood why.

I grabbed everything else and followed him out into the café. After dumping it all on our table, I re-boiled the kettle to make him a coffee and me another hot chocolate with lashings of marshmallows and cream. Sometimes a girl just needed the boost of calories, and eating an intimate breakfast with the ex you still loved was definitely one of those times.

Amusement twitched his lips when he saw the hot chocolate. "Isn't it a little early for dessert?"

"It's never too early for dessert, my friend, and you should know that by now."

Our gazes met as I said that, and desire ignited between us, the scent so thick and rich that my pulse skipped into overdrive and the deep-down ache woke to fierce life. I knew he was thinking of all the times breakfast had led to the "dessert" of lovemaking; knew because I saw it in his eyes and because I was thinking exactly the same thing.

I wished... but wishing would get me nowhere. Neither would giving in to the attraction that still burned between us.

I pulled my gaze from his, handed him his coffee, and then slid into the seat opposite. "I take it your parents are now at the hospital?"

"Yes." His lips twisted. "And they want to know what the hell is going on."

"You told them about the siren?"

He nodded. "I also told them we have no idea why she appears to be targeting not only our pack, but our line."

I picked up my knife and fork and started in on my breakfast. "Did you mention Katie's warning to your mom?"

"I did." He grimaced. "It did not go down well."

"I'm thinking that means she basically accused me of either spelling or calling this evil into existence in order to get back at her."

And of course, it was utterly possible I *was* the reason for her presence here. I might not have spelled or summoned the siren into existence, but if strong emotions like anger could draw darkness to an area, why not grief? The grief over a breakup might not have anywhere near the pull of loss or death, but if the wellsprings had somehow amplified my emotions?

All bets were off.

"She did say something along those lines. I told her not to be so fucking stupid." A smile tugged at his lips but held very little humor. "It's the first time in years I've seen her come close to launching at me."

I blinked. "Your mother was on the verge of *attacking* you?"

"Dad talked her down, but yes." He shrugged, though I suspected his nonchalance was nothing more than a front, simply because I could see and feel the anger simmering underneath. "It happens quite often when pups are young and being particularly rowdy."

"You're hardly a pup."

"No, but sometimes alpha instinct takes over before the brain can catch up."

I suspected it was more a case of her being unable to think with any degree of clarity when it came to witches in general and me in particular. I picked up a piece of toast, slathered it with butter, then swirled it through my egg yolk. "You need to ask her what happened to make her hate witches so much. It stems from more than just her conviction I'm an unsuitable partner for you, Aiden."

"I'll ask when she's a little less... volatile. It hasn't been a good month for her."

It was on the tip of my tongue to say it hadn't been a good month for *any* of us, but that would have been crass, given she not only had one son still doing rehabilitation, another who was basically refusing to have anything to do with her, and now she'd possibly lost her brother.

Anyone would be a little volatile after all that.

No, most wouldn't, came Belle's comment. *You're being altogether too generous when it comes to that bitch.*

Of course I am—if fate decides to toss me a miracle, she'll become my mother-in-law. I quickly finished my toast and

125

reached for another piece. To say I was hungry was some-thing of an understatement. *What are you doing up at this hour? It's not even six yet.*

Monty wants to get an early start on hunting down your granny killer, and I might as well go see Aiden's uncle before we open up for the day.

But it's still dark out there.

Magic works at night just as well as in the day, Belle said, amused.

Yes, but Monty and early starts have never been bosom buddies. Of course, that was before Belle had started sharing his bed....

She didn't say anything, but the wisps of satisfaction washing down the line all but confirmed *that* thought.

"I take it," Aiden said, his voice dry, "that you're in conversation with Belle? Dare I ask what about?"

"Monty wants to get an early start hunting down our granny killer, and Belle said she'd go see Josh this morning, if you want."

"Sounds like a good plan to me."

"You can't be in two places at once, Aiden."

"No, but Belle doesn't need my help at the hospital."

"She will if your mom's there."

"She's not. Mac's on guard, and I've already instructed him to give Belle access."

I frowned at him. "Even so, shouldn't you be resting? Tala or one the other rangers is perfectly able to accompany us on this search."

"They certainly are, but it's not like I'll be able to sleep anyway, so I might as well keep going."

"Even werewolves need to sleep sometime, Aiden. The last thing we need is you—"

"As you keep telling me, I'm fine." His smile held little humor. "Right now, I just need to work."

I understood that need perfectly, given I was basically doing the same thing. But him working himself into the ground was far more dangerous than it was for me.

Not really, Belle said. *He might be a ranger and he might deal with plenty of lowlifes, but you're this reservation's conduit. Your fall could endanger everyone.*

I think you're being overly dramatic.

Not given what Gabe and Eli have said.

They said nothing along those lines.

It was implied.

I snorted. *I think you were listening in to a very different conversation.*

Perhaps it's more a case of me being more open to conversational undercurrent. In many ways, you're still fighting the merger—

I can't fight something I can't stop, Belle.

There are different ways of fighting, and we both know that. We'll be there in fifteen minutes. Monty said he expects bacon and eggs to be waiting.

Tell my dearest cousin he knows where the kitchen is.

She laughed. *I did tell him you'd say that. He said he'll settle for cake and coffee instead.*

I smiled and, as the mental line went dead, said to Aiden, "They're on their way."

He picked up his coffee and leaned back in his chair, his expression giving little away. "Will you be coming with us?"

I nodded. "Monty said it's possible he could track my spell once I explain its construction, but it's simply easier if I do."

"And the siren? Any idea how we're going to stop it hitting any more members of my family?"

I hesitated. "If they can't hear the song, they can't respond to it. Is it possible for you to order the men in your pack—including you—to start wearing earplugs?"

Amusement ran through his expression. "Really?"

I nodded. "In all the legends, not hearing a siren's song is the only way to avoid them. It would only be at night, given that's when she seems to be active."

"I'll tell them."

"It would probably have to include kids as well. She hasn't sung to them up to this point, but that doesn't mean she won't."

"God, I hope she doesn't. Things are fraught enough as it is."

I couldn't help the tight smile. "If your mother attacks me, Aiden, I will defend myself."

"I would expect nothing else. But she won't."

"I wished I shared your positivity."

"Mom is... complex, I'll grant you that, but she loves this reservation and won't do anything to endanger it. She's well aware of your family's standing and won't risk bringing your father's wrath down on us."

Once I would have laughed at the thought of my father in any way caring what someone said or did to me, but now that he knew about my ability to manipulate the wild magic, he deemed me a valuable asset.

Once—when I was very young and foolish—I would have welcomed such a development. Now I saw it for the gigantic pain in the ass it was. I did *not* need or want my family stepping back into my life. I had a found family here in the reservation, and they were all I now needed.

"I still think you need to talk to her about her hatred," I said flatly. "Because if this situation gets any worse, it may well blind her to reason."

Whether it would make any difference to the bloodshed I was seeing in my dreams was another matter entirely.

"I will. I promise."

I nodded and, without looking up at him, swished another bit of toast through the last of my eggs. Then, after snagging the last bit of bacon on the plate and munching on it, I pushed to my feet and returned to the servery to make Monty's coffee and cut a slice of the banana and walnut cake. It was the closest thing to a breakfast cake we currently had in the fridge.

The two of them came in a few minutes later, so full of brightness and energy it made me feel old.

Well, Belle said, in that "mother knows best" tone she had a habit of taking on lately when she was about to lecture me, *if you got some decent rest and took some time off, as we've suggested, you'd be feeling a whole lot better.*

Rest doesn't cure heartache.

No, but it'll stop you collapsing at the wrong moment if either of the current investigations goes south.

I snorted mentally, put everything onto a tray, and carried it over to the table.

"You are the best," Monty said, immediately picking up the spoon and digging into the rich cake.

"Anyone would think you don't feed that poor man," I said.

"I think he was a hobbit in a past life," Belle said, her voice dry. "He needs first and second breakfasts."

"Are we talking about food here?"

She spluttered into her coffee but didn't reply. She really didn't need to when Monty's Cheshire Cat grin said it all.

I reclaimed my seat next to her and picked up my hot

chocolate. "Have we got a search plan or are we just going to randomly drive around until I pick something up?"

"Given he was heading north up the highway," Aiden said, "we'll start there, then sweep around the reservation's borders and work in from there if necessary."

"What if he's left the reservation entirely?" Monty asked.

Aiden hesitated. "I don't think he has. Call it a gut feeling, but I think Liz is right and he's bunkered down in an out of the way place somewhere in the bush."

"Isn't *that* just what this reservation needs," Belle said dryly, "yet someone else working on instinct."

"Ranger work always involves a degree of gut feelings and instincts." Aiden's phone dinged. He pulled it from his pocket and glanced down. "The council have called a general meeting at one and want me there to give an update. If we haven't found anything by twelve, we'll take a break and resume tomorrow."

I frowned. "The council meeting shouldn't take that long, so why not resume after that?"

"Because I've seen the toll magic takes on you, and five hours searching is long enough." He put his phone away then rose. "I need to make some calls—meet you out in the truck in, say, ten minutes?"

I drank my chocolate and watched him leave. Knew I was going to have to get used to the sight of him walking away on a permanent basis even if my heart currently refused to entertain any such thought. Belle touched my arm, drawing my attention. "You're doing well."

"It's not my relationship with him I'm worried about," I muttered. "It's the one with his mother."

Monty raised an eyebrow. "Meaning?"

"Nothing." I grimaced and pushed up. "I need to get into some warmer gear. Shall I meet you in the truck?"

He nodded, though his suspicions followed me up the stairs. Belle didn't enlighten him, though she was well aware I'd dreamed again last night, even if she didn't know the specifics.

I kicked off my Uggs, then pulled on a thicker sweater, woolly socks, and my hiking boots. While there was a good chance we'd find absolutely nothing, the boots were a precautionary measure. Aside from the fact they were waterproof, they'd also give me plenty of grip if we had to go cross country again.

I shoved my phone and keys into my pockets, then grabbed my coat and headed out. Monty was sitting in the truck's front passenger seat beside Aiden, which was a relief. I really didn't want to be that close to the man for the better part of the morning. It would be just too... distracting.

We headed out of Castle Rock and onto the highway, cruising along at a good clip until we reached the town on the reservation's northern boundary. I had no sense that our target was close, so we tossed a coin and headed left, working our way toward Maldoon and then on to Carin-brook. Dawn rose, sending her flags of pinks and oranges across the sky, but the first drops of rain were now drifting across the windshield, and the storm the weathermen were promising didn't look all that far away.

None of us talked, but the silence wasn't tense, and that was a good sign. The three of us needed to be able to work together for many years to come.

We were sweeping the western edge toward Creswyn when I felt the first faint pulse along the magical lines. I straightened abruptly. "Got him."

Monty's head snapped around. "Seriously?"

I nodded. "It's a very faint signal, so he's still some distance away."

"Faint is better than absent," Aiden said. "There's a left turn just ahead—we taking it, or continuing on?"

I hesitated. "Straight."

He flicked on the emergency lights but not the siren, and we sped through Creswyn and out the other side.

"Next left," I said, as the locator's pulse grew stronger.

"That road," Aiden commented, "just happens to skim the Sinclair pack's boundary."

I frowned, instincts twitching, though I wasn't sure why. "He seems to have an affinity for pack grounds, doesn't he?"

Aiden made the turn, then glanced at me through the rearview mirror. "June wasn't found near pack grounds."

"No, but his first victim was." I paused. "Did you get an ID on her?"

"Yeah, her name was Doris Brown, and she ran sheep out Moolort way."

"Where's that?"

"Between Maldoon and Carinbrook."

"When was she reported missing?" Monty asked.

"Three days before June was snatched. We found her car abandoned just past the Moolort turnoff, but there was no trace of her."

"No scent trail?" I asked.

Aiden shook his head. "By the time we got there, the storm had washed away any possible trace evidence she or the man who snatched her might have left."

"If there wasn't any damage to her car—"

"And there wasn't," Aiden said.

"Then she must have known her attacker."

"Or he flagged her down for help. Folks in that area wouldn't have thought twice about stopping."

"Most country folk don't," Monty said. "But if the time between his attacks on June and Doris is anything to go by, its likely he's already on the hunt for another victim."

"Which is why it's vital we find him today," Aiden said.

No pressure then, I thought grimly.

We entered an area of thick forest, the right side being the boundary line for the Sinclair compound while the wilderness to the left was public ground. I couldn't help but wonder if the pack had trouble with hikers trespassing, as there didn't seem to be much in the way of signs warning they were about to enter wolf territory.

The locator's pulse continued to gain strength, its voice so loud in my head now that it felt like a second heartbeat.

"Right turn coming up," I said. "We're close now."

Aiden found the turn, then slowed the truck and turned off the lights.

"Are we still cruising the compound boundary?" I asked.

"Yes," Aiden glanced back at me. "Why?"

"I don't know, it's just ... given he was able to walk around the edges of the Marin compound with impunity, and now he's here, skirting the edges of the Sinclair compound, I'm thinking it's looking more and more likely he's a wolf."

"If he was a wolf, someone would have scented the blood and the violence on him," Aiden said.

"Maybe someone has," I said. "Maybe it's simply a case of pack protecting pack."

"Or even," Monty said, "it being explained away by roo hunting."

"A roo has a very different smell to a human," Aiden said, voice bland. "Trust me on that."

"Yes, but scent can be concealed," Monty said.

"Have you any idea how sensitive a wolf's nose is?"

"Yes, but magic has been used to hide all sorts of scents from wolves—and others—for decades," I said.

"If he *was* using magic to conceal scent," Aiden said, with another glance back to me through the rearview mirror, "it would surely have also concealed his personal scent. Besides, wouldn't you have noticed the traces of magic after he broke into your truck?"

I smiled. "Maybe, once the panic had eased. Take the next left, then slow right down."

"That road leads into the reservation."

"Meaning we *are* dealing with a wolf," I said.

"I can't see a wolf doing what he's doing," Aiden replied. "Respect of elders—especially *female* elders—is ingrained."

And yet there are some females who make disrespect utterly easy... like your mom. But I kept *that* thought to myself. I hadn't grown up in the wolf culture, so I had no right to judge. "But we're obviously dealing with someone who is mentally ill. Werewolves are no more immune to that than humans or witches, Aiden."

"Again, someone in the pack would have noticed."

"What if he's a loner?" Monty said. "What if he and his mom were ostracized from the pack for some reason? The lone wolf legend has its base in fact, doesn't it?"

Aiden hesitated. "Yes, but it's extremely rare for outliers to remain on pack grounds. Generally, they move on to another pack."

"Couldn't that be what has happened here?" I said. "Maybe they've come here and have permission to stay on pack grounds but, for whatever reason, have decided not to fully integrate?"

"Possible," Aiden said. "It does at least give us another line of enquiry if we don't grab him today."

"Fingers crossed we *do* grab him today, though," Monty said.

"Amen to that," I muttered. We had a siren to hunt down before it went after any more of Aiden's family. We really didn't need to be worried about a psycho wolf taking out any more grannies. "There's a slight turn to the right just on the crest of this hill. Head down there."

"That's little more than a damn goat track," Monty said as Aiden turned. "Are you sure this is where he is?"

"It's where the truck is. Whether he's there with it is the unknown factor right now."

We continued down the rough dirt lane, the trees drawing closer, casting the day into a patchwork of shadows and light. Thankfully, all the rain we'd had over the last couple of days meant we weren't leaving a dust trail, but the downside of that was the multiple rivulets that had carved up the surface, making it extremely difficult to traverse.

"I can see why he needs a four-wheel drive," Monty muttered, holding the grab handle tightly as we bumped over a particularly rough patch. "A normal car would have been bogged half a kilometer back."

"Which could be why he's ditched the Ford," I said.

"He would have done that anyway, given he more than likely saw me chasing after him at the tower," Aiden said.

We crested a small hill. Barely visible in the valley below was a partially rusted tin roof. The rest of the building was hidden by the trees, but it was at least an indication that the locator was leading us somewhere.

Whether that was to our killer or simply his vehicle was something we'd soon find out.

We wound down the other side of the hill, and the old house gradually revealed itself. It was a rather large building with two main sides and an inset center. The tin roof was more rust than anything else, and the weatherboards had long ago lost whatever color they'd been painted. The two sash windows either side of the front door appeared to be boarded up from the inside with cardboard, while the two on the end of either wing were covered by lace curtains.

Sitting at the front of the building was a black Toyota.

As we entered the small clearing, the curtain covering the right wing's window twitched, and a man briefly peered out at us.

He wasn't, as I'd been imagining, a pale, gaunt figure. Instead, his features were strong-looking, his hair long, his beard neatly trimmed.

"Fuck," Monty said, "he's spotted us."

"Yeah." Aiden stopped the truck and threw open his door. "Stay here while I check it out."

He was out before either of us could argue. I undid my seat belt and leaned forward, watching as he raced onto the inset porch and over to the front door. No one answered. Aiden stepped back and then cocked his head, obviously listening to something.

He swung around to face us. "He's on the run. Stay here in case he doubles back."

With that, he raced off to the left and disappeared around the side of the building. I drew in a deep breath and fought the instinctive urge to run after him. We were most likely dealing with a wolf, and Aiden was perfectly capable of capturing him without any sort of magical help from us.

And yet... instinct was nagging.

I shoved open the door and climbed out. The wind whipped around me, running chill fingers through my hair then tossing it behind me. I shivered and dragged my hood over my head. It was then I noticed the threads of wild magic. They were from the older wellspring rather than Katie's, which made their presence here even odder, given how far away we currently were.

I reached out. Several gossamer threads immediately raced toward me and looped around my wrist. The minute they did, my senses exploded. The day became sharper and the wind so full of soft sound that for a moment it felt like I was drowning in it all.

Then, as my senses acclimatized to the din, I heard them.

The running steps of two people—two *wolves*—one moving away from the house, the other more distant but slowly looping around and coming back.

The latter wasn't Aiden. It was the man he'd been chasing. He was definitely a werewolf.

"The bastard has doubled back," I said to Monty. "He's going to get away."

"From Aiden? Unlikely."

"The wind is going the wrong way for Aiden to scent track properly." I slammed the door shut. "Stay here and keep an eye on that truck, Monty."

"Liz, don't—"

I ignored him and ran, as hard and as fast as I could, into the scrub, following the sound of those footfalls, letting the threads guide my steps even as the wind swept my scent and sound away from my target. I flew over the ground, my steps strong, showing none of my usual noisiness. I might be running on two rather than four legs, but for this moment in time, with the wind in my face, the wild magic pulsing through my veins, and the exhilaration of the chase in my heart, it very much felt as if I was wolf in all but form.

His scent drew closer, and I absently created a cage spell around my fingers. If I did get close enough, I needed a means of stopping the bastard.

Of course, if he had a gun or a knife, I was in deep shit. The wild magic might have protected me from a gunshot once before, but I couldn't rely on it. Better to avoid that situation if I possibly could.

I leapt over a fallen log and ran on. The ground trembled under the weight of my target, and his unpleasant scent was stronger in my nose. Then, up ahead, I saw a flash of gray.

He must have seen me at the very same time because he did a sharp turn and raced diagonally away from both me and the house.

I swore, shifted direction, and continued after him. Slowly but surely, I gained ground, but the trees were so thick that casting the cage spell was a waste of time. I needed a clear shot of the bastard to have any hope of this working.

Then, from the corner of my eye, I caught movement.

It was another wolf, coming straight at me.

Chapter Eight

I twisted around and released a hastily constructed repelling spell. It hit the wolf and sent him tumbling away... revealing a second wolf right behind him.

I threw up my hands and shouted, "I'm Lizzie Grace. I'm here with Aiden O'Connor, and I'm chasing a murder suspect!"

The second wolf—a female—skidded to a halt and shifted shape. She was tall and slender, with the black skin and hair of the Sinclair pack. Her eyes were the most startling shade of gold and her expression disbelieving.

"If that's the case, why are you here and not Aiden?"

"I can explain, but please, we need to go after that gray wolf first—"

"That wolf has permission to be here; you do not." The second Sinclair wolf stopped beside his companion and brushed the dirt and leaves from his body.

"For fuck's sake," I growled, "you're letting him get *away*."

"Pack rules—"

"You can shove your fucking rules where the sun doesn't shine." I threw the cage spell at them. "This is more important, and I have no time to debate it."

As the net settled around them, I spun and raced after the suspect. Awareness flickered across my magical senses as my captives tested the boundary of their prison, but I ignored it, concentrating on the scent of my quarry.

But it was fading fast, and while my senses might have sharpened, he was now running across the wind. I just didn't have the experience or knowledge to follow him. I briefly debated sending the wild magic after him, but it never seemed to move with any great urgency.

I crested a rise and then stopped. There was nothing but trees below me and he could have been anywhere.

I blew out a frustrated breath then turned and made my way back. As I neared my captives, I pulled out my phone and called Aiden. I had no doubt my captives had made their own calls, and I was going to need his help, because the shit would no doubt hit the fan over what I'd done.

"Lizzie," he growled by way of greeting, "what the hell have you done?"

"I'm guessing you've already been informed of that." I stopped a couple of meters away from my captives but didn't release them. Their expressions were thunderous, and they paced the confines of their magical prison like, well, caged wolves. "They wouldn't listen to reason, they wouldn't believe I was with you, and the murderous fucker was getting away. What the hell did you expect me to do? Hang around and wait for Tweedledee and Tweedledum to get their act together?"

He made a sound that was halfway between a growl and a laugh. "Stay where you are. I'll be there in a few minutes."

"I'm not moving anywhere, but also not releasing Dee or Dum. I've got a feeling they want a little retribution."

The two of them glowered at me when I said that, all but confirming my statement.

"Fine. I'll deal with the fallout when I get there."

"Just make sure you get here before whoever they called in does, otherwise you're likely to find more caged wolves."

He snorted and hung up. The woman growled, "You can release us. We won't attack."

"Yeah, and tomorrow it'll snow." I gave her a sweetly false smile. "Sorry, but I can see the anger in your aura, and there's no way known I'm going to let you anywhere near me until Aiden gets here."

She made a low sound in her throat, but the other wolf lightly touched her shoulder, and she took a step back, making a visible effort to calm herself.

"You say the wolf you were chasing is a murder suspect," he said. "If that's the case, we would have heard something. The wolf council would have provided an alert to the three packs."

"Except the council isn't meeting until one today, and we didn't know it was a wolf until we tracked him here."

"And how did you do that?" he asked.

"Via magic." I waved a hand. "You know, the same stuff that has you caged."

"You're the witch who runs that cake café at Castle Rock?" the woman asked.

"One of them, yes."

I was a little surprised that she mentioned the café rather than the fact that Aiden and I had been an item. But then, they both looked to be in their very early twenties, and I guessed the topic of who was and wasn't going out with the head ranger really wouldn't factor into their lives or social media scrolling.

"Then why the fuck would you be running around after potential murderers?" she growled.

"Because," Aiden said as he stepped through the trees, "she also happens to be the assistant reservation witch."

My stupid heart did its usual little happy dance at the sight of him, even though we hadn't been apart that long. It was a reaction that might get old one day, but today was not that day.

"You okay?" he added, his gaze scanning me critically.

"I'm pissed that these two enabled our suspect to get away but, other than that, perfectly fine."

A smile twitched his lips. "You'd better release them, then."

I deactivated the spell and then said, "Done."

The two of them stepped somewhat hesitantly forward; relief crossed their expressions when nothing pushed them back.

"The rescue party has been called off," Aiden said. "The next time Lizzie, or indeed Monty Ashworth, tells you they're racing after a suspect, please help rather than hinder them."

They made a low, somewhat grumbly sound of agreement and disappeared into the trees. I frowned after them. "Why didn't you question them? They said our wolf had permission to be here, so they must know who he is."

"Because I've already spoken briefly to the alphas but will talk to them more fully later."

"Because I ruffled pack feathers and you need to smooth things over?"

He smiled. "Yes."

He turned and led the way back through the bush. Rather surprisingly—and unlike all the other times I'd gone bolting through the bush—I hadn't left a clearly visible trail. That suggested I'd not only run with the speed of a wolf but also the lightness of one.

I glanced down at the threads still wrapped around my wrist. Had they helped? Had their power somehow reinforced the changes my inner wild magic appeared to be making?

It was possible.

Of course, until we got a clearer picture of what to expect from the book Eli was still transcribing, anything was possible right now.

"According to Jackson," Aiden was saying, "there're currently eight outliers living within the compound's grounds. He needed a description to pin our boy."

Jackson being one of the Sinclair pack alphas, no doubt. "Well, he's a gray wolf, and big, but he's not likely to stay here in this compound now that we've tracked him down."

"No, but once we get a name, we can put out a BOLO. It won't take us long to find him after that."

"There's plenty of places to hide in this reservation."

"Yes, but with the three packs on alert, his hiding options will be restricted."

I hoped he was right. I suspected he wasn't.

As we reached the clearing and the house, Monty appeared from around the far corner.

"There's a newish grave in the backyard," he said. "If our theories are right, that could be dear old mom."

"I've already called in Ciara and her team, so they can investigate that when they get here. You haven't gone inside yet?"

"No. Figured you wouldn't approve."

"You're learning." Aiden got his kit from the back of his truck, handed us gloves and booties, and then said, "This way."

We followed the overgrown path to the steps that led up to the rather rickety porch. The solid-looking front door was mostly bare wood, though the flecks of paint visible in two of the four paneled sections suggested it had once been a rather cheery yellow. After putting on the gloves and booties, Aiden carefully tested the handle and then pushed the door open.

The air that rushed out was stale and odorous. Much like the wolf who'd been staying here.

"Ranger Aiden O'Connor here," he said loudly. "Anyone home?"

His words echoed, but there was no response. He walked in cautiously, the bare floorboards creaking under his weight. Monty and I followed, forming a single line behind him.

Two rooms led off the small entrance hall; on the left was a study that hadn't been used in quite a while if the amount of dust covering everything was anything to go by. To the right was a small living room. It held an overstuffed leather recliner, a coffee table, and a monstrous TV that looked almost as old as the house. The dust was evident here, too, although the scum on the half-finished mug of coffee didn't look more than a day or so old.

We moved on and came to a junction with three hallways going in different directions. The place might have appeared to be a squarish U-shape outside but inside it was more a weirdly shaped Y, and it was far bigger than it had first appeared.

"Why don't we split up?" Aiden said. "Monty, you take

the left, Liz can take the right, and I'll go straight. If you find anything, shout."

His gaze came to me when he said that, and I couldn't help smiling. "I promise not to run after anything if it bolts."

A smile tugged at his lips. "Good."

As the two of them moved down their respective halls, I cautiously went right. There were several dusty old photos hanging on the walls, most of them of a rather strong-looking boy with short-cropped pale hair and oddly opaque black eyes. There was also a family shot that looked to have been taken on the front porch—the woman had a severe bun and a stern expression, the man was whip-thin and some-what glum looking. Two boys stood on the step below them; one was obviously the kid in all the photos, while the other was tall and gangly. He looked so awkward and out of place in the photo that it made me wonder if he was even part of the family.

It would certainly explain why he hadn't featured in any other photos so far. Either that, or I simply hadn't gotten to his wall yet.

I moved on and came to a T-intersection. There were two doors down each end, and I hesitated briefly before going right. I could see sunlight coming through the window in the room at the far end and it looked far more inviting than the shadows down the other end. Besides, the man had been standing in that room, so it was more likely I'd find something there.

I pressed my fingertips against the door and pushed it all the way open but didn't enter. It was a bedroom—a woman's rather than a man's. A flowery pink comforter covered a bed stacked high with decorative pillows and, opposite this but to the left of the central window was a mid-height chest of drawers. A jewelry stand stood atop of these, the various bits and pieces large and somewhat gaudy. On the other side of the window was another set of drawers, this one holding an old-fashioned wash bowl and jug. A flannel was folded over the basin's rim, suggesting it had been in use at one point.

The only other bit of furniture was the antique-looking freestanding wardrobe that sat against the left wall.

My gaze went to the back window and the motes of dust that danced in the pale beams of light shining through it. Our fugitive might have stood here checking our arrival, but those motes should have settled by now.

That they hadn't meant something else had stirred them.

I glanced back to the hall. I had no sense that anyone or anything lay in wait, but there was definitely a presence within this room.

A presence that was filled with cold fury.

I shivered and backed away. I needed to check the other rooms before I entered this one, just in case the source of that fury was not alone.

The other door on this side of the hall led into a bathroom—it was basic and ancient-looking, but it did at least have a toilet. Many of these older places that hadn't been renovated in years still had them located outside.

I moved to the far end of the hall. The other two rooms were bedrooms—one of them obviously hadn't been used in years, if the dust on the bed and the few bits of wooden furniture was anything to go by, while the other looked as though it was still being used by a child. There was still plenty of dust but, like the first bedroom, it was only a thin layer and that suggested it had accumulated over weeks rather than months or years.

But the room also felt oddly empty. There was no resonance of life here, no love. There was only emptiness and grief.

Because the boy who'd once slept here had left long ago, and his room was now a shrine....

I frowned at the insight and walked back down the hall to the front room, hesitating briefly in the doorway before stepping in.

That's when I saw her.

Or rather, her ghost, though in truth she was nothing more than a slight shimmer that stood between the wall and the chest of drawers that held the jewelry.

I hesitated and walked over. She moved as I approached, motes of dust trailing behind her filmy figure like a fine train. On the floor where she'd been standing was a dark stain.

It wasn't ink or mud or anything else.

It was blood.

"Aiden," I called out. "You need to come in here."

His footsteps echoed, then he appeared in the doorway. "What have you found?"

"What I believe is a bloodstain and a ghost."

His gaze jumped to mine. "A ghost?"

I nodded. "She's standing near the bed at the moment."

"Is she dangerous? Some ghosts can be, can't they?"

I hesitated and studied the shimmer. "I'm definitely getting a feeling of rage from her, but it's not aimed at us."

"Then who is it aimed at? The man we were chasing?"

"Most likely. He was in this room before he ran off, after all."

He squatted and touched the edge of the stain and sniffed it. "It's definitely blood."

After scraping a few samples into a bag, he shifted his weight and studied the edge of the dresser and then the wall to the side of it, where a dark smear stretched to the floor. "If I have to guess what happened, she fell into the dresser, which cracked her head open, then slid down the wall and hit the floor."

"Could she have been pushed?"

He hesitated, looking up at the dresser. "If she'd been pushed from behind, she would have fallen headfirst. The strands of hair on the dresser's edge suggests she hit either side on or fell back somehow."

I frowned at the blood on the carpet. "There's not enough blood for her to have bled out."

"No, but if she hit hard enough, it would have caused all sorts of brain trauma. I'm guessing we'll uncover the truth once we exhume the body—presuming, of course, the grave Monty found is hers." He pocketed the sample. "Will you and Belle be able to talk to our ghost?"

"Hang on while I check." I reached for Belle and asked, *You available to chat with a ghost?*

Yes, as the midday rush has apparently rushed right on past us today. Her mental tone *was* amused. *Whose ghost am I talking to? That of the victim you found in the fire tower?*

No, we think it's the mother of our murderer.

Meaning we guessed right. Go us. Let me get upstairs and comfortable. You got your spell stones?

That depends on whether my stolen backpack is still in our felon's truck. We haven't had time to check yet.

Then just get Monty to make a protection circle for you. Better to be safe than sorry when it comes to ghosts.

Will do. I glanced around as Monty came into the room.

"There's a bathroom and two bedrooms in the other wing," he said. "One is obviously our felon's because, oh boy, was it rank. Anyone doing a search will need a full hazmat suit. You two find anything?"

"Yeah, a ghost. Will you be able to create a protection circle for me?" Most ghosts generally weren't violent, but it was always better to be safe than sorry.

"Sure. I'll just go out and grab my spell stones."

As he spun around and disappeared, Aiden said, "Will you be all right here alone? Ciara and the team are almost here, and I'll need to organize the various searches before we head back to Castle Rock."

I touched his arm, a reflex action that was electric enough to make the small hairs at the back of my neck stand on end. He must have felt it too, because awareness echoed brightly through his eyes.

"I'm fine." I dropped my hand but found myself clenching my fingers in a vague attempt to hold on to that electricity just a little bit longer. "If our ghost intended any of us harm, she would have done something by now."

"And you'll record your interview with her, as per usual?"

I nodded and smiled, though it felt a little tight. Felt a little sad.

"Good. Thanks." His gaze dropped to my lips, and then he leaned toward me, the heat of his body washing over my senses, and his lips so close I could almost taste them. And I wanted to taste them. *Desperately.*

Then he made a low sound in the back of his throat and straightened.

"Sorry," he murmured. "Old habits are hard to break."

"I hope I was more than just a habit, Aiden."

"Of course you are." He scrubbed a hand through his hair, frustration evident. "I hate this whole situation, Liz. I want to be with you, damn it."

"Then sort out the situation with your pack."

"That is nigh on impossible."

"Only if you never try, Aiden."

"I am bound by the ruling of my alphas," he growled. "It has been made very clear that I will never be given dispensation to marry you. If I did, I would face exile."

I stared at him for several long seconds. Then I swallowed and croaked, "You asked?"

He absently ran a finger lightly down my face and rested it on my lips. The heat of his touch rolled through me, making my pulse skip and my heart tremble. "My mother made the ruling when it became obvious you were more than just a casual lover to me. She is my alpha; even as an alpha in waiting, I cannot negate it."

Did that mean he could change the ruling when he became alpha? Was that what Katie had meant when she'd said he was now playing the long game?

It was possible. More than possible.

But did that fact change our situation any?

Not unless I was willing to waste years waiting for that eventuality while still running the risk of a more suitable wolf walking into his life.

I was nearly thirty. If I wanted children, I needed to start thinking about that in the next couple of years. And sure, there was nothing stopping me from having them with Aiden right here and now, but if we did, and he found his wolf mate, it would just make the situation even worse. I couldn't—wouldn't—do that to any kids we might have.

I forced myself to step away from his touch and the treacherous emotions it evoked. No matter what burned between us, no matter how real and honest and precious it was, in the long run it was the best thing I could do for both of us.

"Then we need to move on, Aiden. You need to stop this. You need to let me go."

"But I don't want—"

"Once again, this *isn't* about what *you* want," I cut in, perhaps with a little more savagery than was necessary. "This is about what is best for us both given the situation we find ourselves in. One which—given what you just said—won't change."

Not short-term. Probably not long-term.

He drew in a shuddery breath, then stepped away. His eyes were full of the turmoil I could see in his aura, even if his expression was impassive. "I know, and I'm sorry. I just miss you. This"—he waved a hand, indicating the room but meaning investigating a crime—"is *not* enough."

I wholeheartedly agreed with that, but it was pointless saying anything. It was what it was, and we both needed to get past it.

"It will be. Eventually."

He obviously disagreed with that but nodded sharply and strode out, every bit of him vibrating with unhappy frustration.

Monty came in a few seconds later. "What's wrong with our ranger? He looked thunderous."

A smiled tugged at my lips. "He's unhappy with the current state of our relationship and my continuing refusal to give in to his wiles."

He unzipped his backpack and pulled out the small silk bag holding his spell stones. "Good. Make the bastard suffer."

I raised an eyebrow. "Is Belle aware of this savage streak you have?"

He grinned. "Of course. She witnessed me knocking out your ex on her behalf, remember."

How could I forget when seeing Clayton all bloody and splayed on the floor had been one of the best moments of my life?

I crossed my arms and watched as he placed his stones in a circle on the floor. Once he'd finished, I stepped inside and sat cross-legged while he activated them. As his power formed a shimmering dome around me, I said, "You'll have to record what I'm saying for Aiden."

He nodded and dropped onto the bed. A pillow immediately flung itself at his head, and I couldn't help laughing. "I'm thinking she doesn't want you sitting there."

"I'm thinking you could be right. But it also means she's been dead for a while—very few new ghosts have the ability to throw things."

"I've got the feeling we're not dealing with your average ghost here." The waves of cold fury hitting my psychic senses were to be expected, given she was forever stuck in place now rather than being able to move on. It was the emotions that lay *behind* the fury that gave me some sense of her character; the ghost, like the woman in the photo, was stern, unforgiving, and didn't suffer fools or weakness gladly.

Monty moved across to the window and propped somewhat tentatively on the sill. When that drew no response, he relaxed and said, "Right, ready when you are."

I reached out for Belle. There was a rush of warmth as her being flowed into mine and fused us as one. The glimmer that was the soul immediately jumped into focus. The only thing that gave away her ghostly status was the slight shimmer running around her outline—a rare thing for a newish ghost. Usually, they remained translucent until they'd had time to adjust to their situation.

And some never did.

She was rangy in build, with short, well-kept silver-gray hair, and blue eyes that shone with the cold fury I could sense. She was wearing a black skirt, a white top, and a pale pink cardigan, which made me think she'd been getting ready to go out when she'd died.

She was a neat-looking, well-dressed woman, and—at least externally—very much reminded me of the two women her son had attacked.

"What is your name?" Belle asked through me.

Florence Seagrave. Her expression was sour, her blue eyes dark points of fury. *Why are you here? Where is the fool I call a son?*

I quietly relayed her reply to Monty, though my attention remained on the soul.

"We don't know just yet," Belle said. "How did you come to be in this state?"

Tripped, didn't I? Tried to catch my balance, but the side of my head caught the edge of the dresser, and then I smacked into the wall behind it. It was pretty much lights out, curtains closed after that.

Which meant Aiden had been right. Her son hadn't pushed her.

"When was this?"

A couple of weeks ago. She shrugged, briefly making her outline shimmer. *Hard to be sure when time seems to have no meaning here.*

"Was your son home when it happened?" Belle asked.

No. He wouldn't have been much use anyway.

"What did he do when he discovered you?"

He yelled and screamed and said I couldn't do this to him. It wasn't like I did it on purpose, but that's Harry for you. Every time something goes wrong, he claims it's not his fault or it's a plot against him.

"You tripping could hardly be his fault," Belle said, with just the slightest hint of annoyance, "so why would you imply that?"

But it was, because I'd asked him multiple times to fix the goddamn carpet. He never did, so here I am.

"What happened once he calmed down?"

He dug a hole out the back and shoved me in it, didn't he?

"He didn't notify anyone? Why not?"

She snorted. *Ask him. I'm sure you'll get a long and complicated tale of woe about how goddamn awful his life was and how I didn't deserve the comfort of last rites. He even spat on my grave, ungrateful sod that he is.*

"Why would he do that?"

Probably because I hold him responsible for Ryland's death. He said it was an accident, but he was always jealous of his brother—he was everything Harry never would be or could be.

That right there was one very good reason for him hating his mom, but that did raise another question—why on earth would he stay here with her? Why not leave? It didn't sound as if she'd have put any barriers in his way.

When Belle asked her that, Florence snorted again. *Where else would he go? It's not like any decent wolf in this reservation would have him, and he hasn't the balls to go off somewhere by himself.*

"Is your other son buried here on the farm?"

Of course not. He's in the Sinclairs' cemetery, alongside his father. It's where I wanted to be, but the bastard wouldn't even give me that.

There was a part of me that totally understood her anger. The same part that had stepped back and allowed a vampire to exact bloody revenge on my ex.

"Can you tell us anything about your son that might help us track him down quickly?" Belle asked. "Has he any friends he might go to for help?"

He has no friends. As I said, the boy is a loser.

Made that way by his mother, it seemed.

"And there's nothing else you can suggest that might help us find him?"

She hesitated. *There is a place we used to go before Ryland was killed—a caravan park out past Argyle. Big Blue or something like that. Been abandoned for years, but he loved that place. He's been saying since his father's death that when I carked it, he was going to sell this place and buy the business and get it going again. He wouldn't, of course— aside from the fact he's too damn lazy for such an undertaking, I wrote him out of the will ages ago. This place goes back to the pack.*

Maybe he'd found out about the will. Maybe that was why he was—and is—so damn angry

"Have you got a recent photo of him?"

She snorted. *Why would I? What has he ever done for me lately?*

I think the more pertinent question, Belle said to me, *is what has she done for him? And not just recently.*

If their relationship was so antagonistic, would he really have stayed here with her?

Given what she said about the will, I really don't know. To Florence, she said. "What about a description, then?"

About five-nine, with brown eyes, curly brown hair that hangs to his shoulders in rat tails, and a thin brown face. She paused, and then added somewhat grudgingly, *He does a bit of body building, so his physique is a bit stronger than what is usual for a wolf.*

"Thanks," Belle said. "We appreciate you talking to us, Florence."

She sniffed. *I don't suppose you can remove the barriers that tie me to this place, can you? I might not be buried next to my beloved boy, but it would be nice to at least be able to watch over his grave.*

Belle hesitated, and her power expanded, gently testing the restrictions that afterlife had placed on Florence. "I'm afraid I can't. You've simply been here too long to be moved on anywhere."

Then you can both get out of my room and leave me alone.

"The rangers will need to investigate your death, Florence, and that means they'll have to come in here. No throwing cushions or anything else."

She sniffed again, a disparaging sound if ever I'd heard one. *Fine. I'll move over to Ryland's room. They don't need to be touching anything in there, because no one but me goes in there.*

"I'll let them know," Belle said, then added to me, *Well, she's a character.*

Putting it mildly, I said. *Are you really unable to move her on?*

Yes, but even if I could, I doubt she'd go. If she can't visit the grave, she wants to be here, in the house where the shrine to her beloved firstborn is.

No wonder Harry is acting out his hatred of her. Her sudden death left him without any means of retribution.

Which still doesn't explain why he only acted once she'd died.

I'm sure a psychologist could give you a very detailed explanation of that one.

And it would be one I have no interest in. Tell Monty

not to get so caught up in the investigation that he forgets our dinner date.

Oh yeah? Where are you going?

Just to the Maurocco.

Which was a local wine bar that also did great cocktails and food. Aiden and I had planned to go there at some point but had never gotten around to it. I ignored the twinge of regret and said, *See you soon, then.*

I broke the connection and then glanced up at Monty. "Belle said you're not to forget your date tonight."

"As if I would."

I gave him "the look." "Because you never have before, have you?"

He grinned. "I didn't forget. I was just a little late."

"I think your definition of little is different to hers."

He laughed, dismissed the protection circle, and offered me a hand up. "Don't forget to grab your backpack from our felon's Toyota before we leave. Good silver knives are hard to replace these days."

"I'll check with Aiden first, just in case he wants it for evidence or something. But I want to check Harry's room before we leave. You never know, I might find something that will let me track him and make everyone's job easier."

"If you really want to submit yourself to that torture, sure." He picked up his spell stones and returned them to their pouch. "This way."

We walked down the long hall and turned right. This wing mirrored the one I'd investigated, and the minute I turned the corner, I knew Harry's room was down the far end.

Monty was right. The smell was horrendous.

I tried breathing through my mouth, but that only left my tongue and throat coated with the stench. It wasn't just the smell, though, but also the emotions. They were so thick and strong that even with my shields up on full, I could feel the press of them.

The closer we got, the more my stomach churned. I had a bad feeling that if I didn't find something quick smart, I'd be fouling any possible evidence with a colorful assortment of my stomach's contents.

I clapped a hand over my nose in the vague hope it would help and followed Monty into the room. It was a mess. There were clothes, shoes, plates of old food, and various drink containers all over the place. There was also what could only be described as an array of computers, which suggested that Harry was either a gamer or a programmer. That area also happened to be the only clean spot in the entire room. I picked my way through the grime and swept my hand across the two desks without touching anything, looking for anything that twinged my psychometry. There was a very faint pulse on the mouse, but it wasn't strong enough to use as a tracker. I spun around and moved on, but the smell increased in intensity, until it felt like I was swimming in his stench and emotions. I just had to get out.

Now.

I spun and ran out of the room, my footsteps echoing in the stillness as I raced for the front door.

"Lizzie? What's wrong?" Monty asked.

I didn't answer. I bolted out the front door, leapt off the porch, and lost the contents of my stomach behind a scraggly rose bush.

Monty stopped behind me on the porch, but it was Aiden's hand that touched my back, Aiden's scent that washed the foulness from my lungs, Aiden's water bottle that appeared in front of my nose.

"Here," he said softly, "wash your mouth out with this."

"Thanks." I drew in a deeper breath to erase the lingering remnants of foulness, then took a drink, swished it around, and spat it out.

"I take it you went into that room?"

I smiled. "I thought my stomach was made of sterner stuff. I was wrong."

"Unsurprising when your olfactory senses are sharpening. Even *I* won't be going in there without a counterscent to balance things out."

"I forgot about that." Although Vicks VapoRub wouldn't have been much help against the press of his emotions, and they drove me out here just as much as the smell.

"I'm betting you won't next time."

"No."

He capped the water bottle and stepped back. "Did our ghost give us anything useful?"

"Our killer's name is Harry Seagrove, and there's an abandoned caravan park near Argyle that he might hide in," Monty said. "She also warned that going into the nursery would piss her off."

Aiden raised his eyebrows. "Does that matter when she's a ghost?"

"She's capable of throwing things," I said. "But she did say Harry didn't go in there at all; only she did."

"Anything else?"

I hesitated. "She blames Harry for the death of her other son, but I'm not sure how useful that is."

He nodded. "I'll go warn Ciara about entering the nursery, and then we can head off."

"Can I grab my pack from his car?"

He nodded. "Just make sure you keep the gloves on."

He turned and strode for the far corner of the house. Monty leapt down from the porch, tucked my arm through his, and then escorted me to the Toyota, grabbing the pack and handing it to me before guiding me across to Aiden's truck.

I couldn't help smiling. "I'm okay now that I'm out of that room."

"I know, but you're looking a little peaked, and I figured a little cousinly support couldn't hurt."

I nudged him lightly. "You are a good man, Monty Ashworth. You're going to make Belle a most excellent husband."

"I keep telling her that," he mused. "And I do believe she is starting to believe me."

I laughed as he opened the door and ushered me into the back seat. "The day the council's original pick for reservation witch missed the plane, giving you the job instead, was a fortunate one indeed."

For me, as much as Belle.

"He didn't miss the plane, no matter what story the council told you," Monty said. "He was talked out of going."

I raised an eyebrow. "And you were the one who talked him out of it?"

"No, though I certainly would have had I realized you and Belle were here. It was his wife. She didn't want to be stuck in some godforsaken country town in the middle of nowhereville. Her words, not mine."

"I take it you know him?"

"I do. He was the one who prodded me into applying when the call went out again. He knew I was looking to escape."

"Then why didn't you apply the first time?"

"Because I was younger than what they were asking for. That stipulation wasn't in the second advertisement."

Aiden climbed in a few minutes later, and we headed back to Castle Rock. Monty stayed to help Belle in the café —not that there was that much to do, as there were only two customers—while I went upstairs to do some stock ordering and other bits of necessary paperwork.

When they headed off just after six to get ready for their date, I ordered Thai for dinner and settled in to do a little investigative work.

A confrontation with Karleen was coming—I felt that in every fiber of my being—and I needed to understand why. Needed to understand what had happened in her past if I was to have any hope of defusing the future.

I typed in "Axton, Flintshire, North East Wales," which gave me pages of information about the county and not a whole lot about the pack or its territory. I added "pack" to the search criteria and got a pretty generic page.

I finished the rest of my Pad Thai and then searched for newspaper archives. That gave me the North East Wales Archives, The National Library of Wales—though it only went up to 1910, and I needed more recent dates than that —and the National Archives, all of which were free to search.

I made myself a hot chocolate, grabbed a bag of cheese and onion potato chips, and settled in for a long night.

It was close to midnight when I found the first hint of what might have happened—several newspaper articles that mentioned attacks on two sixteen-year-old girls in the Axton area. It was originally thought some sort of drug had been used because the girls had no memory of the event, but after a third girl was attacked, they discovered the remnants of a seduction spell on her.

Digging deeper didn't produce any more information about the girls, but I did find a brief description of the witch they were searching for—he had crimson hair and green eyes.

The same as me before the wild magic had started making its changes.

I scrubbed a hand across my no-longer-green eyes. No wonder she'd hated me on sight. I was a reminder of a bleak chapter in her life.

More searching uncovered the fact that nine months after the event, multiple royal witches were attacked and killed. The article went on to say that James Axton, who was the father of one of the girls attacked, was arrested and charged with the murders. He was released on bail— suggesting he had someone powerful in his corner—and he and his family subsequently disappeared before the trial date. It wasn't hard to guess that that's when the whole family emigrated to Australia.

I blew out a breath and switched to checking the death notices for that year. Katie hadn't said that Bryanna had died, but it was a logical guess given the sequence of events and the depth of Karleen's hatred.

That's when I found multiple death notices for Bryanna Axton.

The date on the notices was just over nine months after the date of the attacks on the girls but a few weeks before the ones on the witches. Though none of them mentioned that she'd died in childbirth, there *were* further notices for a Nia Axton. She was listed only as Bryanna's daughter, and all of them said gone from this world too soon. It wasn't hard to put two and two together.

I swore softly and leaned back. It all made sense now. Not just Karleen's hatred for us, but also her conviction that any child born of a witch and werewolf union would not survive.

How I was going to use the information, I had no idea. If she'd wanted her family to know about her sister and what had happened, she would have mentioned it. Me blabbing about it could possibly only make an already bad situation worse.

Maybe what I needed to find was proof that such unions could produce viable offspring—though even if I could, it was unlikely to change her mind or her edict.

I rubbed my forehead wearily, then shut down the computer and went to bed. I could worry about the next step when I wasn't so damn tired.

Darkness still held the room deep in its grip when the first refrains of the otherworldly song filled the air.

I scrambled out of bed, threw on my jeans and shoes, then grabbed my coat, keys, and phone and raced downstairs. I grabbed the backpack on the way through, though it was unlikely to be of any use when I didn't have a bronze knife and had no idea if holy water would work on a creature who lived in water. I raced outside, jumped into the Suzi, and sped out of the parking area. Once on the road, I hit Aiden's number.

"Where are you?" I asked the minute he answered.

"At the ranger station—why?"

"The siren has just started to sing. I'll be out the front in less than a minute."

He swore and hung up. I slid around the corner, then came to a sharp halt outside the ranger station, sending a cloud of rubber smoke drifting past the vehicle's nose. He appeared a few seconds later, shoes and coat in his hand and his shirt undone, suggesting he'd been asleep in the station's bunkroom when I'd called.

The minute he was in, I drove off.

"Where is she this time?" He hurriedly shoved his feet into his shoes, then pulled on the seat belt. "Still up near the compound?"

I nodded. Thankfully, the signal was coming through loud and clear, and I could reserve some of my attention for the road and getting us there safely.

"Here's hoping she doesn't snare anyone this time," he growled. "I did order everyone to use earplugs."

I cast him a quick glance. "I don't see any in your ears."

"They're in my pocket. I'll put them in when I need to, but right now, I need to be able to converse with you."

It was more a case of "want" than "need," as I didn't know anything more than him at this point. "Are you positive the council will relay the order back to everyone?"

I couldn't imagine Aiden's parents wouldn't, given they'd already lost at least one family member, but there were four other O'Connor lines in his pack, and it was impossible to guarantee the other alphas had understood the urgency. The same could be said about the different lines in both the Marin and Sinclair packs.

"I would presume so, but I haven't checked."

I didn't say anything. I drove through the quiet streets, pushing the Suzi for all the speed she had.

This time, the song led us into the reservation itself.

I slowed as we approached the entrance. A gangly-looking wolf appeared, and Aiden wound down the window to show his badge—it was the only way I was going to get in. The guard immediately waved us on. As he stepped back, I saw the bits of yellow poking out of his ears. He, at least, was protected.

I hit the accelerator and zoomed on. It wasn't the reservation's main entrance, so the road was little more than a dirt track barely wide enough for the Suzi to get through, but it was at least drivable and didn't have any potholes or corrugations.

I wasn't seeing any water, but given the thickness of the forest on either side of us, that really wasn't surprising. We were close, though, because the song no longer held a distant feel. I glanced at Aiden. "You'd better put those earplugs in."

"I'm not hearing anything, Liz."

"Doesn't mean you won't once we're closer."

"If she was targeting me, surely I'd know by now."

"Probably, but the last thing I need is you getting ensnared. I'd rather keep you alive than dead."

"Pleased to hear that," he said, voice dry.

He pulled the plugs out of his pocket and shoved them in his ears. I swung left onto an even narrower track but didn't get very far down it before we came to a tree blocking it. There was no way to get around it, so I stopped, grabbed my backpack, and scrambled out. Aiden followed suit and motioned me to lead on. I leapt over the tree's trunk and ran up the track, only half of my attention now on the siren's call. Dawn was little more than half an hour away, and the forest was coming to life. Magpies warbled, small animals crawled through the undergrowth, and from deeper in the distance came the soft footfalls of a wolf.

Running toward the dam I could now smell. Answering the call of the siren.

I increased my speed, desperate to intercept him before he could launch into the water. Aiden ran beside me, his aura a tumble of emotions—fear, uncertainty, and, rather oddly, surprise.

I briefly wondered why, then pushed it aside and

concentrated on reaching the wolf who drew ever closer to death.

Then, through the trees, came a flash of silver. I spun a containment net around my fingers, but once again the trees were too thick, and he was going too fast. If I unleashed it, it'd probably snare nothing more than a tree trunk.

I swore and pointed. While the earplugs Aiden wore were foam and meant he probably would hear me if I shouted, so too would the other wolf *and* the siren. I couldn't risk her changing her song and perhaps forcing her prey to self-harm or even kill himself. I had no idea if that was possible, of course, but given this reservation's tendency to attract off-center beings, we couldn't take the risk.

Aiden obviously understood what I wanted, because he leapt ahead, his form flowing from human to wolf as he wove through the trees with speed and grace. A stream of ethereal, luminous filaments chased after him, while others now stirred around me. The former came from Katie's wellspring. The latter were from the original—mine, as I was now starting to think of it.

I changed direction, leapt over a fallen tree, and ran for the dam I could smell but not yet see. If, for any reason, Aiden failed to stop the wolf, I needed to be there, ready to prevent him from diving into the water.

I raced up a steep incline, then slid to an abrupt halt as the ground fell away and dark water stretched ahead of me. I couldn't see the siren even though I could still hear her song. I studied the water through narrowed eyes and, after a moment, caught the faint shimmer of magic near the center of the dam. It was obviously some kind of concealment spell, but from the little of it I could see, its construction was extremely unusual.

Unsurprising, given what had constructed it.

A deep howl of anger cut across the fading darkness and was quickly followed by growls and snapping teeth. The wolf was fighting Aiden's attempts to stop him. I clenched my fingers against the need to go to his aid. This might be my only chance of stopping—or at least, capturing—the siren. I might not have the right weapon on hand to try the former, but I could at least try the latter.

I hurriedly created a cage spell—one that had been designed to hold a Soucouyant so should contain a siren—then cast it at her. The net of glowing threads tumbled across the water, hit her invisibility shield, and fell away.

She'd woven some sort of spell diffuser into her conceal-ment spell.

I swore, created a second cage, and flung this one under the water, vaguely hoping I could come up underneath her and snare her that way.

Once again, the spell hit a wall and fizzled away.

Fuck, fuck, *fuck*.

Her song was increasing in intensity, and the sounds of fighting were growing more desperate. Aiden was obviously having trouble containing whoever had answered the siren's call. I had to do something, but what?

I wrenched the backpack from my shoulder and tugged my knife from its sheath. Silver could cut through most spells, but I had no idea if it would work when it came to magic created by an otherworldly creature.

The other problem was the fact I normally couldn't throw that far, but at least *that* was one easily enough solved.

I called several threads of wild magic to me, wrapped them around the knife, and directed them to hold and guide. Then I drew back my arm and threw the knife as hard as I could toward the concealed siren.

It arrowed across the water so fast it was little more than a blur of silver. The knife's tip hit the concealment spell and stopped abruptly. For a heartbeat, nothing happened. The knife merely hovered in the darkness with little more than a centimeter buried in the protective wall, its silver blade gleaming brightly under the wild magic's gently pulsing light.

Then her spell exploded, and a wave of dark energy rolled across the dam, gathering water as it raced toward me. I threw out a hand, raised a barrier spell, and braced. The wave hit hard enough to send me sliding back several feet; water washed over the top and sides of my barrier, but the dark energy didn't make the leap from water to land. Maybe it couldn't.

It took me a moment to realize the song had stopped.

My gaze leapt to the middle of the dam. The wild-magic-wrapped knife continued to hover, the remnants of the siren's concealment spell fading limpets that clung to its hilt. The siren wasn't visible, but my "other" senses told me she was diving deeper and moving away. From me, and from this dam. She *was* using the creeks and the underground springs to get around.

I was briefly tempted to send the knife plunging after her, but even if silver could kill her, the wild magic was attached, and I couldn't risk fouling the purity of either it or the wellspring.

I recalled the knife, released the threads, and tucked it safely back into the pack. Then I turned and ran down the hill. The sound of fighting no longer filled the air, but the fact I couldn't hear any conversation worried me.

I caught Aiden's scent a few seconds later and followed it through the trees. I saw the luminous threads of wild magic first. They hovered above the two men sitting side by side on a fallen log. Their profiles were so similar that for a moment the only way to tell them apart was the difference in hair color.

The siren hadn't gone after any old O'Connor.

This time, she'd called Aiden's father.

Chapter Nine

Aiden's clothes were shredded, and there was a deep and bloody scratch running down his cheek. His father was covered in mud and his clothes were torn, but I couldn't immediately see any wounds. It suggested Aiden had been making a concerted effort to restrain rather than fight back.

They glanced around as I appeared out of the trees, their eyes twin spotlights of vivid blue.

"The siren?" Aiden's voice was soft, and rough with exhaustion and emotion. Restraining his father had taken it out of him in more ways than one.

"She'd woven a protective barrier around her body. By the time I figured out how to dismantle it, she'd fled."

"At least you stopped her song." He pushed to his feet. His jeans were torn and bloody, and he wasn't putting much weight on his left leg. He must have fought his father in human form even though his dad had been in wolf. I wondered why but didn't ask. I didn't have the right, especially now. "We'll get you back to the Suzi, then I'll help Dad get home."

"That's not necessary, son," Joseph said. "I'll be—"

"Don't say fine," I said, "because you won't be. Not if the siren starts her song again."

Aiden glanced at me, his expression troubled. "How likely do you think that is?"

"Dawn isn't that far away, and while she's restricted her calls to night, we just don't know enough about her to be certain she can't do so during the day." I hesitated and glanced at Joseph. "It is, however, very possible she'll target you again tomorrow night."

He scraped a hand across his bristly jaw, his expression a mix of angst, regret, and anger. I suspected the latter wasn't aimed at either me or Aiden but rather himself. For answering the call few could have resisted, and for fighting his son. "How she managed to target me tonight is the question that desperately needs answering. I was wearing the earplugs, as suggested. The next thing I know, I'm out here chewing the hell out of my own son."

Aiden gripped his dad's shoulder. "It's fine—"

"No, it's not." It was flatly said but his gaze, when it came to mine, was determined. "Is there a spell you can use to stop me answering the call if she does sing again tomorrow night? The earplugs obviously didn't do a great deal."

"There is." But knowing what I now knew about Karleen, how likely was it that she'd ever allow me to spell her husband? "The real worry is, if I cage you in magic, will she force self-harm once she realizes you physically *can't* answer her song?"

Aiden frowned. "I thought you said sirens died when no one answered their call?"

"That's what most of the legends say, but it wouldn't

apply here because he would answer the call if he wasn't being prevented."

"Then we try a two-prong approach—cage and drugging me senseless." Joseph shrugged. "It's the safest way."

It might be the safest, but I was still betting Karleen would have a whole lot to say about the idea—and me. "It would probably be best we did it early in the evening, just in case she changes her timing."

He nodded. "I'll arrange for someone to pick you up—"

"I'll do that," Aiden cut in. "We both know how Mom feels about her. I'll not risk—"

"Son, I'm not about to allow any harm—"

"I'll still be there to ensure it."

Joseph stared at Aiden for several seconds and then said, rather abruptly, "Fine."

It was obviously anything but fine, but Joseph looked at me and added, "Thank you for your help. I know it can't be easy given the situation."

"I'm just doing my job."

"Yes, and we *all* appreciate it, even if it doesn't always seem that way."

I didn't reply to that. What could I say, given we all knew he was referring to his mate? Aiden caught my elbow and said, "This way."

I gently tugged free of his grip. "How about you shift shape first so you're not leaving a bloody trail? Besides, I know where I left the car."

"You do?" Joseph said, surprised. "How, when we are deep within pack grounds?"

I motioned to the luminous threads they couldn't see. "The wild magic guides me."

"The wild magic through which Katie speaks?" he asked.

172

I glanced at him. "Some of it, yes."

"Then she *has* become the reservation's guardian?"

It was said with just the slightest trace of incredulity. Despite everything that had happened, he really hadn't believed. But then, Karleen still wasn't a hundred percent convinced, even though Katie had not only spoken to her through me but also appeared before her.

At least I now knew why she distrusted all things witch.

I nodded then turned and headed off through the trees. Aiden shifted shape, padding beside me for a couple of seconds in wolf shape before shifting back to human, while Joseph remained a few steps behind. Neither man said anything, but tension still simmered between them. I wished I knew why, but it wasn't like I could ask.

But I damn well wanted to.

Dawn was painting the sky with glorious shades of pink and gold by the time we reached the Suzi. I slung the backpack onto the rear seat and then climbed in. Aiden gripped the door to prevent me closing it and leaned in. For a moment I thought he was going to kiss me and couldn't help the twinge of disappointment when all he did was simply tug a twig from my hair and flick it behind him.

"I'll give you a call tomorrow once a time has been arranged."

"Meaning once your mom has calmed down and agreed to me spelling her husband."

I said it as neutrally as I could, but a wry smile touched his lips. "Basically, yes."

"And if she doesn't?"

"She will. No matter what she thinks about you personally, she's aware Dillon's only alive thanks to you, and she certainly won't risk Dad's life simply to spite you."

I nodded and, once he'd stepped back, slammed the

door shut. I reversed the Suzi down the track until I found a spot clear enough to turn around, and then drove out.

I was halfway home when my phone rang, the tone telling me it was Ashworth. I flicked the answer button on the steering wheel and said, "Did Eli kick you out of bed for snoring or something?"

He laughed. "No, I got a damn call from the RWA. They want me to check an incident up on the border. Just thought I'd let you know I unearthed my bronze knife, and it's here if you need it."

"I will. She's still targeting Aiden's family."

"Then I'd have to say she was definitely called here by your anger and grief."

"That being the case, why would she target the men rather than Karleen? That's who I'm angry at; no one else."

"Sometimes the best form of revenge lies not in death but rather suffering."

And Katie had warned her mother that she would suffer... I swore and rubbed my eyes. "Is there any way I can stop her? I mean, if I'm the reason she's here, there should be some way for me to get rid of her."

"You could try a banishment spell—Eli will be able to guide you through that one—but you'd need to find where she's hiding first."

"A mite difficult considering she's using the waterways to get around."

"She'll still have a safe place, lass. Not even the supernatural can remain alert twenty-four seven."

"Finding it is going to be tricky in a reservation well known for the sheer number of its mineral springs and dams."

"If monster hunting was easy," he said, "there would be no fun in it."

I snorted. "You're crazy."

He laughed. "So Eli has said, multiple times. Which reminds me, he got a call from the professor's family. They found his notes and are expressing them down to us. Should be here by tomorrow."

"That was fast."

"Apparently they were glad someone might finally find them useful."

"Even if we do, we can't tell them. We can't risk it getting back to the High Witch Council."

"Oh, trust me, I doubt anything we tell his family would escape their lips. Apparently, they're not on great terms with the council after the way they treated Malcom's life work."

"Maybe, but I'd still rather—"

"Rest easy, lass, nothing will be said. Eli and I no more want the high council hordes descending on this place than you do. Eli will give you a call once they arrive and he's had a chance to look at them."

"Thanks. You be careful monster hunting, won't you? I don't want anything happening to my surrogate grandfather."

"Ha, don't you be worrying about me, lass. I'm intending to be around long enough to bounce the wee babes you eventually have on my bony old knees."

I laughed. "Given there's currently no man in my life, I like your optimism."

"There was that Kang fellow. According to Belle, he was quite keen."

"And unlikely to ever settle for a quiet life here in the reservation," I said dryly. "If you start matchmaking me, the scones will go off the menu."

He laughed. "Consider the matter never mentioned again. I'll see you in a couple of days."

He hung up, and I continued with a smile on my face. I really, *really* hoped his plan eventuated, and that he did live long enough to bounce babies on his knees. Although at the rate things were going, Belle and Monty would start producing way before I ever did.

God, don't wish motherhood on me came Belle's comment. *We're not even married yet.*

You can have babies without getting married, you know.

Of course, but we're still at the "learning to live with you" stage. Babies would only throw a spanner in the works and maybe even wreck things.

At least you're no longer denying marriage and babies do lie in your future.

She sighed. It was a very put-upon sound. *It's hard not to fall for a well-built, good-looking man who is not only open about his wants and desires, but who also cleans. I mean, do you know how rare that is?*

I laughed. *I'm sure Monty will be pleased to know the reason you finally fell for him is because he's so adept at housework.*

People have fallen for less, she said.

True. I paused, waiting for a truck to go past so I could turn right. *How'd you do at the hospital yesterday?*

Not good. His soul was more than partially consumed—he will never wake up. He'll simply fade and die, even on life support.

Ah, fuck.

Yeah.

Have you told Aiden?

I haven't seen him since I did the reading at the hospital, and it's not the sort of thing you can put in a message.

True. An odd sound caught my attention, and I looked into the rearview mirror.

All I could see was the grill of a big Toyota Hilux.

Coming straight at me. Accelerating rather than stopping.

If I didn't get out of his way, he'd push me into the path of the oncoming truck.

I was *not* going to lose another damn car... especially not one that I loved driving.

I hauled the steering wheel hard to the right and hit the accelerator. The Suzi's wheels spun briefly, then gripped, and she slewed around and shot past the Hilux in the opposite direction. I had a brief glimpse of the driver and realized it was the man who'd peered out from his mother's bedroom window. Our granny killer, Harry.

In the rearview mirror I saw the Hilux's rear lights flash as he braked, but he was going too fast and shot past the stop sign, straight into the path of the oncoming truck. The two hit nose to side, the big truck pushing the smaller vehicle in front of it for several seconds before it speared off into the grassy verge.

I pulled over and ran back. The truck driver had stopped, but I couldn't see any movement in the cabin. I leapt onto the running board and hauled the passenger door open.

"You okay?" I asked.

He was shaking, pale, and rubbing his chest, but he nodded. "He just came at me, you know. I couldn't stop in time."

"I know, I saw it. Stay in the cab while I go check him."

"You want me to call the rangers?"

"And an ambulance, please."

I jumped down and ran around the front of the truck. It

had a massive bull bar, which would explain why the side of the Hilux looked crumpled. They were generally tough old vehicles.

It was sitting nose-first in a ditch, facing away from the road so that I couldn't see if our killer was still inside.

Be very careful came Belle's warning. *Just because he should be unconscious after a crash like that doesn't mean he will be. Werewolves are tougher than humans.*

They could also shift shape to heal any major trauma, even if trapped. He just had to have some level of consciousness for instinct to kick in.

I approached the back of the vehicle warily, a repelling spell buzzing around my fingers. The Hilux's engine was making a god-awful racket, and smoke poured from under the engine bay, though the color was white, suggesting it was simply steam coming from a smashed radiator rather than something more serious.

I couldn't see a figure in the driver seat, but maybe he was unconscious and had collapsed sideways. I hesitated near the broken rear lights and scanned the immediate area, looking for any sign that he might have been thrown clear before moving slowly on.

The driver side of the vehicle was basically destroyed. Had it been anyone other than a wolf inside, they'd probably be dead. Hell, even a damn wolf's instinct to shift shape and heal might not have been fast enough for an accident this bad.

I edged forward past crumpled metal and broken glass and peered into the front of the vehicle. He wasn't there.

I blinked in shock for a moment, then spun and looked around again. If he'd been thrown out through the front window—and that was possible given the state of it—he should be visible. The grass wasn't that long....

The thought died as a scuff of sound was followed quickly by a shouted warning.

Before I could unleash the repelling spell, something hard smashed into the side of my head and I knew no more.

* * *

Waking was a slow, painful, and very cold experience. There was an army of madmen armed with jackhammers happily drilling into my head, and tremors racked my body. My teeth were chattering so damn hard, my jaw ached.

The reason why was immediately obvious—I was partially submerged in water. It lapped around my waist, but both my hair and coat were sodden, suggesting that at some point I'd been fully submerged.

I had no memory of falling into water. No memory of getting out of it.

I reached for Belle, but it felt like I was wading through mental glue. There weren't many things that could break our telepathic connection, but concussion was certainly one.

I just had to hope she still had some sense of me. Otherwise, getting out of here was going to be tricky.

Not that I had any idea where "here" was.

I warily looked around. I couldn't initially see anything other than the odd looming shape, but as my eyes grew used to the darkness, it became obvious I was in some sort of underground cavern.

I twisted around to look behind me, but the movement was too quick and set off the idiots in my head. The pain was so bad that my eyes watered and stomach rolled. I concentrated on breathing evenly and, after a few seconds, both calmed down.

I gingerly felt my head. There was a cut at least two inches long on the left side, and while it didn't appear to be bleeding, it was hard to tell when everything was wet. But my fingers didn't come away bloody, so that was at least something.

I had no idea what the bastard had hit me with, but it had obviously been heavy enough to split my head open. I guessed I should be thankful that he hadn't seared out my eyes or sewn my lips closed, but maybe I didn't fit his target profile.

Or maybe he just needed me out of the way so he could continue his murderous backlash against his mother.

So why hadn't he just killed me? Why dump me? Had he expected that doing the latter would lead to the former without him putting in too much extra effort?

Maybe. His mother had said he was a lazy bastard.

I took a deeper breath but regretted it almost instantly. The air was stale and foul-smelling, and it caught in my throat and sent me into a coughing fit that lasted entirely too long for comfort.

I scrubbed the resulting tears from my eyes with the heel of my hand and kept to shallow breaths. Which was hard when I needed to move and moving bloody hurt.

Slowly, carefully, I climbed out of the water. The idiots in my head still protested, but not as vigorously this time. I hugged my knees close to my chest, trying to warm my body and stop the chills from getting any worse.

Other than my head and the ice that had settled deep into my bones, I wasn't hurt. I had absolutely no idea where I was or how much time had passed, but I had no doubt Belle would have raised the alarm the minute the connection between us had snapped. Whether they'd find me before hypothermia got me was another matter entirely.

I shivered and studied the vast cavern. The lake was a mirror of black that gave little clue as to its depth, and I couldn't immediately see its source, though there was steadily dripping water somewhere off in the distance. Stalactites of various lengths hung from the roof, but it was the deeper shadows dotting the walls and parts of the shoreline that caught my attention. Though the darkness made it hard to be sure, those darker spots appeared to be horizontal mine shafts—an impression strengthened by the old wooden beams that framed at least half of them.

If they *were* shafts, then I'd obviously been dumped in some sort of old mining complex. I did seem to have an affinity for the things.

I scanned the ceiling again but couldn't see an entry point, which suggested Harry had carried me in here and thrown me into the water rather than simply dumped me into a vertical shaft. Why I hadn't drowned was a bloody good question. The lake was obviously deep, given it had flooded some of the lower tunnels. But even as those questions stirred, so too did memory. The shock of immersion, of cold. Fighting inky blackness, and of lungs burning with the need to breathe, the desire to just let go fighting the desperation to live, swimming. Then kicking to the surface and onto the shore....

Harry obviously hadn't stuck around after he'd thrown me in, because if those memories were anything to go by, I wouldn't have been in any state to fight him.

But I wouldn't have been when unconscious either. Perhaps, I thought slowly, it wasn't so much a case of him *not* wanting to kill me but rather, being unable to. Was it possible that my inner wild magic had kicked in and instinctively protected me? It certainly wouldn't be the first time it had happened, but it might perhaps be the most important.

Speaking of wild magic... I looked around again but had no sense of its presence, which was unusual, given these days it seemed to be everywhere.

I shifted to see if my phone was in my back pocket and wasn't surprised to discover it gone. Given how little evidence Harry had left behind in his previous two crimes, he obviously had some working knowledge of police procedures and would surely be aware that the rangers could have used my phone to track me.

I scanned the walls again, wondering which of the many tunnels might lead back to the surface. While I had no doubt everyone would be out searching for me, I also had a bad feeling I might have to get myself out of here.

And there was no better time to start than now. If I stayed here hugging myself, I might just turn into an icicle.

I rolled over onto my hands and knees, waited for several minutes for the madmen to calm down again, and then pushed slowly upright. My legs wobbled, and my knees felt ready to give way, but I didn't fall, and that was definitely a bonus.

I drew in a cautious breath and then created a light spell and tossed it above my head. Pale silvery light filtered through the darkness, glinting off the dark water and throwing the crumbling remains of the nearby mineshafts in stark relief. None of them looked safe to enter. If I was going to get out of here, my best bet would be one of the tunnels much higher out of the water.

I shuffled forward cautiously. The surrounding rocks were slick with moisture, and I had no desire to slip and fall. If I did, I might not have the strength to get up again.

It was slow going. The ice that had settled into my bones seemed to have sapped my strength, and I barely managed to walk a third of the way around the lake before I had to stop and rest, my breath a harsh rasp that echoed loudly across the still darkness.

At this rate, it'd be Christmas before I reached the other side of the lake.

I pushed upright again and continued. After what seemed like forever, I slowly climbed an old path hacked out of the rock by hand tools and reached a wide plateau that held the metal remains of what looked to be tracks. Cart tracks—the sort that miners used to haul waste out.

I swallowed heavily and tried to ignore the leap of hope. Just because there were tracks didn't mean they'd lead me anywhere. Didn't mean the tunnel was safe to use or hadn't collapsed.

I motioned the light spell closer to the ground and followed the rusting snake of metal to the tunnel sitting on the far-left edge of the plateau. I paused in the entrance, warily studying the struts and what little my light showed of the interior. Water dripped steadily from the tunnel's roof and ran past my feet, but the wooden supports appeared to be in reasonably good shape—at least in this section. The air wasn't any fresher in here than in the cavern, which was a little alarming, given it should have been if there was an exit somewhere ahead.

I wrinkled my nose and pushed forward. If it turned out the tunnel was blocked, then I could just turn around and try one of the other ones. It wasn't like I didn't have plenty of other options.

My light bounced along several meters ahead of me, highlighting the rough-hewn path that appeared to be sloping upward. I once again tried to curb the rush of hope. Just because it was going up didn't mean it was leading out.

Twenty minutes later, I hit a partial collapse. The left side support had given way and fallen toward the right and, in the process, had bought down half the roof. But the way the left support had lodged against the right meant it had prevented a total collapse. I could still get through, but I guess the question was, should I?

I sent the light spell into the triangular gap and squatted down to peer after it. Rubble lined the tunnel for a good two or three meters past the collapse, but it otherwise seemed pretty clear. That didn't mean there couldn't be other collapses I couldn't see, of course.

But I could taste fresh air now. More collapses or not, there was an opening somewhere ahead. I had to take the chance and continue.

I eyed the gap a second or two longer, then got down on my hands and knees and crawled through. Dirt and stones sprinkled across my back, and my pulse rate leapt, but I resisted the urge to hurry, wary of bumping into anything and bringing the whole lot down on top of me.

The tension eased a little once I was out from under the collapse, but I wasn't out of trouble just yet. I climbed back to my feet and continued. There were two more partial collapses, the last one so bad that I basically had to crawl through on my belly.

It was only the growing freshness of the air that kept me going.

I wasn't sure how much later it was when I saw the first glimmer of light. It was pale and insubstantial, but it sang with power and presence.

The moon.

It was the goddamn moon.

And that meant I'd been missing and/or unconscious for at least a minimum of twelve hours.

Fuck.

I trudged up the last bit of steep slope to the vertical

slash in the tunnel's roof. It wasn't an exit—not a manmade one, at any rate. That was a few meters farther ahead, if the rail tracks disappearing into the huge pile of rubble was anything to go by. The entrance had obviously collapsed a long time ago; there was no way I was ever going to get out that way.

I stopped under the overhead slash and breathed deep of the fresh, clear air.

And felt a sharp twinge of awareness across the psychic line.

Belle? I said instantly. *Can you hear me?*

Lizzie? Oh, thank god.

Her voice seemed to be coming from a very great distance, but relief nevertheless surged through me. Its force was so strong that my knees wobbled, and I had to place a hand on the wall to help keep me upright.

How badly are you hurt? she continued. *I'm getting the impression of pain, but our connection is so fuzzy, it's hard to tell how badly.*

I was hit on the head and probably have concussion.

That would explain the fuzziness. Anything else?

I'm bone cold and soaked to the skin, but otherwise fine.

Where are you? Can you tell?

I gave her a quick description of the mine and then added, *Right now I'm standing under a horizontal slash in the roof. I can see the moon but little else.*

Now that our connection is active, I should be able to track you down. You able to hold on?

Stay conscious, she meant. *Yes, but bring food with you. I'm famished.*

I'm not surprised. You've been missing for nearly twenty hours.

Meaning my guess had been on the conservative side. *Has the siren struck again?*

Maybe.

My stomach dropped. *Meaning what?*

She sighed. *Aiden's father has gone missing. No one knows where he is, but we haven't found a body yet.*

Oh fuck....

Yeah. Belle's voice was grim. *But let's worry about that situation once we get you out of there and home safe.*

Let me know when you're close. I'll send my light spell through the hole so you can see where I am. Oh, and bring ropes.

Will do. She paused. *Try not to fall asleep.*

I'm well past the three-hour danger zone for concussion, Belle.

Always better to be safe than sorry

She disconnected but not fully. A warm static-type buzz continued to flow down the line, and it made me feel both safe and connected.

Safe. Who'd have thought *that* hours ago.

I blinked back the tears of relief, then sat under the slit and stared up at the stars. Aiden's father going missing was not a good development, and I couldn't help but wonder if my disappearance had scuppered the plans to cage him. But even if they had, he could have still drugged himself unconscious—surely a siren's song couldn't counter medicine's influence.

I leaned my head against the rock behind me and sent a silent prayer to whatever goddess might be watching for his safe return. I hated to think what would happen if he died. Hated to think what Karleen's reaction might be—although given my dreams, maybe I already knew.

A luminous sliver of moonlight moved across the slash

above me. I raised a hand, and it spun down and wrapped around my wrist. Almost instantly, the creeping tiredness washed away and the shivers that still racked my body eased. Not totally, but enough that it was no longer unpleasant.

The thread was from my wellspring rather than Katie's, and while she did have a connection with it, it wasn't strong. I still tried to reach her through this thread, but she didn't answer. I guessed that was to be expected; her attention would be on her pack and her missing father rather than a missing witch, even if that witch was her only earthly connection.

I wasn't sure how long passed before I heard the first snippets of noise. A heartbeat later, Belle came back online and said, *I think we're close.*

I pushed to my feet and cast my spell light through the slash.

Seeing that, she immediately said. *We're probably five minutes away. Hang tight.*

I closed my eyes and fought the stupid desire to cry. I was safe; tears were not necessary.

But they are understandable, Belle said.

Maybe, but I've shed too many of them of late. It's a habit I do not want to get set in.

She laughed softly. *I'm decidedly more comforted by that statement than all your earlier assurances that you're okay.*

I smiled and continued to stare up. After a moment, she appeared close to the slash's edge, relief in her expression and her thoughts.

Monty appeared beside her, his expression echoing hers. "Goddamn it, woman, don't do something like this ever again. You gave us all heart attacks."

"Sorry," I said dryly. "But it wasn't like I planned for that bastard to attack me."

"What happened? How did you end up—"

"Monty, you can ask all the questions you want later" came Aiden's comment. "Right now, move aside so I get the harness down there and get her out."

My pulse rate stuttered and then began to gallop. Aiden was here, searching for me rather than his father. And while that made my heart want to sing, it also worried the hell out of me. Karleen wasn't going to be happy about his decision.

He appeared above me, blue eyes bright but ringed with shadows. "If I lower the harness down, you okay to strap it on?"

I nodded and watched as he connected the rope and then lowered the harness down. I grabbed it once it was close enough then hurriedly put it on with shaky fingers. I checked everything was connected and tight before looking up at him again. "Ready to go."

"Grab the rope and hold on."

As I did, the luminous thread detached itself and drifted back into the moonlight.

A heartbeat later, my feet were off the ground, and I was pulled slowly but safely out of the shaft. I gripped the edge, then climbed up and stepped away. I didn't have time to do anything else, because Belle's arms wrapped around me in the biggest, fiercest hug.

"I thought I'd lost you," she said softly. "It was the worst twenty-four hours of my entire life."

I wrapped my arms around her and held on tight. I had some sense of what she must have gone through, having gone through sheer and utter panic when the realization that Clayton had kidnapped her had hit. But at least our connection hadn't been severed. I'd always known she was alive—indeed, that was part of Clayton's grand plan, because he'd known that everything he did to her would echo back through me.

Belle hadn't had that comfort. All she'd had was silence.

"Sorry," I whispered. "I didn't mean to scare you like that."

She laughed, though it was a little brittle-sounding. "We need to work on another means of contacting each other just in case something like this ever happens again."

"I'd rather we plan on it *not* happening again" came Monty's comment.

"So would I," Aiden said quietly.

I pulled free from Belle and met his gaze. His expression gave little away, but his face was drawn and his aura a tumble of conflicting emotions. I opened my mouth to thank him, but he cut me off with a brusque, "Don't you dare."

I didn't. I simply dropped my gaze from his.

Belle squeezed my arm and said into the somewhat tense silence, "Why don't you sit down on that rock over there while we have a look at that wound on your head. That way, we can decide whether to move on or wait for the paramedics."

"We wait," Aiden said. "It's possible she's got hypothermia, given all that shivering, and she needs to be warmed up slowly before we go anywhere."

"Did anyone think to bring a spare set of clothes? Because I'm not going to warm up in these ones."

"Good point," Belle said. "Monty, strip off your socks and your sweater. Aiden, we'll need your coat."

As the two men obeyed, Belle inspected my head wound and made a tsking sound. "I think it's going to need stitches."

"Just pour some holy water over it."

"That's not going to stitch it back together."

"No, but it should stop any infection."

She grunted, cleansed the wound, then ordered Monty to turn around while she helped me strip off my sodden clothes and get into the borrowed ones. Aiden's jacket fell to my knees, and his scent lingered, warming me in a myriad of ways.

My gaze rose to his again. He was standing to one side with his arms crossed. I wanted to hug him, comfort him, but that was no longer my place, and I couldn't keep blurring the boundaries between friends and lovers.

Though even friends hugged each other in times of need. And he did need. Desperately.

Before I could say anything, though, Jaz appeared with two paramedics behind her. She walked over and gave me a quick but fierce hug. "Glad to see you're alive and well."

"Glad to be alive and well," I returned, and fought the urge to ask her all the things I was reluctant to ask Aiden. With him in earshot, that wasn't practical. Or wise.

The paramedics did a thorough check and decided I did indeed have a concussion and mild hypothermia, and it was decided I should be taken to the hospital so I could be monitored for twenty-four hours. As always, I protested the decision, but this time I was outvoted and basically ignored.

Belle handed me several chocolate bars in commiseration, and I munched on those as I was carried through the bush on a stretcher.

It took us nearly an hour to get out. Monty and Belle said they'd follow the ambulance to the hospital, but Aiden gave me a gruff, "We'll talk later," and disappeared.

I wasn't surprised. He had a duty to his pack and his alpha, and that had to take priority now that he knew I was safe.

After going through a whole bunch of scans and checks at the hospital, my head was patched before I was finally taken to a private room. Belle and Monty appeared a few minutes later.

"Eli and Ashworth send their love," Belle said, as she strode in. "They wanted to come and see you, but I convinced them you needed your rest."

I frowned. "I thought Ashworth had been sent up to the border to investigate an incident?"

"He was, but in his own words, 'I canna investigate a goddamn grave robbing when my adopted daughter has gone missing.'" Monty grinned. "He and Eli have been crafting all sorts of spells in an effort to locate you."

"I was so far underground that regular location spells were never going to find me."

"Oh, they were trying irregular ones, too. I've never seen either of them so worried."

"You were Aiden's priority, you know," Belle said. "He delegated the search for his dad, but he was on the ground with the rest of us looking for you."

"I've never really doubted that he cared for me—"

"Oh, I think it's safe to say he loves you," Monty cut in. "That has been blindingly obvious to everyone over the last twenty-four hours."

"Yes, but love isn't enough. Not when he can't gainsay the ruling of his alphas." I hauled myself up into a sitting position. "Enough of that for now. When did Aiden's father disappear?"

Belle pulled the visitor's chair closer to the bed while Monty perched on the windowsill. "Just before dusk yesterday. He said he was going for a run but never returned. He's not answering his phone, and his scent trail abruptly disappeared about a kilometer from his house. The O'Connors put out a compound-wide alert at nine and made it reservation-wide at midnight."

"I take it the lakes in and around the reservation have been checked?"

Monty nodded. "They've ordered extra divers on the off chance she's weighted him down. They'll start searching in the morning."

Belle glanced at him. "We don't know that he's dead yet."

"The siren missed him once. She's not going to let that happen again."

I scrubbed a hand across my eyes. "Karleen will find a way to blame this on me."

"Undoubtedly," Belle said, her voice dry. "I mean, you did promise to cage the man and keep him safe, and then you had the audacity to get kidnapped."

Sad thing was, that was likely to be her exact thought line. "What about Harry? More importantly, what about the Suzi? Is she okay?"

Belle laughed. "Yes, she is. She was found unharmed and in mint condition—aside from a blood stain on the back seat that pretty obviously came from your head—on the other side of Creswyn."

I could imagine what everyone had been thinking when *that* had been discovered. "How did she get there? That's not where I left her."

"According to the truck driver—"

"Is he okay?"

Monty nodded. "He tried to help when you were attacked and got a broken arm for his trouble."

"He told the rangers that Harry carried you to the Suzi, threw you in the back, and took off," Belle continued.

"When it was found in Creswyn three hours later, it was presumed you were both in that area."

"So where was I found?"

"Up Fryer's Ridge way."

Which wasn't that far from the O'Connor compound, if memory served me right. "I wonder how he knew about that mine? It seems pretty odd that he went out of his way to dump me there when there were a multitude of other options closer to where he snatched me."

Belle shrugged. "Maybe he was simply aware how hard it would be for a passerby to hear or scent you in that one."

Maybe. It had been a long way underground, that was for sure. "I take it he's still on the run?"

"Yes," Monty said, "and if he has any sense, he'll run right out of the reservation."

"I don't think any of us believe he'll do that," I said. "He wouldn't have tried to get me out of the way if that were his plan."

"Aiden said the same thing. They've placed a watch on that abandoned park his mom mentioned, and they're running a check on all abandoned buildings."

"How? They're only a small team—they haven't the manpower."

"They've conscripted the other packs to help out."

"If those two Sinclair idiots hadn't sidetracked me, we would have already caught the bastard."

Monty grinned. "I believe Aiden said something along those lines but a lot less politely to the Sinclair alphas when you were kidnapped. They've certainly gone out of their way to help ever since."

"And so they damn well should." I yawned hugely. "Sorry. Nothing personal. You're not boring me or anything."

Belle laughed and caught my hand. "Get some sleep, and we'll pick you up in the morning once they give you the all-clear."

She dropped a kiss on my cheek, then rose, caught Monty's arm, and escorted him out. I smiled and settled back down in the bed. Unsurprisingly, I was asleep in minutes.

Awareness stirred me many hours later. I cracked open an eye and saw the figure slumped in the chair. My heart did a little jump.

Aiden.

I didn't move, didn't say anything. I just watched him sleep, knowing he probably needed it a whole lot more than me. But even in sleep he looked stressed and worn out. The last few days had probably been harder on him than anyone else, and my heart ached for him.

He must have sensed the weight of my gaze, because he opened his eyes and studied me. Neither of us said anything. We didn't need to. Not in that moment.

Then I shifted, breaking the spell. "Any news on your father?"

"No. As impossible as it should be, he has completely disappeared." He grimaced. "We've now started checking abandoned mines that we know have been flooded. She could have lured him underground."

That was more than possible, especially if she was intent on preventing me from stopping her before she could make her kill. "How's your mother taking the situation?"

"As well as you could expect." His lips twisted with bitterness. "I daresay there will be an explosion once we get a conclusion one way or the other."

"Would she agree to me helping you find him?"

He nodded. "She can be many things, but she's not stupid."

"I never said she was."

"I know that." He rose, walked over, and sat lightly on the edge of the bed. "When you disappeared, it felt like my whole world was falling apart. And it gave me some insight into what you must have felt when Mia appeared. I'm sorry you went through that. Sorry I just didn't take what it must have been like for you into account."

I drew in a shuddering breath and fought the goddamn tears that were threatening again. "I appreciate the apology."

He waited a heartbeat, as if expecting me to say more, but what else could be said? It was an apology, not a declaration of intent.

His lips twisted. "Until our situations change, and as much as I absolutely hate admitting it, you walking away was for the best. I can't keep putting you through this stress; I understand that now."

Not the words I wanted to hear. Somehow, though, I kept my voice even. "And if I find someone else?"

"I will resist the temptation to rip out his fucking throat and wish you both the best."

Which was probably as close to a declaration of love I was ever likely to get. I resisted the urge to throw myself into his arms and never again let him go, and said lightly, "No more sneaky kissing attempts?"

He smiled. "It may take a little while to get over that particular habit."

I echoed his smile. We had a truce, one that would make things easier in the short term. Long-term? Well, that remained to be seen.

"Once the doctors give me the all clear, I can start the search for your father."

"I'm not sure either Belle or Monty would agree to you jumping back into the chase so soon. Hell, Ashworth and Eli would probably have a word or two to say about it, too."

My eyebrows rose. "That sounds as if they've already had a word or two."

"Ashworth has never been one to mince words," he replied dryly.

No, he hadn't, but I was a little surprised he'd unleashed on Aiden. He'd promised he wouldn't. I guess my disappearance and possible death had voided that promise.

"The longer we leave it," I said, "the less likely it is that we'll find him alive."

"I know that—"

"Then get your pack's clearance and find me something that has his echo on it, and we'll start in the morning."

He hesitated and then nodded. "I'll come by the café, then. At the very least, it'll give you time to grab some breakfast."

"Appreciate that. Even after all those chocolate blocks I consumed earlier, I'm famished."

"If I'd known, I would have brought you in something." He hesitated and then rose. "I'd better let you get back to sleep."

He caught my hand and kissed my fingers. I smiled. "I thought the kissing was going to stop?"

"Fingers are a step down from lips. Can't expect me to give up my drug of choice cold turkey."

I laughed and suddenly felt a whole lot easier about the future. Which was weird when he'd just agreed we were better apart than together. "I take it you've retrieved my car?"

He nodded. "I returned the backpack to Belle, but we're still doing forensics on the car. You should have it back in a day or so."

"I can survive that long without her." It wasn't as if I needed to tootle back and forth from Argyle anymore, after all.

"I'll get a mate to give her a cleanup before we return her—he's a detailer and should be able to get the blood stain out."

"That would be brilliant. Thanks."

He hesitated briefly, then nodded and left. I drew in a deep breath, snaring the last remnants of his scent, savoring it as I would chocolate. Then I settled back down and went straight back to sleep.

The doctors checked me over and released me a few hours later. Belle brought in fresh clothes and shoes, and once I'd dressed, drove me home. I spent a good twenty minutes in the shower, not only washing away the last remnants of inner ice but also the foul staleness that seemed to have ingrained itself into my skin.

By the time I got back down, Belle had breakfast ready, and Aiden had arrived. He looked up with a smile, and my heart did its usual little dance. "Did you get your pack's clearance?"

"I did. Mom gave me this for you to use." He reached into his pocket and drew out a plastic bag. Inside was a sturdy-looking gold watch. "She told me to thank you for making this attempt to find him."

I raised an eyebrow. "She expected me to be vindictive and not?"

"She did." He hesitated. "There are some in the family who believe this is some sort of twisted means of getting into her good books."

"Some" meaning Karleen herself, no doubt. "Has it not occurred to any of them that if I *did* want revenge for either your mom's active destruction attempts on our relationship or her stance on witches in general, I'd go directly after her? I wouldn't be picking off innocent members of her family."

"Picking off family members causes greater pain than a direct attack ever would."

"I didn't call this siren into the reservation, Aiden. Not intentionally."

"I know that." He paused. "But I'll give you fair warning, it's the unintentional part my mother has fixated on. If this goes wrong, if Dad dies..."

"She'll come after me," I finished for him.

"Not physically. But legally? Through the reservation council? Yes."

I thought again of those bloody images in my dreams and wondered how well he truly understood his mother. She'd lost her sister and would eventually lose her brother; if she lost her husband as well, it might just break her mentally.

If he *was* dead, it was all bets off.

I took the bag holding the watch, but before I could do anything further, Belle took it from me and placed it on the counter.

"How about we all eat something first before we start worrying about finding Aiden's dad." There was a hint of censure in her voice. "Lizzie's not the only one walking the fatigue line. You're not looking so great yourself, Ranger."

His lips twisted. "I'll be fine."

"Ha," she said. "Heard that before—usually before Lizzie does something dumb like collapsing in a heap."

His quick grin was an acknowledgment of her truth. "Does Monty know about this bossy streak of yours?"

"Since before we were teenagers." She placed their coffees and my tea down on the table before sitting. "He swears the first time I bossed him around was the moment he fell for me."

"I wouldn't have picked him for a man who likes to be dominated."

"Oh, he's not, but you've got to remember he's from a high-profile royal witch line, and even as a kid, had been burdened with the weight of great expectations. According to him, I was the only one at school who treated him as just another kid." She glanced at me with a bright smile. "Well, me and Lizzie, because I wouldn't have been there without her."

"Then why is he here if his future had been planned from such a young age?" Aiden asked. "He's obviously not lacking in power, so why was he working in cataloguing before accepting the position here?"

"The problem with expectations is living up to them," I said.

He glanced at me. "Meaning?"

"Everyone attending witch university is graded power-wise before entry. The tests revealed he was lower on the scale than expected. His family did not react well."

Aiden frowned as he began to eat. "These tests—is that what you'll have to undergo when you head back to Canberra for the trial?"

"Yes." And I was not looking forward to it.

"Will they detect the wild magic in your DNA?"

I hesitated. "Unknown, but the wild magic has ramped my native magic, and they will detect that. And my father is well aware I can use wild magic."

"Do you think it'll play into either of the court cases?"

It was a question that surprised me, if only because I

really hadn't thought about it. "I wouldn't have thought so, but who really knows. It's been a long time since either of us have been up there."

"If your father can use your power boost to his advantage for either case, he will," Belle said grimly. "The man is a power-hungry monster."

And I was hoping that, like all monsters, he'd eventually get his comeuppance. If I had a hand in that happening, so much the better.

The conversation moved on and, once we'd finished our breakfast, I retrieved the watch and pulled it out of the bag. There was no pulse, no indication of life.

I raised my gaze to Aiden's and saw the hope in his blue eyes fade. "It's dead, isn't it?" he said, his voice tightly controlled.

"That doesn't mean he is," I said. "It could simply be a matter of the connection fading faster than normal or him being too far away for the connection to activate."

All of which were true, but not the truth in this situation. He knew that as much as I did.

"We could always try a locator spell, using the watch as a base," Belle said.

"Locator spells didn't work finding Liz, though."

"No, but she was deep underground."

He frowned. "Why would that affect anything? That type of spell isn't normally restricted by physical barriers, is it?"

She hesitated. "According to Monty, it depends on the density and composition of the earth, as well as the depth of the item or person being sought. If such constraints weren't considered during the casting, then, yes, they can."

"Ashworth and Eli would have been aware of those restrictions, though."

"Yes, but none of us had expected him to dump her down a mine shaft. We were all working on the presumption that he'd do to her what he did to the two older women."

Red flicked across Aiden's aura at that comment. Harry would pay for what he did to those women and to me. Aiden might be a law-abiding man, but if Harry was stupid enough to resist arrest or even attack, Aiden would retaliate. "I guess we have nothing to lose by trying."

"And if I fail, we can ask Monty, Ashworth, or Eli to try." I paused. "I'm surprised they haven't already been asked, to be honest."

He raised an eyebrow. "Knowing my mother as well as you do, why would you think that?"

"Because she's desperate to find her husband and canny enough to overcome prejudice if necessary."

He laughed, though it was a somewhat bitter sound. "That's certainly a truth. But in this case, even if she *had* requested help, you were their priority, and I can't blame them for that."

Because you were also mine. He didn't say those words, but he was thinking them. I could see it in his eyes and in the wash of his emotions.

I dropped my gaze to the watch in an effort to control my own treacherous emotions. "It would also be worth talking to Katie. She'd be aware that Joseph has gone missing and would surely be searching for him. If he *is* in a mine, though, it's likely she wouldn't have any more luck than anyone else."

"What makes you think that?" Belle said, surprised. "Wild magic is formed deep in the earth, so why would it be restricted?"

I hesitated. "When I woke in the cavern, I had no sense

of the wild magic. It was dead, just like our link. It was only when I neared the surface again that it came to me."

"Katie's threads? Or the original?" Aiden said.

I glanced at him. "Original. I think Katie's attention was probably on the search for your dad."

"Which is odd, when you think about it," Belle said. "I mean, you're the only one she can interface with, so you'd think she'd at least have some of her threads looking for you."

I shrugged. "It's possible that by the time she realized I was missing it was already too late. She was present when Joseph answered the siren's song the first time, and I'm thinking she would have kept a pretty close eye on him for the rest of the day."

"If that's the case, why isn't she looking for you now to communicate where he is?" Aiden asked.

"The siren's magic can block Katie's sight of people, but rather than sit here and theorize, why don't we just go and ask her?" I rose and picked up my mug of tea. "At the very least, we'll know whether we'll need to do the locator or not."

Aiden's chair scraped as he rose and followed me up the stairs. His emotions washed over me in waves and were a mix of hope and dread. I suspected the latter was not so much due to the possibility of Katie telling us their dad was dead, but rather her not knowing his location at all.

I drank more tea and then placed the mug on the kitchenette's counter as I moved toward the balcony. The day was cool, but the wind was mild, and the clouds didn't look as if they were going to unleash any time soon.

I stopped near the balustrade and raised a hand. Almost immediately a thread of wild magic deviated toward me and wrapped itself around my wrist. The damn stuff really was everywhere these days, and it made me wonder if my connection to it and its growing sentience had something to do with that. Was it keeping close to me in order to protect itself?

It's possible, Belle said. *Even the most basic forms of life have a self-preservation mode.*

Wellsprings are powerful, but they've never held any sort of awareness or agenda that we're aware of—until now—and they've always had to be protected by external spells.

It's the "that we're aware of" portion of that statement that's important, especially given what Gabe has told you.

True. I put out a silent call for Katie, and the thread wrapped around my wrist pulsed, as if amplifying the call. *Do you think that means our spells might not be necessary one day? That it might eventually be able to protect itself?*

It's not beyond the bounds of possibility given what's happening. And there had to be a reason witches of old risked destruction to create the Fenna.

Barely visible slivers of moonlight floated down the street toward us. As Katie had said, the threads didn't hurry anywhere for anyone. Once they were close enough, they wrapped around my wrist, over the thread already there.

You disappeared, Katie said, almost accusingly.

Yeah, sorry, the nutter killing the grannies snatched me.

Ah shit, are you okay?

Yes. Did you follow your father when he went for his run yesterday?

Of course, but then the siren's magic washed over him and stole him from sight.

"Any luck?" Aiden asked from behind me. He was standing in the doorway, his arms crossed.

I held up a hand for silence and said to Katie, *Were you able to track him via the magical static?*

For a while, but she must have realized something was happening, because the interference changed and then both Dad and that faint buzz disappeared.

Where was he when that happened?

Near Louton.

He was out of the O'Connor compound?

Well and truly.

Obviously, Belle said, *our siren wasn't going to risk you interfering with her prey again.*

Which suggests she doesn't know a lot about me. Maybe she thinks I'm a wolf.

It's possible. I doubt sirens are up to date when it comes to werewolves and magic.

I returned my attention to Katie. *I take it you've done a thorough search around that area?*

Yes, but he could have gone anywhere, and there are a lot of old forests and mines in that region.

Were you able to check any of the mines?

Some of the shallower ones, yes. I am restricted when it comes to the deeper ones.

Which meant I'd been right about that. It also meant our siren might have based herself in a mine, given many of them were flooded.

Aiden and I are about to head out and search now.

Then I will keep close in case I am needed.

She'd be keeping close anyway, we both knew that. Her family was under attack, and I was her one means of not only finding the threat but dealing with it.

I turned and headed back in. Aiden stepped out of the way, then slid the door shut behind me. "Was she able to provide any useful information?"

"She lost him near Louton, so we can try the locator spell from there." I walked into my bedroom to put on my boots and grab a coat. "We'll have to drop by Ashworth's first, though. I need to pick up the bronze knife."

He leaned against the door frame. "Using a knife puts you entirely too close to her, in my opinion."

"Trust me, using the knife will be an absolute last resort."

He moved aside so I could get past him and then followed me down the stairs. Once I'd grabbed his father's watch from the table, I headed for the reading room to create the locator.

"You want my help?" Belle asked.

"Definitely. The two of us jointly weaving should increase the spell's range and power."

And if Belle activated her portion of it here, then she wouldn't need to be with us. Better to be safe than sorry when it came to dealing with a basically unknown entity.

Once we'd shifted the table and rolled up the carpet, we sat on the floor in the middle of the protective symbols, our knees touching. It wasn't really necessary for this sort of spell work, but the siren had proven to be quite adept at magic, so it definitely came under the heading of "better safe than sorry."

I motioned Belle to start the spell. She wove her threads quickly and efficiently around the gorgeous old watch while I looped my portion of the spell through hers so tightly that it was almost impossible to distinguish the two. The result wasn't only a much stronger locator, but also one with a far greater range. Once Belle had finished, she tied off her spell threads and activated them. I tied off mine a few heartbeats later but left them inert; that way, the overall spell remained inactive and wouldn't immediately pull on either her strength or mine.

Although given the wild magic pulsed through the

entire thing, there was a distinct possibility *it* would support the spell, and neither of us would be physically affected.

Belle pushed to her feet, then offered me a hand up.

"Did it work?" Aiden asked.

"Yes, and it's a pretty damn awesome spell, even if I say so myself," Belle said. "Whether or not it'll find your father is another matter entirely given what we're dealing with."

"You think she might permanently conceal him?"

"Until she's ready to leave, it's a definite possibility," I said, "especially now she's aware my magic can penetrate hers."

Besides, if she'd sensed Katie's presence—and the mere fact that the spell concealing Joseph had been adjusted midway through the song certainly suggested she had—then there was no reason to believe she wouldn't start concealing her kills. It would certainly make it harder for us to track her down. Hell, she might even tweak her song so that I *couldn't* hear it. She would have gotten a feel—however brief—for my magic when the knife had cut through her shield.

Aiden helped us shove the carpet and table back into place, then I grabbed the backpack and followed him out to his truck. It didn't take us all that long to get around to Ashworth's.

"I'll wait in the truck," Aiden said. "Otherwise, we could be here all day while they fuss around you."

I laughed at the thought of Ashworth "fussing" over anyone. There was no doubt he spoiled Eli, and these days he pretty much considered me family, but the man did not "fuss."

I jumped out of the truck and ran down the path to the door of their pretty miner's cottage. The bell chimed softly, and the sound of approaching footsteps echoed before the door opened, revealing Eli's handsome features. His expression lit up, full of warmth and relief. "Lizzie! Good to see you're not only up and about, but not carrying any injuries."

I smiled. "Only the usual emotional ones, and they're getting better every day."

"Tell that to someone who doesn't know you as well as we do." Ashworth shouldered his partner aside, then hauled me into a brief but fierce bear hug. "You worried the hell out of us, you know."

"I worried me, too," I said dryly. "Being stuck deep in a mine without a phone or my connection to Belle is not an experience I want to repeat."

"Amen to that. Are you coming in for a cuppa?"

"I can't." I kissed his cheek then pulled back. "We're heading out to try a locating spell to find Aiden's dad."

"Ah." Ashworth's gaze went past me. "I should really apologize to the lad. I did give him a bit of an earful, and he really wasn't deserving of it."

"Hopefully," Eli added, "your disappearance was something of a wake-up call for him."

"Oh, it was," I said. "But not quite in the way I was hoping."

Ashworth's eyebrows rose. "Then you'll definitely have to come back once the search is done. We can't be grandfatherly shoulders to lean on if we haven't got all the relevant information."

I smiled. "I will. In the meantime, I need the bronze knife. I don't think we'll find her today, but on the off chance that we do—"

"It's always better to be prepared than not," Ashworth finished for me. "But you're not going to need it. Your regular silver knife should do the job nicely."

My eyebrows rose. "I take it you've talked to the knowledgeable bods up in Canberra?"

He nodded. "The consensus is that we're dealing with a rusalka rather than a siren—they're a cross between a demon and a water nymph."

I frowned. "I thought rusalka were the souls of women who'd committed suicide over an unsuccessful love affair?"

"They can be, but they're generally tied to the area where they committed suicide. The demon-based ones can travel and are drawn to—and can feed off—darker emotions such as anger and grief. They're also gender neutral when it comes to who they call." He grimaced. "Basically, if it's humanoid and has a soul, they will consume it."

I scrubbed a hand across my face. "That's a confirmation I did not want."

"They also said the best way of getting rid of her is to banish her," Ashworth continued. "Apparently, this can only be done by the person responsible for her presence. You must confront her and recant the desire for revenge."

"I can't recant what I didn't knowingly call for. Besides, how the hell are we going to find a being who is using underground springs to get around?"

"You do a summoning," Eli said.

"*We* do a summoning," Ashworth corrected. "We can't risk the wild magic getting involved in such an action."

"Can this summoning be performed anywhere? Like our reading room?" I'd feel a whole lot more comfortable about performing the spell if it could.

"It is better to perform it either close to her nesting point or at least somewhere close to where she has recently killed."

"I figured that might be the answer. I mean, when has anything ever been easy in this reservation?"

Ashworth laughed. "Life would be boring if summoning demons was easy."

"And yet, humans have a long history of doing just that without any trouble at all," Eli said, voice dry.

"Only because many of those humans have a scrap of witch blood, and it does make all the difference." Ashworth glanced at his partner. "And just because they do it doesn't mean they pay no price."

"I'll come around tonight," I said. Though Aiden had made no move to hurry me up, I could feel his increasing need to get going. "We can discuss the finer points of the summoning over cake and coffee."

Ashworth nodded. "I got some notes from the Canberra bods, but we'll do a bit more research while you're out. Now, you'd best be going before the ranger gets too annoyed at us for delaying the search."

I laughed and ran back down the path to the truck.

"No knife?" Aiden said, as I jumped in and did the seat belt up.

"No need. Apparently, what we're dealing with is demon-based, and she needs to be banished rather than killed. They're researching how to go about that today and will get back to me."

"Us," Aiden said. "You're not confronting this thing alone."

"I won't be alone, and given you're a member of the pack and the line she is targeting, we can't risk you being present. Just because she hasn't called on you yet doesn't mean she won't if cornered."

He made a low sound in the back of his throat that told me exactly how he felt about *that*, but otherwise didn't comment.

Mainly because we both knew I was right.

We continued in silence to Louton, and while he radiated tension, it was based more on what we might—or might not—find rather than what was going on between the two of us. And that was a relief, even though I had no doubt choppy waters still lay ahead.

As we neared Louton, I activated my portion of the locator, and the spell came to life. Unsurprisingly, there was no immediate signal direction. Our singing demon wasn't likely to stash her prize close to a township where discovery was more likely.

Still, it would have been nice to get instant results for a change rather than spending hours aimlessly driving around.

"Anything?" Aiden said, with a quick glance at me.

"Not yet."

"There's a right turn coming up—do we take it, or keep going straight?"

"Right," I said, for no reason other than the fact it would lead us out of the more inhabited areas quicker.

But as we headed toward Fryer's Town, I couldn't help thinking it would be the mother of all ironies if the siren turned out to be hiding in the same mine system that I'd woken up in.

The locator continued its low-level pulsing and for what seemed like ages there was nothing else. But just as we swept into the bush the other side of Fryer's Town, the locator came to life. My heart skipped a beat, even though the response was faint and certainly didn't mean Aiden's father was alive. We wouldn't know *that* until we found him.

"Take the next left," I said.

"You've got a signal?" He glanced at me, his expression a mix of surprise and hope. "Is it a strong one?"

"No, but that might change, and any signal right now is better than nothing."

"I'm not about to dispute that."

He slowed and turned into what was little more than one of those goat tracks that were standard fare in the thicker forests around the reservation. It was rough and potholed, and the truck bumped and rolled along, barely scraping past the many trees crowding either side.

Slowly but surely, the signal got stronger. We came to a four-way crossroad and Aiden braked, waiting for directions. There was a secondary pulse under the original one now, but it was much fainter, and I suspected it was nothing more than an indication that going either left or ahead would eventually get us to the same point. At this point, though, it was better to stick with the stronger signal.

"Keep following this track," I said.

He released the brake, and the truck crawled forward again. "I'm pretty sure the track narrows up ahead to the point of being unpassable."

"I'm thinking we'll end up walking anyway. It's unlikely she'd stash him somewhere that could be easily reached."

"I would hardly call *this* easy."

I smiled. "For those in a truck, no. But for werewolves? Simple."

He didn't say the obvious—that I wasn't a wolf and being on foot wasn't likely to be easy for me even if my muscles had gained some of a werewolf's stamina. The terrain was just too rough and hilly, and I wasn't exactly fit.

But it wasn't like we had any other choice if we wanted to find his dad.

We continued down the windy path, but it wasn't long before the trees crowded the track so closely it was impossible to push through any further. I grabbed the pack and climbed out of the vehicle. Katie's threads briefly stirred around me, but more to let me know she was here rather than to make a connection attempt.

Once Aiden had retrieved the harness and ropes from the back of his truck, we moved on, but we'd barely gone half a kilometer when the signal started pulling toward the left. The amount of rubble scattered about the steadily rising ground suggested we were about to enter an area where there were lots of old mines and tailing piles. I mentally crossed all things and hoped I didn't fall into another shaft. I'd survived three of the things now. I wasn't sure my luck would hold for a fourth.

The undergrowth was thick despite the denseness of the forest and tall enough to tear at my shoulders and face. I protected the latter as best I could, but it was tough going.

"There's water up ahead," Aiden said after ten or so minutes. "I can smell it."

I couldn't, but that might just have been because I was sweating so much. "River or dam?"

"I can't hear water movement, so dam. In this area, it's likely to be related to old mine diggings."

I glanced briefly at him. His face was set, giving little away, but he couldn't so easily control his fear and worry. He reeked of it. "How many mines are in the area?"

"Plenty of small ones, but if we're looking for a large body of water, then the Nuggetty Creek mine is probably our best bet. They were a small open cut operation before they tunneled in."

"Isn't that rather unusual?"

"Yes, but in this particular area, it did pay off."

Meaning they found enough gold to make it worthwhile. "I take it that's the one we're heading toward?"

"Yes."

Given the signal's strength, it was pretty obvious we were going to find Joseph in either the mine or the dam. I hoped it was the former, because that meant there was still a chance of life. I feared it would be the latter.

The trail got steeper as we climbed toward the ridge. I paused at the top, more to catch my breath than anything else, but there was little to see. The trees were thick, and they dominated the skyline even as they swept back down the hill. The Nuggetty Creek mine might be close, but it wasn't visible.

But I could at least hear the trickle of water now, so there was a creek somewhere close—maybe the same one responsible for the dam. Not that it meant anything when we were dealing with a water demon rather than a siren; she wasn't restricted to using the waterways to get around and logically could be anywhere.

I drew in a deep breath filled with the sharp scent of eucalyptus, then half walked, half slid, down the slope until we reached the valley floor. The creek was tiny, but there was plenty of evidence that it had in the past been panned for gold—there were small piles of river stones and the remnants of wooden rocker boxes scattered right along the visible length of it.

I glanced down at the spell-wrapped watch. Its pulsing was almost frenetic. We were close now. *So* close.

I took another of those deep breaths that didn't do a thing to ease the gathering tension and headed upstream. The terrain was even rougher along the creek bed than it had been in the surrounding hills, forcing me to scramble over and around numerous rocks, scratching my fingers and knees multiple times in the process. We finally reached a slope that had all the hallmarks of the bank of a dam and, once on top, discovered the creek's source—a long, wide stretch of black water.

There wasn't a body in that water—at least, not one we could see—but there *was* magic present. I could feel the foul wash of it.

Katie's threads moved past me and skimmed the surface of the water. It soon became evident that she was unable to sense the magic, and that was interesting. It meant the rusalka really *had* picked up the presence of the wild magic and was now reacting to it when she was creating her spells.

But if that were the case, why was I still feeling it? The wild magic was an inseparable part of my spell work these days, and she surely would have noticed its presence when I'd cast the knife at her.

Aiden stopped beside me. "The shaft is situated behind that scree pile to the left."

I glanced over. The entrance's timber supports definitely looked as if they'd seen better days, and that didn't bode well for the condition of those deeper in the mine. I really hoped we didn't have to go in there—especially given the dam's water wasn't only lapping at the base of the scree pile but trickling down into the shaft itself. Even if the inner supports hadn't rotted away or collapsed yet, any sort of disturbance might tip them over the edge.

I glanced down at the watch again, even though it wasn't really necessary now. The pulsing said the man we were seeking lay straight ahead—in the same area, in fact, where the magic waited.

I took a deep breath and exhaled slowly. "I'm going to have to go into the water."

Aiden stilled briefly, then closed his eyes and drew in a breath. The brief wash of fear and sadness faded from his expression, but I could nevertheless see it in his eyes and in the emotive swirl of his aura. He didn't say anything, though. He just nodded.

I handed him the watch, then swung off my pack and stripped off. The air caressed my bare skin, a chilly teaser for what was to come.

Aiden took the harness from his shoulder and helped me into it. It was damn uncomfortable to wear when naked, but I wasn't about to go in the water without it.

Once he'd connected the rope and tested the knot, he said, "Be careful. God knows what lies at the bottom of this dam."

"As long as it's not our rusalka, I'm not overly worried."

"Getting caught in old equipment could prove just as dangerous, and given the amount of crap that's lying around the banks, the bottom is likely to be riddled with it."

"Even if it is, it won't be actively trying to kill me."

He frowned, worry evident. "If you're sensing her presence, then maybe it would be better to call in help."

"I'm not, but that doesn't mean anything when we're dealing with a demon able to move through water and across land. I'm more worried about you getting caught in her song."

"It's not practical to wear earplugs when I'm manning the ropes, because I need to be able to hear your directions. But I have them in my pocket; the minute you sense her presence or hear the first strains of her song, warn me."

I nodded. I would have preferred he wear them now, even if it had become fairly clear they didn't exactly work.

I pulled my knife out of the backpack, then took a step into the water. Everything immediately clenched. Crap, it was even *colder* than I'd thought it would be. I shivered but forced my feet on, edging slowly but surely deeper into the water. The dam's bottom was rocky and covered with wood and sharp bits of metal, but there was nothing big enough to get tangled in. At least, not yet.

The water crept over my hips, and a gasp escaped; by the time it reached my breasts, my teeth were chattering. The dam's bottom still sloped steeply, meaning the water would be over my head sooner rather than later. I bit the bullet and swam on, keeping the knife in front of me just in case there were spell traps I couldn't see or feel.

But it was the one I *could* see that started causing problems. The closer I got to it, the more intense the buzz of its magic became, until it felt like I was surrounded by hundreds of stinging gnats. My skin twitched and crawled, and it was all I could do to keep swimming.

The spell itself remained invisible, which meant she *had* learned enough about my magic to apply some concealment. But while I might not be able to see its construction, its overall shape wasn't hidden from my senses. It was pod-like and maybe a foot and a half high and little more than six feet long—in other words, roughly the height and length of a body.

When I was close enough to touch the spell, I stopped, treading water for several seconds. The buzz of it was so fierce, my face burned under its intensity. I silently prayed for luck, then raised the knife and, with a short, sharp movement, thrust it deep into the spell.

This time, the response was instant.

It exploded, the force so strong that it tore my grip from the knife and thrust me back and down. For several seconds there was nothing but blackness and fear, then the rope on the harness snapped taut and I was being dragged backward. I kicked hard with my feet and broke the surface, gasping for air even though I hadn't been under all that long.

The remnants of the rusalka's spell fell around me like rain. What I couldn't see was a body. Or my knife.

Maybe the spell had pushed him under, as it had me.

Or maybe it had simply erased him—though surely if that had happened, there would have been some physical evidence of it. Bits of flesh floating in the water, perhaps.

"Liz? You okay? What happened?"

"I defused the concealing spell," I shouted. "I'm okay. Just give me some more slack."

"Have you found anything?"

"Not yet."

The pull of the rope immediately eased, and I kicked forward warily. The water was choppy, washing past me in waves that slapped at my face and stung my eyes. Swallowing the muck probably wouldn't be a great idea.

When I neared the point where I'd attacked the spell, I paused, once again treading water as I studied the area. I couldn't see the knife or any indication of a body.

I cast a retrieval spell, and a few seconds later, the knife was back in my hand. I gripped it tight, feeling safer even if I wasn't.

She would have felt that explosion. She'd know I was here.

Whether she'd react or not was the million-dollar question.

As I turned toward the mine, my feet brushed against something solid. A squeak of fear escaped, and wild magic burst from my skin, forming a protective circle around me—which was rather awesome and made me feel a whole lot safer even if it was a bit excessive, given there wasn't a repeated touch from whatever the hell it had been.

I sucked in another of those deep breaths that did nothing to ease my accelerated heart rate and created a light spell around my free hand. It illuminated the dark water in a small circle around me but quickly faded about a meter out and down.

But it was enough to reveal the body.

I briefly closed my eyes, hoping against hope *and* reason that it wasn't Joseph, that it was someone else. Which of course would only mean heartbreak for another family, and that wasn't something anyone should wish for.

I ducked under and, without opening my eyes, reached for that figure and dragged him back to the surface.

Turning him over confirmed the worst of my fears.

It was Aiden's father.

Chapter Ten

A heartbeat later, a howl ripped across the silence. It was deep and mournful, and it spoke of death, sorrow, and pain. The goose bumps that crawled across my skin had nothing to do with the chill slowly sapping my strength but rather the anguish in that lone sound and the way it echoed on and on....

It would be heard in the O'Connor reservation.

They would know their alpha had been found.

That death had been his fate, not life.

But that death might not be as simple as it first seemed, thanks to the ragged bit of metal sticking out of his chest.

If the spell's explosion had pushed him deep enough for him to get speared by whatever that metal had come from, then his body would have gotten stuck there rather than floating back up.

But if it had happened *before* the explosion—maybe even before he'd died—how? Why? The rusalka dined on souls, and it was *that* act that killed them. It didn't make sense that she would stab Joseph first, because doing so meant his soul would move on before she could take it.

Had he killed himself? It was a possibility that couldn't be discounted.

But I fought the instinct to reach for Belle and ask her opinion. I needed to get out of the icy black water first.

I caught Joseph under the armpits, then shouted for Aiden to haul us back. He waded into the water once we were close enough and helped me upright. I wrapped my arms around his neck and pulled him close. "I'm so sorry, Aiden."

He returned the hug but didn't say anything. After a too-brief moment, he stepped back, grabbed his father, and dragged him clear of the water. Katie's threads hovered above him, and if her energy could have wept, it would have. As it was, both her and Aiden's anguish washed across me in waves, threatening to drown me in their sorrow.

I tightened my shields and managed to mute their grief, but there was little else I could do. Once I'd stripped off the harness, I used my T-shirt to dry off and then dressed.

By that time, Aiden had gotten his emotions under some control, though his expression when he looked up at me was bleak. "This is going to break my mother."

And her breaking would be the precursor to her breaking me—or at least attempting to. "She's a strong woman, Aiden—"

"Not this strong. Not on top of her brother."

And her sister decades ago.... I rubbed my arms, but it didn't do a lot against the gathering chill—one that was based on what would soon be coming at me. But I couldn't say that. It would only make an already stressful situation more so—for him, more than me.

"She might surprise you."

The smile that twisted his lips held little humor. "I like

the conviction in your voice when you say that, even if I suspect you don't believe it."

Oh, I totally believed she *would* surprise him, just not in the way he was thinking. But again, that wasn't something I could really say. "While you're calling your team, I'll have a look around and see if there's any indication the siren is staying in the area."

"Look for Dad's clothes while you're searching, as that'll tell us which direction he came in from. But don't stray too far. While there's no vertical shafts in the immediate area, they do exist."

I nodded. "If I find anything, I'll give you a shout."

"Good." He dragged out his phone to start making the necessary calls.

Katie's threads continued to hover over her father, and I couldn't help but see the swirl of guilt through her grief. Her soul had been infused into the wild magic so she could become the reservation's guardian and protect the people she loved, and yet she'd been unable to save the lives of her uncle or her father. That she didn't yet have the capacity to act on her own wouldn't in any way ease that guilt.

I slung the backpack over my shoulder but didn't immediately move out. Instead, I reached for Belle.

I take it from the waves of unhappiness washing down the link that you've found him.

Yes, but I'm not entirely sure he died at the rusalka's hands. You able to do a quick soul check for me?

Sure. Her being flowed into mine and my gaze jumped back to Joseph's body. After a moment, she said, *He definitely wasn't soul stripped.*

And his soul isn't lingering around the area?

Not that I can see or sense.

Which meant this death was ordained, and that was at

least something. He might be dead in *this* life, but he could move on and enjoy others. The rusalka's other victims did not have that option.

That means he was able to resist her call long enough to take matters into his own hands.

Aiden would have told him what this demon was doing to those she called, and he'd have known there was only one way to escape such a fate.

It looks like it, Belle said. *But to know for sure, I'd have to talk to his spirit.*

Can you?

Yes, but to what point? It's doubtful he'll be able to tell us anything more than we already know. In truth, it might be better—especially given the situation with Karleen—to not give them the option. It'll only rip open an already wide wound.

That was undoubtedly true. I glanced at Aiden, but he was still on the phone. His expression was all business, and he obviously had a tight leash on his emotions right now, because there was very little leakage through his aura.

I sighed. *He's well aware you can spirit speak, so let's wait and see if he asks.*

Good plan.

I broke our connection, then followed the dam's banks around to the scree pile. The dark water trickling over the ground made it slippery, forcing me to place each foot carefully or risk falling on my ass as I moved toward the mine's entrance. When I was a meter away from it, I stopped. The beams supporting the entrance smelled as rotten as they looked, and there was a steady creaking and groaning coming from deeper within the old shaft. Entering the thing was definitely out of the question—especially when I was getting no immediate sense that the rusalka hid inside.

But was that really surprising? No self-respecting demon or spirt would dump their victim on their doorstep—not unless it was a trap, and this hadn't been.

Even if she'd been confident her magic would successfully conceal him from both eyesight and magic, she'd been canny enough to change her song midstream to counter the presence of wild magic and would be unlikely to take any sort of risk.

I continued on up the hill. Near the far end of the dam, close to the point where it met the upper portion of the little creek, I found a pair of socks. Like her other victims, Joseph had stripped off before entering the water. I wondered if she simply preferred them to be naked or if it ensured the weight of their clothes didn't pull them down before they reached her.

I gave them a wide berth to avoid fouling any possible evidence and continued on, following the creek line for a few minutes before coming across a boot. I had no idea where the other one was and wasn't about to trudge around to find it. That was neither my job nor important right now. His jeans lay a few meters farther up, and his shirt hung from a low tree branch several more beyond that. Given I was now a good distance from the dam and he'd obviously still been in her thrall, did that mean it been the water that had woken him? Had its iciness stirred enough realization of what was going on and what was about to happen?

It was possible. After all, this was the second time he'd been ensnared, so a flash of comprehension would have been all he'd need to take matters into his own hands.

I trudged on up the slope. After a few more minutes, awareness leapt tenuously across the psychic lines. I stopped and carefully put out some feelers. It was coming from the left, from somewhere behind the thick stand of trees. I spotted a path and moved across, stepping past several trees into deeper shadows as a shiver stole across my skin. The air was a whole lot colder here, though it was probably imagination and fear more than any real drop in temperature.

I cast another light spell—more to make myself feel better than from any real need to light the faint path I could see quite clearly—and tossed it in front of me. It bobbed along at knee height, throwing out light in a semicircular arc. I'd barely gone ten meters when, on the very edge of the light to the right, I spotted timber. It was another horizontal mine entrance—one that looked to be in far better shape than its mate near the water.

I directed the light spell toward it, then grabbed a fallen branch and followed cautiously, testing the ground before each step. Previous experience had taught me that it was utterly possible for a vertical mineshaft to be positioned right in front of a horizontal. Thankfully, that wasn't the case here, and I reached the entrance safely.

I motioned the light globe into the mine but didn't follow. The shaft was wide and in reasonable condition, though the air leaching from it smelled of mold, and that suggested there might be some timber rot deeper down.

The rusalka's presence remained faint, but that might simply be because she was deep underground. It wouldn't matter for a summoning—as long as we were in her general area the spell should work—but it did mean I'd have to remain here with the rangers just in case she attacked.

I stepped back and then hesitated, half wondering if I should place an alarm spell across the entrance. But that would only tell her we'd found her lair and was the last thing we needed right now.

I turned and headed back to the little stream. But before

I followed the trail back down, I created a little marker spell and attached it to a tree. While it was possible she'd sense its presence if she came out this way, she wouldn't from inside the mine. It was worth the risk, as it would make it easier to find the trail into the forest and to the mine again later.

Tala and Luke—another one of the rangers—had arrived by the time I got back to the dam; Luke was taking photos of the body while Tala did a line search around the dam. Aiden was walking toward the top of the dam but stopped as I came out of the trees.

"Any luck?"

I nodded. "There's a trail of clothes following the creek."

"And the rusalka?"

I grimaced. "Nothing definite."

He swore and scrubbed a hand across his face. Just for a moment, the depth of his grief showed, and my heart broke for him. I stopped and placed a hand on his arm. I might have been touching steel, his muscles were so tense. "I know this isn't much comfort, but his soul has moved on. It wasn't stolen."

He stared at me for a second then looked away. His lashes were wet when his gaze met mine again. "The metal bar in his chest—he did that?"

I nodded. "It was the only way he could have escaped her. It means he can move on and live other lives. Her other victims do not have that choice."

"I won't be mentioning *that* bit to my mother."

"Best not to." It was bad enough that this demon had snatched the lives of her husband and her brother. To learn that her brother's soul would never again grace this earth?

If the deaths didn't break her, that surely would.

He caught my hand, twining his fingers through mine as he led the way back down the hill. Warmth trembled through me, and I somehow resisted the urge to hold on tight and not let go.

Ever.

"Do you want me to call in someone to take you home?" he asked.

I shook my head. "While I don't get a definitive sense of her location, it would be better if I stay, just in case she decides to sing again."

"That hasn't been her pattern so far."

"No, but this is the first time she's missed her prey."

"True." He pulled a couple of chocolate bars from his jacket pocket. "I asked Tala to grab these on her way up here."

Meaning he'd been expecting me to hang around. "Thank you."

I rose on my toes and dropped a kiss on his cheek. He didn't move, didn't try to capture my lips with his, but the muscle ticking along his jawline suggested he wanted to.

"You're welcome." He hesitated, then nodded and walked away, his every movement filled with tension and sorrow.

And there was nothing I could do to ease either, no matter how much I might wish to.

I found a log to sit on and watched the proceedings as I munched on the chocolate bars. As the morning drifted into afternoon and the smell of rain began to taint the air, Aiden finally wrapped things up.

He offered me a hand and pulled me up easily, but once again didn't release my fingers. I didn't really mind; he was warmth and familiarity, and his touch went some way to easing the chill gathering in my soul. "I've asked Tala to drop you off. I've got to pick up Mom and take her down to the morgue."

"You told her?"

"Didn't need to." He grimaced. "There are some things a wolf innately knows, and the death of a mate is one."

"And yet she held on to hope—"

"We all did. None of us wanted to believe the decimation of our family could be so complete."

I wouldn't be so certain it was complete. Not when the rusalka still remained in the reservation. But that did prompt the question—why? If my grief was the reason she was here, why would she remain when, for all intents and purposes, revenge had been fully taken?

Or was revenge merely the starting point? Would she now go after the cause of that grief?

It was possible.

More than possible.

As much as I hated Karleen, I didn't want her dead. There'd already been far too many deaths attributed to my grief. I couldn't be responsible for more.

"I think you might need to keep her under guard, Aiden. If this demon is here because of me, she might well be the next target."

"Fuck, I hope not."

"So do I, but it's a possibility we cannot ignore."

"No."

We came out of the trees and walked toward the two remaining trucks. Tala waited in hers, the engine already running.

Aiden squeezed my fingers, then released me. "I'll make the arrangements."

"It could also be worth asking her to wear earbuds tonight, just in case."

Bitterness twisted his lips. "That didn't help Dad."

"No, but if she's also being guarded, then they'll be able to stop her leaving."

"In theory."

My eyebrows rose. "Meaning as an alpha—even one under threat from a foreign entity—she could order them aside and they'd obey?"

"No, but an alpha can get violent if disobeyed, especially if they're not in their right mind."

Or when they were struck by a grief so great nothing mattered anymore.

Nothing except revenge.

Another shiver stole across my skin. I ignored it and, as Aiden opened the passenger door, climbed in.

"I'll talk to you later," he said, then slammed the door shut and walked back to his truck.

As there was no immediate turning point in the area, Tala reversed back to the crossroad and then drove out. Neither of us spoke. Tala's grief wasn't as fierce as Aiden's, but her anger burned my skin. It was aimed at the situation and, I suspected, at us witches for not stopping this thing in time. Which we both knew was unfair and was undoubtedly why she didn't say anything.

By the time she dropped me off at Ashworth's, big fat drops of rain were beginning to fall. I tugged on my coat's hood and raced for the front door, but it opened before I could ring the bell.

"Belle sent word you were on your way and would be needing this," Ashworth said, and handed me a hot chocolate

There was no whisky in it, but it was piled high with cream and marshmallows, providing not only warmth but the sort of sugar hit I needed right now.

I smiled, wrapped my cold fingers around the mug, and took a sip. "Perfect. Thank you."

He ushered me inside and closed the door. "There's also a hearty stew sitting on the stove. We figured you'd be needing that before we head out again."

"Meaning you've worked out the appropriate summoning spell?"

"Oh, we had that," Eli said as I appeared in the kitchen. "It was the protections against her song we were worried about."

"Is it even possible to weave auditory protections through a spell?"

"It can be tricky, but I believe we've found a spell that will achieve the desired result."

"I hope so, because I don't want to be knocking either of you unconscious."

"Given the hardness of Ira's head, that would be a difficult thing to do," Eli commented.

I laughed and sat down at the table. "Will you or Ashworth be doing the summoning? Or will I have to?"

"If it *is* your emotions that have called her here, then you'll have to perform the ceremony." Eli handed me a bowl of delicious smelling stew. "We've written it down so all you'll have to do is read it."

Which was a good idea, because learning what I suspected would be an intricate spell in a such a short space of time wouldn't be easy or indeed wise. There'd been plenty of warnings given to us in school about the risk of disaster, injury, or even death from a misunderstood or misapplied summoning, and I had more than enough problems on my plate already.

I scooped up a bit of the stew and discovered it tasted

even better than it smelled. "Have you advised Monty about all this?"

"Aye, lass," Ashworth said. "I daresay he'll be here any moment. That lad has a nose for a good meal."

The doorbell rang just as he said that, and I couldn't help another laugh. "Are we taking bets on that being him?"

"I wouldn't." Eli's voice was dry. "He'd be the shortest-priced favorite ever."

Ashworth headed back down the hall. A heartbeat later, Monty said, "Unless you want to listen to my stomach grumbling for the next two hours, I hope you're dishing me up a bowl of whatever is creating that divine smell."

"Yes, laddie, we are. If there's one thing we don't need is you fading away, especially in the middle of a spelling." Ashworth's voice was dry. "I mean, it's not as if Belle or Lizzie ever feed you now, is it?"

"Spelling is an extremely taxing business, as you all know." His eyes twinkled as he pulled out the chair next to me, then accepted the bowl Eli handed him with a nod of thanks. "And a young lad like me does need a steady supply of fuel."

"But not just for the spelling, I'd wager," Ashworth said.

Monty grinned but, for a change, didn't take the bait. He took a mouthful of stew, made appreciative noises, then glanced at me. "I take it you've found the rusalka's location?"

"I found a possible location, but she's deep underground, so it's hard to pinpoint her precisely."

"As long as we're close, it shouldn't matter in the scheme of things," Ashworth said.

"What happens if she answers the summons but refuses to be banished?" Monty said. "I've heard tales of that happening."

"Anything is possible when you're dealing with a demon, but it's unlikely in this case because of the nature of the one we're dealing with and the fact we know who and what likely drew her here."

I ate more stew and tried to ignore the guilt that stirred. "If a summoning works for this demon, why haven't we tried it for the others that have come here? It would have made getting rid of the bastards a whole lot easier."

"Because for the most part, we haven't known for certain what sort of demon we're dealing with, and summonings need precision to work."

"Not to mention plenty of protection for the summoners," Eli added. "That's why we invited the laddie here. The combined might of four protection circles should be more than enough to contain her and protect us."

I had no idea if he was crossing mental fingers as he said that, but I certainly was. "I don't suppose you've had a chance to look through the *Earth Magic* book for any mention of the Fenna?"

"I did," he said. "And Gabe was right. The Fenna were indeed a witch-wolf hybrid created specifically to guard the wellsprings."

"Why werewolves?" Monty asked. "Especially given the current belief that mixing our DNA with theirs is problematic."

"It's a belief that doesn't stand up well in the light of good research," Ashworth said. "There have been hundreds of hybrids who have lived full and healthy lives over the centuries."

"Hundreds isn't all that many over the course of history, though," I pointed out.

"No, but you've got to remember werewolves were insular societies for a very long time. It's only in the last few hundred years that outsiders have been allowed into reservations."

"Then why the current thinking that the two don't mix?" Monty asked.

"Because hybrids aren't capable of shifting or healing," Ashworth said, "and often not accepted into the pack."

"There must be records of birthing problems for hybrids, though," I said, thinking of Karleen's sister and the baby that had lost her life only hours after birth. "Otherwise, the belief wouldn't have held for so long."

"*Any* birth can be problematic, be it human, wolf, or hybrid," Eli noted. "Remember, up until the development of modern medicine, childbirth was considered one of the most dangerous threats to not only the mother's life, but also the child's."

I scooped up more stew. "Did the text say why werewolves were used as sperm donors in these conception binding ceremonies?

He nodded. "A wolf's ability to shift and heal meant the offspring had more of a chance of surviving the forces they would one day control."

"Which doesn't make sense if the hybrid can't shift or heal."

"That might be where the wild magic comes in," Ashworth said. "Perhaps it is the key—the link that binds the two different genetic materials into one."

"Which would mean," Monty said, "if you and Aiden ever did get around to having kids, there's a damn good chance they will become Fenna."

"An interesting but somewhat unlikely scenario at this point of time," I said, even as my heart leapt at the thought.

The little girl I'd seen so often in my dreams could still

be Aiden's. We just had to get past his mom attacking me, him being alpha, and his pack not accepting me.

Should be a walk in the park, I thought wryly.

"If the Fenna were vital for protecting the wellsprings," Monty asked. "What happened to them?"

"Two things, I suspect, given the date of the final record in the book," Eli said. "The first was the Black Death, which wiped out a good proportion of human and witch. Many of the witches who survived the disease were subsequently burned at the stake—and had their homes and temples torched—thanks to the mistaken belief that the plague was a result of a curse."

I harrumphed. "Humanity were always blaming us for something."

"Still are in many third-world countries," Monty mused. "Hell, even today in Australia, the US, and many other countries, there are backwaters with a deep and abiding suspicion of all things witch."

From what I'd seen over my life so far, it wasn't always confined to backwaters. "What's the second reason?"

"A war between witches and werewolves. It created a schism that only recently started to heal."

I scooped up the last bit of stew, then picked up my hot chocolate and leaned back in the chair. "As important as this information might be to my future kids, it doesn't really explain why *my* link with the wellspring is strengthening. I'm not a hybrid."

"Is it possible that there's Fenna blood in Aunt Eleanor's family?" Monty asked. "Just because the Fenna stopped protecting the springs doesn't mean their bloodline died out, and she *did* survive the wellspring's surge. By rights, it should have killed her."

"It's possible, and it would certainly explain why

mother and daughter survived full immersion. It would be very hard to check, however, as many records from that period perished in the burnings." Eli grimaced. "And given the upcoming court case, I'm thinking any attempt to check wouldn't be wise anyway."

Monty frowned. "Why? It's not like Lawrence can use the information to justify his actions."

"No, but the high council might well declare such a development of great interest and place an embargo on Lizzie's movements."

"Put me under house arrest and send in the medical community to prod and poke me, in other words," I said sourly. "Then sell me off to the highest bidder so I can breed little Fenna."

"That's unlikely to—"

"When there's the possibility of controlling the wild magic—an unlimited source of power that has eluded every attempt to use it for centuries—do you really think that even if the case goes in my favor, it would prevent them from restraining me?"

"Oh, the council would undoubtedly restrain and examine you were you a minor. But you're not," Ashworth said. "You also have the weight of the Black Lantern Society behind you, and that'll always make them wary."

"Besides," Eli said, a twinkle in his blue eyes, "if all else fails, we'll smuggle you out and bring you back to the reservation—and *that* is a promise."

"One I'll hold you to when the shit hits the fan," I said.

"It won't. Both your father and Clayton's family have too much to lose, especially with the Society by your side." Ashworth's smile was definitely on the wicked side. "The Society is not above playing dirty if it achieves the desired results."

I raised my eyebrow. "Which suggests you have dirt on either my father or Clayton's family, so why hasn't it been used before now?"

"Because sometimes it's better to keep your aces up your sleeves."

"And the Society," Eli said, voice amused, "has mighty big sleeves. The high council steps warily around them for good reason."

"If that's true, I'm surprised the council hasn't tried to get rid of them," Monty said.

"Oh, they have, and multiple times over the decades," Ashworth said. "The trouble is, the Society not only knows where most of the bodies are buried, they're backed by an unidentified board of five. Hard to destroy something if you don't know who's actually behind it."

I raised my eyebrows. "I thought your sister was the Matriarch?"

He glanced at me. "She is, but in her nearly eighty years of service, she's never met the board, only their delegates."

"Delegates can be questioned, drugged, or mind raided," Monty said.

"From what Sophie has said, they're well protected against any of that."

"No protections are one hundred percent effective," Monty said.

Ashworth's smile held little humor. "No, but death is."

I blinked. "The board would kill rather than risk their identities becoming known?"

"Would and have." He shrugged. "You've got to remember the Society's manifesto—to right wrongs and bring justice to those who escaped it, via whatever means necessary."

"Wouldn't killing those who work for them just to keep their IDs secret be one of those very wrongs?"

"Anyone promoted into a delegate position is obviously informed of the risks," Ashworth said. "And can step away at any time under the condition of a partial memory wipe."

I snorted. "Yeah, because that's so easy."

Eli smiled. "In Canberra, it's something of a perfected art."

"Which is why they developed telepathic protections," Monty said, voice wry.

I grabbed a spoon to scoop the last bit of chocolate from the bottom of the mug. "I'm surprised anyone wants to work for the Society."

"Not everyone in Canberra is a self-serving narcissist," Eli noted.

I snorted. "No, but the majority of the high councilors are."

Ashworth laughed as he picked up his empty plate and walked over to the dishwasher. "We'd better get moving. It'd be best if we did the summoning before night sets in and our demon gets active."

I followed him over to the dishwasher and placed my bowl and cup in. "I'm more worried about the storm. It's a pretty remote area, and too much rain will make the ground hideous to walk over."

"Are you sure you're going to be able to locate the mine again?" Monty asked.

I nodded. "And if I can't, I'm sure Katie will help."

She might be in mourning with the rest of her family, but if I reached out through the wild magic from either wellspring, she would answer.

She wanted this demon stopped as badly as we did.

Once Eli and Ashworth had gathered all the necessary

gear, we headed out. Monty drove, as he still had our SUV and we'd need its four-wheel drive capabilities, especially if the storm did hit.

Thankfully, the rain had eased while we were inside, but by the time we reached the point where we had to get out and walk, thunder was again rumbling ominously overhead. I sent a silent prayer to the weather gods to hold off until we at least found the dam site again, but they obviously weren't listening. By the time we reached that first ridge, it was pelting down.

"This is fucking dangerous," Monty said. "We're not going to see any of the mines until we fall into the things."

"As long as we keep to the track, we should be right." And I crossed all mental fingers that we were actually *on* the right track. The rain was making it harder and harder to tell.

We finally found the little creek, and I heaved a silent sigh of relief. From there, it was relatively simple to find the dam and the trail leading up the hill beyond it. The marker I'd left gleamed bright in the day's dullness, making me glad I'd taken the risk.

I led the way into the forest. The trees at least protected us from the worst of the downpour, though it was still decidedly unpleasant. Once we reached the mine entrance, I reached out with other senses. The rusalka's presence remained, no different than before.

"We good to go?" Monty asked, looking wet but not miserable. He was totally looking forward to this summoning.

That's because he's crazy came Belle's comment.

And you're going to marry that crazy.

Her harrumph rolled down the mental lines, but she didn't actually deny it.

"Yes, she's there," I said, and glanced at Ashworth. "You take the lead; we'll follow."

"We'll do the pentagram first and then weave the protection circles around that."

"And then pray like hell the auditory protections work," Eli said, with a twinkle in his eyes that suggested he knew full well they would.

The spells were so complicated that it took us close to half an hour to complete them, with runes replacing the candles on the pentagram. The latter simply weren't practical in weather this bad.

We stood at the four cardinal points, leaving the fifth—the one representing spirit—free, and raised the protection circles. Then I began the summoning ritual. As I carefully read out the spell, power rose around us, shimmering brightly in the gloom and thick with demand.

Just for an instant, the air within the pentagram sparkled and the sense of evil and darkness washed across my senses. The heavy weight of the spell pulled at my strength as the spell rose to its zenith.

The shimmer never became anything more.

The spell had certainly reached our demon, but it wasn't strong enough to pull her fully back to us.

As the echoes of the spell faded away, I glanced at Ashworth for guidance. He didn't say anything, not for several minutes.

Then he sighed. "There can only be one explanation for her eluding the summoning."

"I'm not the reason she's here."

"No," he said heavily. "You're not."

Chapter Eleven

Relief stirred, though in truth, the only thing that really changed was a lessening in the depth of my guilt. "Are you sure I didn't read the spell wrong?"

"You read it perfectly. If she didn't answer, then you're not the source for her presence."

"But who else could it be? No one else here is connected to the wild magic—"

"Demons like her have been answering the call of emotions for eons," Eli said. "Wild magic might have amplified *your* emotions, but no one else's. She's not here because of you."

"Or at the very least, not *solely* because of you," Ashworth said. "It's possible a combination of emotions has drawn her here."

"Karleen has to be one of them," Monty said. "She's been hating on Lizzy for months."

"It's not me, per se, but rather the fact I was going out with her son. Had I chosen a non-related wolf, she wouldn't have cared," I said. "But if she *is* the reason for the rusalka's presence, why appear when I've broken up with Aiden? And why would it be going after her family and not mine?"

"You might not be with Aiden anymore, but you foiled Karleen's plans for a more suitable match, and you're still in the reservation," Monty said.

I snorted. "Karleen foiled her own damn plans by not knowing her son well enough and inviting the very last person he wanted to see back into the reservation. And none of that explains why our demon is going after her family."

"It's because the anger that draws the rusalka also feeds her," Ashworth said. "In killing Karleen's family, the rusalka flames the fires of that anger and sweetens the meal."

"At least that does mean our granny killer can't be the source," Monty said.

Eli nodded. "If he had been, she'd be going after older women. That she's going after the O'Connors specifically basically confirms they are the source."

"Then we need to include Aiden as a possibility," Monty said. "Remember, he's not only grieving a broken relationship, but he's also very angry at Karleen for her interference."

"That's a distinct possibility," Ashworth said, as he and Eli began magically dismantling the pentagram. "And that means we'll need both of them for the summoning to work."

"I don't like our chances of getting Karleen to do anything right now," I said. "Every instinct I have says she's in the mood for a fight and will attack given the slightest provocation."

Ashworth frowned. "She's an alpha. No matter how great her loss—"

"It's not just her mate and her brother she's lost, but also her sister," I cut in. "Even werewolves can be overwhelmed by the weight of grief."

"Wasn't her brother the only direct family she had left?" Monty said.

"Here in the reservation, yes. Her sister's death was the reason they left Ireland."

"I take it she was killed by a witch?" Eli asked.

"Yes, when she was sixteen and Karleen fourteen." I didn't go into greater detail because it wasn't my secret to tell. Besides, the specifics didn't matter, only the end result.

"Well, fuck," Monty said. "That's not going to make things any easier, is it?"

"Karleen is many things, but she's not a fool," Ashworth said. "No matter how much she might revile us—no matter how much she might not believe the reason these deaths are happening—she wants the rusalka stopped as much as we do."

"While that much might be true, I'm thinking her and Liz in the same room is not a good idea at the moment," Monty said. "The council was told about our initial theory that Liz's grief was responsible for this thing being here, and after the deaths of three family members, she's not going to believe anything else."

"On that we agree," Ashworth said heavily. "While we can't escape Liz needing to be present for the summoning, there are protections we can employ. And you, laddie, will have to be the one approaching Karleen with the new information."

He frowned. "Wouldn't it be better coming from Aiden? We have to tell him anyway."

"Except for the fact that, depending on her state of mind, she might believe he's simply trying to divert suspicion from the woman he cares for," Eli said.

"*That* is a certainty," I said. "But there's one other point we need to consider—that the rusalka might go after her next. Is it possible to weave the auditory spell you used here into a protective charm?"

"It's possible, although if Karleen is the reason for the rusalka's presence, she'd be safe from attack until the demon's task is done," Ashworth said.

"This demon was drawn rather than summoned here, though, so the rules might not apply," Monty said. "And auditory spells draw on a practitioner's strength, so couldn't be used for any length of time."

"What if you showed me the spell, and I used wild magic as the power source?"

"That would work," Eli said. "But again, it had better be Monty or one of us that gives it to her."

"Oh," I said with a wry smile. "I'm not going anywhere near that woman unless I absolutely have to. I have no desire to have my throat ripped out."

"She wouldn't dare," Ashworth said.

"Nor would Aiden let her, alpha or no," Eli added.

My smile held little humor. "He has to be in the same room to stop her."

"You don't need him to stop her," Monty said. "You hold the power of the wellspring in your damn hands. You could wipe the floor with the lot of them if you wanted."

"And wouldn't that make living in the reservation so much more pleasant?"

He grinned. "Werewolves respect strength. You need to show them—and her—what you're truly capable of."

I raised an eyebrow. "Since when have you specialized in werewolf psychology?"

He airily waved a hand. "It's a commonly known fact."

I snorted. "Thanks, but I still think avoiding her is the

far better option."

"For the moment, yes. Long-term? No." Monty dismantled his protection circle and began picking up his spell stones. "Now that we have a plan of action, can we please get the hell out of here? If it gets any wetter, we're going to have trouble finding our footing, let alone the track."

I walked behind him, picking up my spell stones. "Not to mention the risk of getting lost with night coming in fast and ending up in a mine shaft."

He glanced around at me sharply. "You *can* find the path, right?"

"Absolutely positive."

"She says, while sounding anything but," he grumbled.

I laughed and touched his arm. "It'll be fine. Trust me."

As it turned out, it was. The rain had definitely made the ground a quagmire and traversing the slopes was on the tricky side, but we'd left a wide enough trail through the forest on the way up here that a lot more than an hour or two of rain would have been needed to wash it all away.

By the time we got back to the SUV, the rain had eased, and the setting sun had set the sky ablaze. Monty reversed back to the same turning point Tala had used and then carefully drove out.

Once we were on the road back to Castle Rock, he said, "If Karleen or even Aiden are possible next targets, we'll need to get those auditory charms up and running pretty quick smart."

"Aye, laddie," Ashworth said. "We'll work on them when we get home. Once we have them created, Liz can weave through the wild magic to fuel them. In the meantime, you'll have to contact Aiden and give him an update. He may be grieving, but he won't be handing over the reins of control to anyone else. Not totally."

I glanced out the window just as a car going in the opposite direction passed by.

The driver had curly brown hair that hung to his shoulders in rat tails and a thin brown face.

Harry Seagrave.

I was certain of it, even though I'd gotten little more than a glimpse of the man.

"Monty, do a U-turn right *now* and chase after that car."

I twisted around to look through the back window. It was an old brown sedan of some sort, but he was going too fast—moving away too rapidly—to get a brand name or any other information.

"Why?" Monty asked, even as he braked and turned. The SUV's tires squealed, and for one heart-in-the-mouth moment, the vehicle threatened to topple. Then we were facing the other way and shooting after the other car at speed.

"Because I think the driver is our granny killer."

"Ah, fuck," Monty said. "Did he have anyone in the car with him?"

"Didn't have enough time to see. If he has, she's probably trussed up on the back seat or in the trunk. He wouldn't risk her being seen if he's snatched her."

"If we can get close enough to the car," Ashworth said. "I'll cast a tracker."

"A spell to blow out his tires or somehow stop him would be better," Monty growled. "Given the speed at which we're approaching him, he's going to suspect we're police."

A comment that proved correct as the car ahead suddenly picked up more speed. Monty swore, and the SUV's engine roared as he asked for every last drop of power. I silently prayed the local wildlife didn't decide to come out en masse. We'd be goners if we hit a roo.

In the back, Eli made a call to the rangers and then left a message. Given what had happened to Joseph, maybe no one was available to take the call or someone had simply forgotten to hit forwarding.

We sped through Fryer's Town and continued on the road that would eventually lead us to Vaughan, a tiny township that held little more than an old hall and a collection of relics from the gold mining era.

Slowly but surely, we drew closer to the sedan. Ashworth wound down the window in preparation, but first grabbed his phone and took a quick picture of the other car. "Not sure how clear that'll be, but the rangers might be able to pull a plate number from it if we lose him."

"Let's hope we don't lose him so that they don't have to," Eli said.

"Or that he's not using false plates," I muttered.

Ashworth tucked his phone away and then began the spell. It was a cage spell at its base, with additional layers that would counter the speed and weight of the car ahead.

I hoped it was enough. Hoped it didn't cause a major crash. The last thing we needed was to kill any captive Harry might have.

As far as Harry was concerned, however, he could go to hell and suffer for all eternity.

"Be ready to dodge, laddie," Ashworth said. "This thing is going to stop that vehicle pretty damn quick."

Monty nodded. I wrapped my fingers around the grab handle and held on tight. This could all go very, very badly....

Ashworth cast the spell. It arrowed through the air, a spear of bright threads that soon caught up with the car. As it crossed over the roof, it began to unravel, quickly flowing down the sides of the vehicle and around each of the tires.

The resulting stop was so sudden smoke erupted from the tires. Monty cursed and tugged the SUV hard to the right, barely missing the sedan's rear end as he braked. Smoke plumed past the SUV's nose as we slid off the road and ended up inches away from several trees.

Eli leapt out and ran toward the sedan. I scrambled out after him, saw the driver side door open and Harry appear. He was holding a shotgun, and it was aimed straight at Eli.

"Gun!" I screamed and cast a repelling spell at Eli.

There was a bright flash, a large bang, and Eli was knocked off his feet. My heart leapt into my throat, and for a moment I couldn't breathe. *Please, please don't let him be dead....*

Another bang, and the back window of the SUV exploded, sending glass flying everywhere. I ducked back beside the vehicle and cast a net spell in an attempt to wrench the gun away. But the spell slewed sideways and hit the edge of the car instead, spinning it around and throwing Harry back inside the car. When it came to a stop, the driver side was facing away from us. Not the result I'd wanted, but at least he'd momentarily stopped shooting.

Monty scrambled out of the driver seat and knelt behind me. "You okay?"

I nodded. "I wish I knew if Eli was."

Another shot rang out, and Ashworth cursed loudly as more glass shattered.

"Ashworth?" I said, voice panicked. "You okay?"

"Yeah, but the door is going to need some patching."

"Like I fucking care about that."

Another shot, and the SUV lurched. Harry had just shot one of the rear tires out.

"Let me leave," Harry shouted, "or I'll fucking kill the bitch I have with me."

"You're going to kill her anyway," Ashworth returned. "So as threats go, that doesn't really hold much weight."

"You're obviously not rangers then."

"No, we're worse," Ashworth said. "We're witches, and all that matters to us is stopping scum like you."

"Oh, I think we both know *that* is an utter lie. Witches have that whole threefold rule thing to worry about, don't they?"

"That only works when it comes to us directly and intentionally harming someone. If you kill her, it takes the weight off our shoulders."

"But not the guilt, I'd wager" came the reply.

He had that right, at least.

Ashworth appeared on our side of the vehicle. "Monty, if I keep him talking, do you want to sneak off into the scrub behind us and see if you can get around him?"

"Why can't we just spell the fucker into submission?" Monty asked.

"Because he's wearing a warding charm."

"He wasn't when he snatched me," I said, "so it's obviously a recent addition."

"Our boy is angry, not stupid," Ashworth said. "Just remember, laddie, that he's got at one gun, if not more, so don't be getting yourself shot."

"See," Monty murmured to me, "he does care."

"He probably doesn't want to face Belle's wrath if you get injured," I said. "And please remember Harry's a werewolf and will hear you if you make too much noise."

As Monty nodded and backed into the trees, Ashworth shouted, "Let your hostage go, and maybe we'll consider releasing you."

"Yeah, and lose any bargaining power? Thanks, but I'm not that stupid."

A comment that made me wonder if he'd heard what we were planning.

"No one said you were," Ashworth said, "but we need some incentive here."

I edged back and said softly, "Do you want me to try and get to Eli?"

Ashworth shook his head. "There's too much open ground between the SUV and him. It's too much of a risk."

"But—"

"No," he cut in savagely. "Eli would never forgive me if you got hurt or killed."

And neither would he. He didn't say that, of course, but he didn't need to, either. I drew in a breath in an effort to ease the growing worry and saw the tiny flickers of light in the shadows of the nearby trees.

Wild magic.

I raised a hand, and it floated over to me. One wrapped around my wrist while the other hovered close. Katie said, *What do you need?*

We think there's a woman in the car, but we're not sure if she's in the trunk or the back seat. I also need you to see if Eli's okay—he's in the trees.

Wait, and I'll check.

"We do this my way or not at all," Harry was saying. "You three leave, or I'll kill her. Plain and simple. You must be aware by now that your magic cannot hurt me."

The luminous thread slipped into the car, and a heart-beat later, Katie said, *She's in the back seat, trussed up tighter than a turkey at Christmas.*

Is she alive?

Yes, and unhurt aside from a bloody lump on her head.

Relief slithered through me. *Can you give me a description? I'll need it to form a retrieval spell.*

Once she'd passed on the information, I added, *And Eli?*

I'll go check on him now.

I glanced at Ashworth and whispered, "His hostage is in the back seat. If you can open the back door, I'll magic her out."

He didn't ask how I knew. He would have felt the wild magic's presence.

While he did a break-in spell, I crafted a retrieval one, using the description Katie had given me to ensure it grabbed the right person. These sorts of spells—or at least the versions I knew—generally needed the item being within sight of the caster or an exact description. I had to hope the latter was enough in this case, because the last thing I needed was the spell making a useless attempt to grab Harry.

"Ready?" Ashworth said softly.

I nodded, body tensing automatically.

Ashworth unleashed his spell. I waited a heartbeat, then did the same. The two traversed the distance between the SUV and the car in the blink of an eye, Ashworth's hitting the back door and ripping it from its hinges even as mine spun in and grabbed the woman who lay on the seat.

Harry's response was instant and furious. He screamed and unleashed his weapons, first into his car, then at us *and* into the trees.

He knew about Monty.

I clamped down on the panic, not wanting to alarm Belle if she happened to be following events. I couldn't feel her, but our connection was so strong these days it was possible she was background listening.

As bullet after bullet hit the SUV and shredded leaves fell like green snow all around us, I scooted the unconscious woman into the scrub on the far side of the road, deep into the trees. Hopefully, she'd be safe there. She certainly wouldn't be safe anywhere else. Not with the metal storm being unleashed.

Ashworth grabbed my hand and dragged me to the front of the vehicle. A heartbeat later, the storm eased. The ensuing silence was eerie, and my nerves crawled. Neither Ashworth nor I moved. While it was possible he'd simply run out of bullets, it might also be an attempt to lure us out.

It's not a trap came Katie's thought. *He's gone,*

Can you send a thread after him?

Already have. Once he's holed away somewhere safe, I'll contact you. She paused. *Eli lives. He's not been shot.*

The surge of relief was so strong that I was suddenly blinking back tears. I gripped Ashworth's arm and told him.

"Ah, that's good news, lass," he said gruffly. "What about our suspect?"

"According to Katie, he's on the run."

"Is she tracking him?"

I nodded. He rose cautiously, but when no gunshot greeted his appearance, he offered me a hand and helped me up. "I'll go tend to Eli. You go find the laddie."

"And the victim?"

"Check her after you find Monty. I'll call an ambulance and see if the rangers are finally picking up. I'm thinking there's no point even trying Aiden right now." He grimaced. "They aren't going to be pleased about this mess."

"Even if we *had* gotten hold of them when we spotted Harry, they wouldn't have gotten here in time to prevent any of this."

"We both know that, but it won't matter in the scheme

of things. Especially when emotions are already running so high."

He turned and ran across the road. As I grabbed my backpack, then walked toward the old sedan, Monty emerged from the trees.

"You okay?" I asked.

He nodded. "One of the bullets hit a tree just as I was passing it, and my hand copped the splinters my face would have got."

"How bad?"

He held up his right hand. At least a half dozen bloody wounds were scattered across his palm, but only a couple of splinters remained embedded. While they weren't large, they were undoubtedly painful.

"What about you?" he said.

"Unhurt." I stopped beside him. There were three guns on the ground—a shotgun and two handguns—as well as numerous shell casings. "Why wouldn't he take the weapons with him? Why leave them here?"

"He ran off in wolf form. Makes carrying anything difficult." Monty squatted beside the shotgun, pulled a tissue from his pocket, and picked something up. "He obviously lost this during the battle."

It was a key. "A house key?"

He wrinkled his nose. "Too small. It looks more like a key to a *specific* sort of lock—a jewelry box or something like that. Could you use it to track him?"

He handed me the tissue-wrapped key. I closed my fingers around it and called on my psychometry. Nothing happened, but that wasn't really surprising. These sorts of keys generally weren't kept on a key ring or used daily.

"There's no life in it." I handed it back, then glanced over the hood at the sound of voices. Eli was standing, though not entirely on his own. Ashworth had one arm wrapped around him, which suggested unsteadiness at the very least. I pulled some silicone gloves from the backpack and handed them to Monty. "While I go check on our victim, can you have a quick look in the car before the rangers get here? Just on the off chance there's some clue as to where he got the charm?"

Monty pulled on the gloves as he moved toward the car. I walked around its nose but didn't immediately go in search of our victim. Eli might have escaped being shot, but he didn't look all that great. His face was pale, there was a bloody scrape across his left cheek, and his left arm looked broken. Ashworth was currently wrapping an immobilizing spell around it.

"Hey." I stopped several feet away and thrust my hands into my jacket in an effort to stop the overwhelming urge to give him a fierce hug. "Sorry about throwing you like that, but I—"

"I'll take a broken bone or two over being gut shot any day," Eli said, voice amused despite the pain that radiated from him. "Don't you ever apologize for saving a life, Liz, be it mine, Ashworth's, or anyone else's."

"But if I'd taken a little more time or care, you might not have broken your arm."

"And if you *had*, it might have resulted in his death," Ashworth said gruffly. "Stop worrying over it. How's the laddie?"

"Unhurt aside from a few splinters. I'm just about to check on Harry's victim."

"Good. The ambulance shouldn't be long. They've only got to come from Louton."

As if to emphasize that point, the wail of sirens bit through the air. I swung my pack around and retrieved one of the pain lotions. "Here, take this. It should mute the pain until the paramedics can give you something stronger."

"That would certainly be appreciated," Eli said.

As Ashworth uncorked the small vial, I moved on. The retrieval spell sparkled in the shadows gathering deeper in the trees and made our victim easy to find. Once I'd dismissed it, I squatted beside her. Like his other victims, she was elderly and slender, with short silvery hair and pale skin. The wound on the right side of her head looked relatively deep, but it no longer bled, which suggested it had been at least half an hour since he'd grabbed her. Dried blood matted her hair and darkened her coat's collar, but as Katie had said, she otherwise appeared unhurt. I lightly pressed two fingers to her neck; her pulse was a little rapid but otherwise strong.

I pulled the knife from the backpack and carefully cut the ropes around her hands and knees, then fished around for salve and rubbed it over the rope burns. It would numb any pain they might cause and hopefully make her more comfortable when she woke.

I glanced up as Monty approached. "Find anything useful?"

He nodded and handed me her purse. "Her name is Janet Whitehall, and she lives in Argyle. She'd got a fair bit of cash in there."

"Which he undoubtedly would have stolen once he'd killed her," I said.

"Probably." He shoved his hands into his pockets. "I'm surprised he's continuing his vendetta rather than getting the hell out of the reservation."

"His mom said he didn't have anywhere else to go."

Monty snorted. "He's a grown man, and she's *dead*. He can go anywhere he fucking wants."

"And just because he can doesn't mean he wants to." I shrugged. "Remember what his mom said about the will—maybe he can't afford to leave."

"Or maybe the increasing risk is all part of the pleasure for him."

Given we weren't dealing with a rational mind, that was certainly possible. "Did you find anything else in the car?"

"A receipt from a place called Witchy Ways over in Trentham. I photographed it and left it in place for the rangers."

I nodded. "We'll need to visit them tomorrow. Although, it has to be a pretty powerful charm to ward off all magic, and that's not something your run-of-the-mill charm and potion witch can generally do."

"Which either means the proprietor is not a run-of-the-mill witch, or the charm is preventative in nature rather than broad reaching."

I raised an eyebrow. "Meaning what? That he's protected against capture spells and nothing else?"

"The type of netting spells we use to capture humans are fairly simple in design compared to the ones we use against demons and the like, and it's easy enough to ward against them." A wry smile twisted his lips. "And remember, none of us attempted stronger magic against him once we realized he had the charm."

"A bluff, and we fell for it."

"It wasn't a total bluff. Your net spell did go awry, remember." He looked around. "The ambulances have just arrived. I'll go grab a medic."

I glanced down as the unconscious woman stirred. Her eyes opened but for several seconds she did nothing more than blink. Her expression was scared and confused.

I touched her arm lightly. "It's okay, Janet. You're safe.

You just need to keep still until the paramedics get here to check you over."

Her confusion increased. "Why am I in the trees? Was I in some sort of accident?"

"You were attacked and knocked out."

"Did he take my purse? I had my pension money—"

"Your purse is here, and the money is untouched." I placed it into her hands and while her panic immediately eased, her confusion didn't.

"Then where am I?" she said, sounding more distressed. "How did I get here? I don't drive, and I don't remember—"

"It's okay," I cut in soothingly. "You were kidnapped by your attacker, but thankfully he was seen. You're in the trees because we had to get you somewhere safe while he was shooting at us."

"Shooting?" she said, even more distressed. "Was anyone hurt?"

"No." I hesitated. "What was the last thing you remember?"

"Footsteps," she said. "They were approaching me from behind and I turned, just to see who it was, because you can never be sure these days. I saw that untidy-looking man—"

"You knew him?" I cut in sharply.

"Not really, but I've seen him in Argyle several times recently, near where I live. Never talked to him, though."

Meaning this might have been a crime of opportunity as much as anything else. "What happened next? Did you talk to him?"

"I didn't get a chance. He hit me, and I don't remember anything after that."

She raised her hand, obviously intending to touch the side of her head, but I stopped her. "You've got a nasty cut.

Best not to touch it until the medics can look at it. Where were you when all this happened?"

"Castle Rock, just near the station there. I was visiting a friend and was walking back to catch a train home."

There should have been too much traffic in that area for an attack to happen, but maybe that was the point. Maybe Monty was right—maybe Harry was getting his jollies as much from the kidnap as the kill. "And you live in Argyle?"

She nodded and winced. Pain flitted through her expression. "Not that far from the lake, close to the old trailer park."

"The closed one?"

She nodded and once again tried to touch her head. I stopped her, then glanced around. Monty and a medic were approaching.

I rose. "She's got a nasty wound on her head, and rope burns around her wrists and ankles. I put some salve on those, but not the cut."

The medic nodded and immediately introduced herself to Janet. Monty and I turned and walked back to the SUV. It was a goddam mess, the rear end sprayed with so many bullet holes it looked like Swiss cheese.

"At least you didn't write it off this time," Monty said, in a philosophical voice. "That's a definite improvement."

"I'm not sure the council will see it that way, especially given their current mood when it comes to me."

"It's not the whole council, just the O'Connor portion of it." He shrugged. "And hey, if they hadn't let the well-spring remain unprotected for so long, the reservation wouldn't keep getting overrun with supernatural nasties, and you wouldn't be writing off cars in the course of protecting their asses."

A smile tugged at my lips. "I'm thinking they're not going to see it that way."

"Probably not, but that doesn't alter the truth of the statement." He shrugged. "Was Janet able to give you any information?"

"Some. She doesn't drive, so the receipt you found is probably Harry's."

"That will hopefully make things easier when we're questioning our witch. Did she say anything else?"

"Only that she lives near an old trailer park in Argyle and has seen him around the area."

"The rangers were putting a watch on the park, so he can't be staying there."

"No, but he must be staying somewhere in that area."

"Maybe the same place the key belongs to."

"Maybe, but that's the rangers' problem not ours."

"A fine sentiment when your intuition keeps making it our business."

I half smiled. "Also true."

A ranger vehicle pulled up behind Harry's car. Thankfully, it was Jaz who climbed out rather than Aiden. I pushed away from the SUV. "I'll deal with the rangers; you can change the tire."

He raised an eyebrow. "Will we be allowed to drive it away? Isn't it evidence or something?"

"I don't know. I'll ask Jaz," I said and headed over.

She was scanning the area, her expression one of horror. "What the hell happened here? Some kind of firefight?"

"A very one-sided one."

Her gaze swept me, then moved over to Monty before settling on Eli and Ashworth. "If a broken arm is the only resulting injury, consider yourselves lucky. You'd better give me a statement."

Once she'd pulled out her phone and hit the record button, I gave her a quick update on the victim and everything else we'd found. "We've basically left everything as it was, except for the woman's purse. She was fretting about it because it has her pension in it."

She nodded. "And what about Harry? Did you manage to put a tracker on him?"

"Yes. The minute I know anything, I'll contact you."

"Chasing suspects is so much easier when there's a witch involved."

I couldn't help but laugh. "I'm thinking there's quite a few in this reservation who would much prefer we witches weren't even here."

She ended the recording and wrinkled her nose. "That's true, but it's mostly confined to the older gen. We rangers appreciate the work you do, and the rest appreciate your cakes."

I laughed. "I'm thinking the latter is the more important."

"For many, that is sadly true." She squeezed my arm lightly, her expression suddenly serious. "I know there's been some grumblings from certain quarters, but I do mean it when I say most of us not only support you, but also your relationship with Aiden."

My eyebrows rose. "I thought werewolves were against crossbreeding?"

"For the most part, yes, but there are always exceptions, and it's pretty obvious to even the willfully blind that you two are meant to be together."

"Gee," I said wryly, "I wonder who you're referencing there?"

A smile touched her lips, but her expression remained

serious. "She may never accept you, but she is not the entire pack."

"She's still their alpha. That's all that matters."

"Again, there are exceptions to all rules."

"Meaning?"

"You could challenge her ruling. You could confront the entire pack and state your case."

"Aiden must be aware that that's a possibility and hasn't suggested it, so he obviously believes it wouldn't work."

She smiled. "He's somewhat hamstrung by the fact he's an alpha in waiting. He must be seen to be doing the right thing by the pack in *all* matters. *You* must prove your worth to his pack. It's not something he dare do."

"It seems being viewed as less than worthy is my lot in this life." I wearily rubbed my eyes. "Even if by some miracle I could convince his pack I'd be a good addition— and seriously, after all I've done for this reservation recently, if they can't already see that, they're idiots—what would it actually achieve? Karleen is not going to change her mind."

Not given her long history with witches.

"No, but if the pack puts enough pressure on her, she might capitulate. Being an alpha isn't a dictatorship, you know."

I raised an eyebrow. "And how often does an alpha get challenged?"

She laughed. "Rarely. But it can and has happened. It's at least something to keep in mind if things escalate."

"If Karleen tries to get us evicted, you mean."

"Well, yes. But she can't do that alone—that would take a ruling from the council itself, and as I said, there are many who support you and the others." She smiled, though it failed to break the seriousness in her expression. "You've also got to remember that, for the most part, the 'common wolf' is unaware of your work with us or indeed doesn't have any real knowledge of magic itself. They have no concept of the forces you can call or the spells you can unleash. Even the council, who are well aware just how much magic has helped us over the past year, don't truly understand it. None of us have ever really had a reason to, and after Gabe was blamed for Katie's death, well, no real desire to, either."

"I'm not sure going in there, all magical guns blazing, will help my cause in any way."

"Maybe it won't but until you try, you won't know. And, let's face it, avoiding the situation hasn't exactly helped, has it?" She touched my arm, as if to take the sting away from the accusation. "I'd better get to work."

"Before you do, are we able to drive the SUV home, or do you need to keep it?"

She hesitated. "In this case, because we already have the guns and multiple casings, I don't think that'll be a problem. But I'll head over now and photograph it for the record."

I left her to it and walked across to the ambulance Eli was being helped into. Ashworth waited to one side. I stopped beside him and said, "I take it you're heading into the hospital with him?"

"Aye, lass. Someone has to hold his hand. His good hand, that is."

From inside the ambulance came Eli's snort. "You know who will be holding whose hand, don't you? I'm not the one who hates hospitals."

"I don't hate them. I just don't want to spend time in the damn things."

I smiled. "You'll keep me updated?"

"Aye. But it's not a bad break by the look of things, so

we shouldn't be in there longer than it takes to set and cast it." He shoved his hand into his pocket and pulled out his house keys. "You'll find an old green spell book on my desk, opened at the page where we found the auditory spell. Use it. I don't think we dare delay in getting the charms to Karleen, Aiden, or even his brothers."

I accepted the key and shoved it in my pocket. "Can I take the book back to the café? I'd feel safer doing a new spell in the protection of our reading room."

Ashworth nodded. "It's my dad's book, so it has sentimental value more than monetary."

"I'll take good care of it."

"I wouldn't have offered it if I thought otherwise." He smiled and touched my arm lightly. "Try to get some rest after your make the charms, lass. You're looking a little ragged around the edges."

"I'm fine. Really."

He didn't look convinced, but he simply nodded and stepped inside the ambulance. I backed away as one of the medics closed the door then gave me a nod and moved around to the driver side.

When both the ambulances had left, I returned to the SUV. Once Jaz had finished recording all the bullet holes and cleared us to go, I climbed into the passenger seat while Monty slipped into the driver side. The journey back to Castle Rock was fairly noisy thanks to all the holes, but the SUV ran okay otherwise. We'd been lucky the engine and petrol tank hadn't been hit.

We stopped briefly at Ashworth's to grab the book, then made our way back to the café. The delicious aroma of roasting lamb greeted us as we walked in the back door.

"Thought you might need a decent meal after the drama of the last few hours," Belle said from the kitchen.

"And there's hot apple pie for dessert."

"A woman who anticipates her man's needs is a woman worth keeping," Monty said as he swept her into his arms and gave her a quick but passionate kiss.

She laughed and pushed him away. "Hate to break your delusions, but the only needs I'm anticipating are those of my witch. Your needs, my dear Monty, come way down the list."

"Seeing as your witch is my cousin, you're forgiven. Especially when everything smells so divine."

She rolled her eyes, then looked at me. "You've ten minutes if you want a quick shower to warm up."

I handed Monty the book and backpack, then raced up the stairs. A quick hot shower eased the physical cold, even if the chill of foresight remained. I tugged on my sweatpants, a thick old woolen sweater, and my Uggs, then headed downstairs just as Monty was carrying the platter of sliced lamb over to the table.

I moved behind the counter and flicked on the kettle. "You want something to drink?"

"A large red wine would be good. I'll need the fortification if I have to confront Aiden's mother later."

"Make that two," Belle said, as she came out of the kitchen carrying the platter of roasted potatoes and pumpkin and the gravy boat.

I was tempted to make it three, but I needed to keep a clear head for the charms, and drinking wine when I was already tired always made me even sleepier. Coffee was safer.

We ate our dinner and chatted about everything and anything other than the rusalka, Harry, and the mess that was my relationship with Karleen and her pack. Once the apple pie—served with several large scoops of cinnamon ice cream—was consumed, we shifted into the reading room and made the auditory charms. By the time we'd finished, my head was booming, and all I wanted to do was sleep.

Even Monty looked weary. He pulled out his phone, put it on speaker, and then called Aiden.

"Hey Monty," Aiden said, his voice flat and emotionless —a sure sign he was controlling himself very tightly. "Is there a problem?"

"Possibly," Monty replied. "We believe the rusalka hasn't finished her kills just yet, but we've figured out a means of muting her call—"

"Too damn late to matter," Aiden growled, then sucked in a breath. "Sorry, that was uncalled for."

"Yeah," Monty said. "It was. Especially when it now appears you or Karleen might be the reason this thing is here, not Liz."

"What the hell are you talking about?"

"We tried to summon her. It didn't work. That means Liz isn't the reason—or at least not the sole reason—for the rusalka's presence."

"It makes no sense that Mom or I—"

"Oh, it makes plenty of sense," Monty cut in. "But I didn't ring to argue over that point right now. We've created a number of charms for you, your mom, and your two brothers to wear."

Aiden sucked in a breath, the sound somehow horrified. "Why would she go after my brothers?"

"At this point, we can't take any chances," Monty said. "Where do you want to meet?"

"Where are you now? Home or the café?"

Monty glanced at me before replying, and I shook my head. Call me a coward, but I really wasn't up to facing Aiden and the sheer depth of his grief right now. He'd spent months keeping his life with me very separate from his pack life, and these deaths were pack business. I might ache to comfort him, to be with him and support him, but that wasn't my place. Not now.

Of course, if Jaz was right, then maybe I could change that by showing his pack I was a worthy mate. But I guess the question was, did he really want that? Was he willing to stand beside me and fight his pack's prejudices and expectations for the sake of our relationship?

I didn't know the answer to that question. Maybe I never would.

"We're just on the way home now," Monty said. "We should be there in ten."

"I'll meet you there." He paused. "How's Lizzie?"

"Home and sleeping, as far as I'm aware."

"Ah," he said. "I'll see you soon."

He hung up, and disappointment slithered through me. Which was stupid. I mean, he *had* asked after me, and what else could he have said, given he was talking to Monty, not me?

Once Belle and Monty had left, I locked up then headed upstairs and climbed into bed. Sleep hit hard and fast, and for a change, I didn't dream. Maybe even the psychic part of me was exhausted.

But that didn't mean I slept the entire night undisturbed, because just after four, wisps of moonlight wrapped around my wrists and gently woke me.

Katie had found Harry's hideout.

Chapter Twelve

I called the rangers, then got dressed and headed downstairs to grab my coat and the backpack. While charms, potions, and magic were unlikely to work against the bastard thanks to the ward he wore, it also held my silver knife, and that might just be enough to deter any attack he made against me.

Though I hoped with all my heart that it *didn't* come down to a physical battle between him and me. It shouldn't, given all I had to do was lead Tala and her team to his lair, but still...

Tala pulled up just as I was stepping out the front door. Jaz was with her, while two other ranger vehicles followed, each holding at least two people. Obviously, nearly the whole team had been at the station, which given the early hour was surprising.

"Where to?" Tala said the minute I jumped into the back of the vehicle.

"He's close to Porcupine Hill."

I had no idea where that was, and Katie hadn't

265

explained it, but it was obviously well-known, because Tala simply nodded and headed off.

I glanced at the luminous threads still wrapped around my wrists. Katie was no longer present, but she'd left her threads with Harry, and I could feel his location through them. "He's in an old mining hut up in the hills, near a creek. His car is parked close by but off road on Middleton Track."

"Clever positioning," Jaz commented. "From the top of the ridge, he'll be able to see us coming."

"It won't matter." Tala voice was cold and determined. "It's six against one. He can't outgun us or even outrun us all."

He'd been doing a pretty damn good job of it so far, but I resisted the urge to say that simply because it was unfair. The rangers, just like us witches, had been doing their best.

We drove through Vaughan, then along a number of rough old dirt roads that wound through thick forest until we reached Middleton Track. Tala ordered the two vehicles behind us to split off to the right and loop around.

I glanced at the threads again. "His car is about half a kilometer ahead, in the trees to the right."

She nodded and drove on at a more cautious speed. After several tense minutes, we spotted the tail end of the car. Tala pulled up behind it, then climbed out, grabbed a knife from the rear of her vehicle, and stabbed the rear tires on our suspect's car several times.

Jaz retrieved weapons and ammo packs from the back of the truck and tossed a set across to Tala. They really weren't mucking about this time.

"Right," Tala said. "We'll head off. Liz, I'm afraid you'll have to accompany us, at least until we're sure he's still in the hut and not roaming about."

If he was roaming about, there was a fair chance he'd either scent or hear us given that, despite recent DNA improvements, I still didn't walk as lightly as a wolf.

We made our way past the vehicle and up the tree-lined slope. Slivers of moonlit magic followed our progress, though these threads were from the old wellspring, not the new.

It took ten minutes to reach the ridge. Tala paused briefly, then moved several yards along until we reached a rocky outcrop that jutted out over the tree line and gave us a clear view of the valley below. No wonder Jaz had said it was clever positioning. Porcupine Hill was an isolated island of trees surrounded by open farmland. The minute anyone approached, from any angle, he'd see them.

"How we going to play this?" Jaz asked.

Tala glanced at me. "He still there?"

I hesitated, feeling my way along the threads, then nodded.

"Good," Tala said. "The other four will approach the hill from the far side and hopefully drive him directly into our path."

"And if he doesn't flee this way?" I asked. "If he decides to make a stand?"

"Then we'll go in and get him." Her smile flashed, fierce and anticipatory. "I'm just itching for a reason to shoot the bastard."

Her expression suggested it would be a good idea never to get on her bad side. "What do you want me to do?"

"Stay up here, out of the way. Aiden wouldn't appreciate you getting caught in the crossfire."

"Rest assured I wouldn't either."

Her grin flashed again, then she and Jaz headed down the hill. I squatted on my heels and tried not to resent the fact that I was being kept safe when the only reason they were even this close to capturing the man was thanks to my connection to Katie and the wild magic. Of course, I was also well aware the resentment stemmed not only from a history of being considered useless and needing to prove otherwise, but also from a slightly fatalist nature—from a belief that if something could go wrong, it would.

And I was nowhere near close enough to help if it did.

Then again, while he might be warded against spells, that didn't mean I couldn't magically impede him in other ways. Especially when the wild magic was at my disposal.

Five tense minutes passed, then a staccato of gunshots bit across the silence, and my pulse rate leapt. I had no idea where Jaz and Tala were, but there was no movement in the valley below, and the shots—which had originated from Porcupine Hill—hadn't sounded aimed this way. He'd been shooting at the rangers on the other side of the hill rather than Tala or Jaz, I guessed.

Another round of shots, but this time there was a sharp response. There was still no movement on this side of the hill, and I shifted my weight, fighting the urge to stand up. That would only present a silhouette that Harry might well spot.

For several more minutes, nothing happened. Then a figure broke from the trees surrounding the base of Porcupine Hill and raced straight toward me.

A single shot rang out. Harry stumbled and briefly went down.

"This is Ranger Sinclair," Tala said, her voice clear and authoritative. "Put down your weapons, then raise your hands, Harry. We have you surrounded. Move, and we'll bring you down."

He didn't move, but for several seconds, he didn't lower

his weapon, either. Blood stained the bottom half of his jeans, but he wasn't favoring his left leg in any way, so the wound had to be superficial. Even if it wasn't, it wouldn't stop him from running, as the process of shifting would heal it.

I waited, tension rolling through me while the wild magic spun lazily around my fingers in readiness.

Then, in what seemed like slow motion, Harry lowered his weapon, stepped back, and raised his hands.

I was almost disappointed. Almost.

"All your weapons, Harry" came Tala's comment.

He laughed. *Laughed*. Like this was all one big game and his life wasn't on the line. The man really wasn't right in the head.

"Slowly," Tala added.

With one hand still raised, Harry reached the other behind his back, and then placed a second weapon on the ground.

But this time, he didn't step back.

This time, he ran, flowing smoothly from human to wolf form. Gunfire chased after him, and he stumbled, his form shimmering from wolf to human to wolf again as he picked himself up and ran on. He was healing the wounds as they occurred, I realized.

Two wolves erupted from the trees below me and chased after him, but he had a good start on them, and he was fast—I knew that from experience.

He couldn't and wouldn't outrun them forever, of course, but that didn't mean I couldn't do something to end the chase here and now. I hastily created a lasso spell, wrapped the wild magic through it, then spun it toward the tree line Harry was headed for. Tala was gaining ground on him, and Jaz was only a few paces behind her, but they wouldn't catch him before he hit the trees, and that was a risk, even if the chance of him escaping them now was minute.

The lasso settled around the top half of a tree. I drew in a deeper breath, then, with every ounce of both magical and physical strength I had, I wrenched the rope back. Hard.

I'd expected to simply tear a number of the big branches free and toss them in his path.

Instead, I tore the whole damn tree out of the ground.

It smashed down meters in front of Harry, giving him little warning and no time to dodge. He hit the thick mass of branches hard, and a howl of pain bit the air. There was a part of me that fervently hoped he'd impaled himself.

Tala plunged into the foliage after him. A few seconds later, she emerged, one hand on his shoulder and a gun pressed hard into his back. The front of his shirt was torn and bloody. He *had* impaled himself.

I deactivated the lasso, released the wild magic, and made my way down the hill.

"I take it the tree was your handiwork?" Tala said when I drew close enough. "If so, thanks for the help."

"Welcome." I reached forward and tore the charm from Harry's neck, breaking the chain of its protection. The tiny threads of disengaged magic floated away on the breeze, quickly fading into the night.

The big man suddenly seemed a whole lot smaller. It was as if, now that the game was well and truly over, his bravado had fled and he'd shrunk in on himself.

The other rangers appeared and loped toward us, gaining human form only when they were close. Tala cuffed Harry, then shoved him toward Mac. "You and Duke take this scum to the hospital and get him treated. Do not, under any circumstances, let him out of your sight, no matter what the doctors say." As the two men grabbed Harry and escorted him away, Tala tossed her car keys to Jaz. "Can you take Liz home? Then go home yourself. The rest of us will run a check on what he was doing here."

Jaz nodded and motioned me to follow. "Can I just say that was pretty fucking impressive? Maybe if you pulled a few trees out of the ground in front the council, they'd be inclined to impart a little more respect."

I laughed. "Or it could just confirm their fears that I'm dangerous and need to be evicted."

She gave me a lopsided grin. "Also possible."

We made our way through the forest, but just as we reached the SUV, the first strains of an ethereal and beautiful song ran along the breeze. The notes of it had changed, and its frequency was very different than before, but horror nevertheless surged.

The rusalka was active again.

I swore and reached for Belle, but for several long seconds she didn't answer. Not because she was asleep—I could tell from the distant wash of fear she wasn't—she just couldn't answer.

Her fear became mine, and all sorts of scenarios ran through my mind, each one more devastating than the previous. I bit my lip and tried to ignore them all.

"Liz?" Jaz said, voice concerned. "Everything okay?"

My gaze jumped to hers. "Sorry, no. The siren just came online again."

"Ah, fuck." She scrubbed a hand through her hair. "Can you track her? If so, get in the damn car, and we'll get going."

I climbed into the front seat and directed her toward the Vaughan Road. Though the song was distant, every instinct said its location was closer to Castle Rock than the O'Connor compound.

I didn't think that was a coincidence.

Not given Belle's current emotional state.

Jaz sped on through the night, the headlights spearing the trees and occasionally reflecting red off the eyes of roos. When we swung onto the main road back to Castle Rock, I couldn't help sighing in relief, even if this road was in reality not that much safer than the tracks when it came to wildlife randomly jumping in front of vehicles.

The mental line finally cleared, and I instantly said, *What's happened? Are you okay? Is Monty?*

He is now, but it was a bit hairy there for a while, and it wasn't until I raided his thoughts that I realized the rusalka was calling him.

I swore softly and scrubbed a hand across my eyes. This was a revenge attack, of that I had no doubt. *You blocked the song?*

It took the combination of the auditory spell and temporarily freezing his ability to walk, but yes.

That Belle had been able to do a workable recreation of the spell on the fly and alone spoke a whole lot to the increase in her magical might. *Keep an eye on him, because her call will strengthen when she realizes he's not answering. I'm chasing her location now.*

Great, but there may be another problem.

What? But even as I said that, I knew and had to fight the sudden urge to be sick.

Neither Ashworth nor Eli are answering their phones, she continued. *I suspect our rusalka is attempting a three-for-one deal.*

I swore. Softly, violently, fearfully. *She must have gotten a feel for them when we tried that summoning spell.*

Undoubtedly, but why go after them and not you? And why now?

She's aware I can interact with the wild magic. Maybe she's wary of getting too close again. As to why now—it's possible she's simply going after them because she can't reach her chosen targets.

Belle's frustration and fear ran down the line, mingling with and strengthening my own. *What are we going to do?*

You're going to stay there and keep an eye on Monty.

You can't go after this thing alone.

I'm not alone. Jaz is with me.

I didn't think that news comforted her any, but all she said was, *Be careful. We can't be sure how deep her control runs, and she may well force the men to attack you magically.*

I hoped she didn't, even as I feared she would. But there was nothing I could do, nothing I could prepare until the worst actually happened.

Hopefully, nothing would. Hopefully the gods would for once be on our side.

Yell if you need anything, Belle added.

I wouldn't, not unless I had no other choice, but she knew that. I directed Jaz to the right, into the back streets and away from Castle Rock. The rusalka lurked in the area between the city center and the O'Connor reservation.

A few minutes later, pinpointed in the gleam of the headlights, we spotted two figures. They were running barefoot along the side of the road, one in jeans and a T-shirt and the other in pajamas bottoms with his arm in a sling. Ashworth, who despite his stockiness was fast, could have left the injured and bruised Eli well behind. That he remained by his side, despite the call he couldn't ignore, spoke of the strength of their bond.

"Holy shit," Jaz said. "Isn't that Ashworth and Eli?"

"Yeah. They're answering the siren's call."

Her gaze shot to mine. "On foot? Why not in the car? It would have been quicker."

"I don't know, but given all her victims have answered her on foot, maybe her control doesn't extend to the workings of a car."

She grunted. "Is it safe to stop them? Or will they attack?"

"Again, I don't know. Stay behind them, and I'll see if I can create a spell to mute her call."

She nodded and slipped the SUV in behind them. Neither man seemed to notice.

I drew in a breath to calm my nerves and then began working on two identical spells rather than just the one. It was very possible that once I activated the muting spell, the rusalka would order the two men to attack each other. She might want to feed on their souls, but I suspected the reason she was calling them was to erase the possibility of them either interfering in her future kills or even banishing her from the reservation. Wrapping them in separate protective spells should counter that possibility.

I used a net spell as a base, built the auditory spell over the top of it, then wrapped the whole thing in wild magic, just to ensure they couldn't physically unravel the spell.

By the time I finished, I was shaking with fatigue and my head was booming. I wiped a trickle of sweat from the side of my face and glanced at Jaz. "Where's the nearest body of water from here?"

"The Golden Point Reservoir—it's about two kilometers up the road. Why?"

"The strength of her song suggests she's close, so that's more than likely where she's calling from."

"It'll take us two minutes to get there."

"Good, because I'm not entirely sure what will happen once I activate these spells." While I had no doubt they would work, the question I couldn't answer was for how long.

"You say the word, and I'll plant my foot."

I wound down the window, stuck out my hand, and launched the spells. The tangled mess of threads and power on which all my hopes hung settled above the head of each man. Ashworth's hand twitched, suggesting he was aware enough to sense my magic but too enmeshed in the song to respond.

I drew in a breath and then activated my nets. The threads unraveled, and a bright curtain of power fell around each man, leashing them to the ground.

They both came to an abrupt stop, and deeper in the distance came an inhuman, ungodly scream of frustration.

Then the power of her song increased, washing over me in a thick wave, making my skin crawl and my feet twitch. Horror slewed through me. She wasn't attempting to break through my magic and force the two men on.

She was attempting to ensnare me.

Why her song didn't have the same immediate effect on me as it had the men, I couldn't say. This particular demon was an equal opportunity killer, so the fact I was female wouldn't be the difference.

Maybe it was the wild magic. Maybe it was the charm around my neck which, while it didn't provide an auditory barrier, had been layered with multiple protections against demons.

But whatever the reason, I couldn't risk it would last. We had to get to her—stop her—*now*.

"What the fuck was that?" Jaz said, her eyes wide as she glanced at me.

"The rusalka. Go. We need to get to that lake."

She immediately swung the SUV around the two men and sped off. A shout followed us, but I didn't look back, and I didn't deactivate the spells around Ashworth or Eli. Until the rusalka stopped singing, I didn't dare.

The rusalka's call strengthened. Sweat broke out across my forehead, and my breathing sharpened. I was drowning under the weight of it; if I didn't do something, she *would* capture me as she'd captured all the others.

I didn't have the time—or the depth of attention needed —to create another auditory barrier on the fly. I needed something else, something that would provide a totally different kind of barrier.

I grabbed the backpack sitting at my feet and wrenched the knife free.

Jaz sucked in an audible breath, and no wonder. Silver was deadly to werewolves and, in a confined space like this, she'd feel the heat and closeness of it.

"What the hell are you doing?"

"The siren is attempting to ensnare me, so I'm battling magic with the one thing that's immune to it." I glanced at her. "Just get me to that reservoir as fast as you can."

She nodded grimly and kept on driving, throwing the SUV around the corners at a ridiculous speed. Through a combination of skill and sheer bloody-mindedness, she kept the thing upright.

I closed my eyes and, not allowing myself any time to think about the consequences, shifted my grip from the knife's handle to its blade.

I didn't grip it hard enough to cut, but it didn't matter. The knife burned bright and hot, and my skin reacted, bubbling and blistering in a matter of seconds. I gritted my teeth against the scream that tore up my throat, the sound coming out as a deep and painful hiss.

The changes in my DNA that had given me some werewolf characteristics—such as sharper hearing, balance, and healing—had also gifted me with a werewolf's susceptibility to silver. It might not be as deep or as deadly to me, but in the long run, that didn't matter. I had the scar of a previous encounter with silver on my shoulder blade, and I would bear the scar of this.

But scars were better than having my soul and life sucked away by a goddamn siren, and this *was* working.

For how long depended entirely on just how long I could stand the deep wash of agony.

That's something I can help with, Belle said.

How? I asked, even as I prayed that she could.

According to Monty, our deep connection means we should not only be able to draw on each other's magical strength but also control the levels of pain. Apparently, it all involves the same area. Hang tight, because I've no time for finesse.

Her mind flowed into mine, but this time she went far deeper than normal. It vaguely felt like she was physically shoving bits of my brain aside as she searched for the right area, and while it didn't hurt, it wasn't exactly pleasant. But a heartbeat later, the pain eased. My skin still burned—I could smell it and briefly wonder just how much damage it could and would cause—but she'd blocked the pain receptors enough that I could not only think but use my other senses.

The rusalka's song was sharp and loud, filled with desperate demand. She knew I was close and she was desperate to ensnare me.

Jaz swung off the road, throwing me sideways into the door, and then crashed through a gate, sending it flying as she came to a sliding stop at the base of the dam's wall.

I flung open the door and scrambled out. Luminous threads of wild magic spun toward me, their glow so bright and their power so fierce, they might have been the moon itself. They wrapped around me, forming a cocoon, muting the rusalka's call even further.

I raced up the hill, the wild magic somehow enhancing my physical strength, lending my feet wings. I paused briefly to get a sense of her direction, then ran around to the left and the top end of the dam, toward the point where the stream fed into it.

The song stopped.

She was fleeing.

I switched the knife from my left hand to my right, this time gripping it by the handle. But I didn't fling it, as tempting as it was to do so. I couldn't risk hitting or maybe even killing her while I was so deeply connected to the wild magic.

But that didn't mean I was about to let her flee unimpeded.

I raised a hand and sent several threads of wild magic tumbling after her. The old wellspring might never gain true sentience, but thanks to our strengthening connection, it seemed to understand what I wanted and went after the disappearing demon at a reasonable clip.

Hopefully, she wouldn't disappear deep into a mine, but even if she did, we would at least have some sense of her position, and that was all we needed to do the summoning.

I stopped running, glanced down at my left hand, and immediately wished I hadn't. It was a blistered, weeping, peeling mess. That I could still move all my fingers was a goddamn miracle, and if it wasn't for Belle's block on my pain receptors, I'd undoubtedly be a screaming mess right now.

There's no might about it came Belle's grim comment. *You'd better get back to the SUV quick smart and get some salve on that burn, because I'm not sure how much longer I can hold the wall between the pain and you.*

I swore and ran for the vehicle, the wild magic still buzzing around me, lending me strength and keeping me upright when the bank's incline threatened to send me tumbling.

How's Monty?

Feeling a little foolish. I had suggested he add an auditory inhibitor through the charm we made him, but he said it could wait until the morning.

No side effects from the song, though?

He said it feels like he's had too much to drink without the pleasure of imbibing, but other than that, no.

At least that's something.

"What's happened?" Jaz asked, as I neared the car.

"She ran, but I'm tracking her." I wrenched open the passenger door, tugged out my backpack, and grabbed a bottle of holy water. After gripping the cork with my teeth, I poured the contents over my hand. The bubbling immediately stopped, but to be doubly sure, I repeated the process with a second bottle. The deeper redness rapidly faded, suggesting the heat had fled. That didn't mean the pain had.

Jaz came around the front of the vehicle and sucked in a deep breath, her expression one of horror. "Fuck, Lizzie—"

"Yeah." I handed her the burn salve. "Can you spread this all over it?"

"You're going to need grafts—"

279

"I can still move my fingers, so the damage isn't as bad or as deep as it looks."

"The scarring will be." She grimly accepted the salve and uncapped it. "I'm not sure any sort of ointment, no matter how good it is at healing, will prevent that, and scars can cause problems if they're bad enough."

"Which is why I poured holy water over it. We used it when Anna Kang was severely burned in the explosion that had been meant for me, and she almost fully recovered."

Jaz grunted, a sound that suggested disbelief, and carefully applied the salve. Once she covered my entire hand, Belle warily eased the strength of her block. Pain stirred, but it wasn't strong enough to immediately reduce me to a screaming mess. It wasn't pleasant, but it was nothing a couple of strong painkillers couldn't help.

"We'd better get back to Ashworth and Eli," I said.

"You don't want me to bandage the burn? You'll need to protect it, or else infection might get in."

"I'll do it. You drive."

She hesitated, then nodded and ran around to the driver side. I climbed in, secured the knife in the pack, and then retrieved the first aid kit. I covered my hand with a sterile burn dressing and then loosely wrapped it in a bandage—a difficult thing to do one-handed.

Ashworth and Eli remained where we'd left them, though they really had no other choice given how well-wrapped I'd left them.

I dismissed the spells as I climbed out of the car, then walked up to each man and gave him a quick, one-handed hug. "So glad you two are okay."

"And I'm glad you were close enough to step in and save us," Ashworth said gruffly. "I hadn't expected her to react against us, which was pretty damn stupid when you think about it."

"What happened to your hand?" Eli said, voice sharp with concern.

I shrugged dismissively. "Burned it."

"At the café? Or somewhere else?"

"It's a silver burn, but it's nothing to worry about."

From inside the SUV came Jaz's snort, but she otherwise made no comment. I turned and motioned toward the vehicle. "Let's get you both home. And please, when you get there, can you take the time to create an auditory barrier? I don't need to be racing out here in the dead of the night to be rescuing your butts again."

"Which raises the point—how did you know said butts needed rescuing? Did you hear her? Because I would have thought she'd modulate her song to ensure you didn't."

"I think she tried, because it certainly sounded different." I opened the back door and helped Eli inside while Ashworth jogged around to the other side. "She attempted to ensnare Monty as well, but Belle managed to stop him before he could leave home."

Ashworth grunted. "This could have gone very badly indeed. Thank god she didn't attempt to call you as well."

"Not until it was almost all too late, anyway," I said, with a somewhat wry smile.

"Meaning she did switch to you once you stopped us answering?"

"Yeah."

"Then you, young lady, had best take your own advice and add an auditory spell to that charm around your neck."

He said it in his best "dad" voice, and I couldn't help smiling. "I will."

"And make sure Monty does the same," Eli said.

"Oh, believe me, Belle's already onto that."

"Good."

It didn't take us long to get back to the cottage. I escorted the pair of them to the door and once again made them promise to do the auditory charms right *now*.

"And you get that damn hand seen to," Ashworth growled. "Don't think I can't see the pain you're in."

"I'll be fine in the morning."

"In case you've forgotten, it *is* the morning."

I laughed, planted kisses on their cheeks, and headed back to the SUV. Jaz rather reluctantly dropped me back at the café rather than the hospital, where I made good my promise to Ashworth and wove the auditory spell into the already overladen charm around my neck.

After taking a couple of the strongest painkillers we had and washing them down with an immune-boosting potion—one that at least tasted better than the foul things Belle generally made—I headed up to bed and fell into a deep sleep.

It was the clatter of dishes and the singsong rhythm of voices that woke me. I opened an eye, picked up my phone, and stared at it blearily for several seconds before the time impacted my consciousness.

It was two in the *afternoon*.

I really *had* slept soundly.

And not without reason came Belle's comment. *I'll be up in a sec. I'll just need to finish dealing with a customer.*

If we were busy, you should have called me.

We coped, and you needed the sleep.

You haven't exactly had a whole lot of it lately either.

Her amusement bubbled through me. *True, but that's mostly for entirely different reasons.*

I laughed and sat up. My hand still hurt, but it was that

sort of itchy ache that came from a wound that was on the mend. *Speaking of Monty, how is he today? I'm surprised he's not here, considering it's scone day.*

He was, but only to collect said scones before he headed over to Ashworth and Eli's.

The stairs creaked as she came up them. She appeared a few seconds later, one of her god-awful potions in one hand and our all-purpose medical kit in the other.

My nose wrinkled. "I really don't need—"

"Oh, yes, you really do." She handed me the swampy-looking drink. "Your energy levels are still low, and I don't want you dropping with exhaustion at the wrong moment. Like when you're battling the rusalka."

Or when I was battling Karleen... I frowned and thrust the thought aside. I really didn't need to be worrying about that right now.

"Was there a reason he loaded up on scones and headed over to the cottage?"

She nodded. "There's a possibility the rusalka could be tracked via her song's resonance."

I blinked. "Surely something like that wouldn't work unless she was actually singing."

"I thought the same, but my guides say otherwise."

"Good god," I said in my best shocked tone. "Your spirit guides actually had something *useful* to say?"

She cocked her head for a second and then smiled. "They wish you to know they always have something useful to say. You just won't hear them."

"That's because they're your spirit guides not mine, and I'm quite happy to keep it that way, thank you very much."

"Oh, that's a sentiment that's definitely returned. But it nevertheless doesn't alter the fact that you could, if you wished, and if you made just a little effort, hear them. Occasionally, at the very least."

I frowned. "What makes them think that, when it's not something I've ever been able to do?"

"Apparently it's due to the deepening of our connection and the changes the wild magic is making." She paused and then added, with a decidedly amused twinkle in her eyes, "They wish to advise they are quite happy maintaining the status quo. They much prefer to deal with someone who takes them seriously."

"If they were a little more forthcoming with pertinent information, I would take them a little more seriously."

"To receive pertinent information," she said loftily, in a voice that was hers and yet held echoes of the ancient spirits who guided her, "one has to ask the correct questions."

I snorted and took a drink of the swamp. Despite the smell, it actually tasted okay for a change. She sat on the bed near my knees and made a "give me" motion. I held out my bandaged hand, and she carefully began to unwrap it.

"Does the fact that they're attempting to track the rusalka through her resonance mean they've given up on the idea of summoning her?"

Belle shook her head. "They'll still need to do that, as it's the only way to banish her. It's just a means of getting a more exact location."

"The wild magic is trailing after her."

"Yeah, but there's no guarantee that will work, because Katie wasn't present when you set the task." She tossed the bandage on the bed and then carefully lifted the sterile dressing. "That is looking surprisingly good."

I leaned forward to have a look. Though there were a couple of blisters remaining, they weren't very large, and the redness had all but gone. It looked more like a deepish scald now than a dangerous, scar-inducing burn. The holy water had once again performed its magic.

"We'll keep the salve, the dressing, and the bandage on, just to be safe, but I'm thinking that in another day or so, it'll be back to normal, aside from a few small scars from the deeper of those blisters."

"I'm not going to be much use in the café with the bandage on."

"You can take the orders. We can handle the rest. It's not as if we're flat out at the moment."

"Hopefully that'll improve now that we're sweeping toward Christmas." I smiled. "Our second in the reservation. Imagine that."

"That's presuming bitch-face doesn't try and get us chucked out before then."

"Oh, she'll try, have no doubt. It's just a matter of whether the rest of the council will comply with her wishes."

Belle replaced the sterile dressing and loosely bandaged my hand. "Do you think Aiden can stop her? He's the alpha male in his family now that his dad is dead, isn't he?"

"He is, but I vaguely remember him saying once that he has to be ratified by the council first. That's not likely to happen until his dad is buried."

"Surely she wouldn't react before then."

"With Karleen, who knows."

She grunted again. "Well, I hope someone has the foresight to warn us if a full council meeting is called. We deserve the chance to state our case."

"We do. Whether they'll offer us that chance is another matter entirely. It's also utterly inconsequential."

Belle stuck the bandage down and then gave me a long look. "I know that tone. It means trouble."

I smiled. "If they start it, I'm more than happy to finish it. I'm done playing their games, Belle."

"We might not know about the meeting or the eviction until it's too late."

"Aiden will tell me," I said. "As frustrating as the man can be, he doesn't want me to leave any more than I want to go."

"A point I agree with, but the truth of the matter is, he may not be informed about the meeting until after the decision has been made."

"True, but there's also Katie. She's keeping a watchful eye over her mom, and she certainly doesn't want me kicked out."

Belle studied me speculatively for a moment. "What has brought on this sudden desire for confrontation? Don't get me wrong—I'm one hundred percent behind it—but it's been a long time coming."

"We almost lost Monty, Ashworth, and Eli to a demon that neither I nor the wild magic brought into this reservation. It's more than past time the council and Karleen accept some of the responsibility for the crap that keeps hitting us."

"And more than past time people start realizing they can no longer push us around."

She wasn't just referring to the council in that statement. At least, not the werewolf council. I smiled. "I'm not entirely sure the bravado will last until we reach Canberra."

"This place has changed you—changed *us*—Liz. We can face them as equals. They need to know that we will no longer put up with their bullshit."

"That *is* the goal." Whether it actually happened was another matter entirely.

She pulled a plastic bag and a tie out of her pocket. "Brought this up in case you needed a shower."

"Thanks. I do."

"Finish that drink first, then."

I downed it in several long gulps, then handed her the empty glass. Once she'd left, I wrapped the plastic bag around my hand, then tossed off the blankets and headed into the shower. Dressing one-handed was a little difficult, and I gave up on the bra, settling for a singlet and wooly sweater over loose-fitting track pants. Not the most glamourous outfit I'd ever donned, but better than causing myself serious injury wresting tighter clothing into place.

Once I'd slipped on my Uggs, I made my way downstairs. The café had closed by that time, so I helped clean up as best I could.

It was close to five when my phone rang, the tone telling me it was Aiden. For no reason at all, trepidation stirred, and my heart began beating a whole lot faster.

I hit the answer button and said, "There's a problem?"

"There surely is." His voice was flat, without inflection, and yet somehow deeply angry.

"Your mom?"

"Yeah," he said. "She called a full council meeting and is asking for a formal eviction vote. She wants you and the rest of the witches off the reservation as soon as possible."

I closed my eyes. While I'd known this would happen, I really had hoped she'd wait until after the funerals.

"Do you think she has the numbers?"

"I don't know."

"And you can't get in there to plead my case?" I guessed.

"Until I'm confirmed as alpha, no. Doing so would jeopardize my position, and being alpha is the only chance—"

He cut the rest off, but it wasn't hard to guess what he'd been about to say. Not given what both Katie and Jaz had told me.

Hope stirred, but I refused to give it any weight. Emotionally, I just couldn't afford to.

"Where and when is the meeting being held?"

"At the O'Connor compound, and it'd be starting now." He paused. "You won't get in, Liz."

"They can't stop me," I said. "I think it's about time your mother and the council confronted some home truths about us witches, the wild magic, and the reason the rusalka is here."

"I've told her Monty's theory on that—"

"It's not a theory, Aiden. It's a truth."

"I know but—"

"Your mother refuses to believe it. Is she at least wearing the charm?"

"Yes, and so are Michael and Dillon."

That was something, at least. "Is the meeting taking place in the great hall?"

"Yes. I'll meet you—"

"No," I cut in. "You won't. You didn't give up our relationship to become alpha only to do something dumb and risk the whole thing."

"*I* didn't give up our relationship."

It was testily said, and I couldn't help the slightly bitter laugh. "No, but you would have, eventually."

"I love the certainty you say that with when you have no idea what I was truly thinking or planning."

"True, but given you kept your cards close to your chest and refused to include me in anything involving your family or pack, it wasn't really surprising I came to such a conclusion."

He growled softly. "I don't want to argue about that right now—"

"You can't be seen with me, Aiden. You can't go into the council meeting uninvited—not without jeopardizing your future. I *have* to do this alone. I have to show your mother she's wrong about me while pleading my case to the council. Your presence will only dilute any impact I might have."

He growled again, though this time it was a sound of frustration. "Fine. We'll do it your way. This time."

He thought there'd be a second time? I seriously hoped he was wrong.

"I'll ring you."

"If you don't, I'll hunt you down."

I half smiled. "I've never been hard to find, Aiden."

He made another of those low growls, but all he said was, "Be careful, Liz, and watch your back. Mom's not exactly herself right now."

"I know. We'll talk later."

With that, I hung up. My gaze rose to Belle's.

"Well, fuck," she said.

"An understatement if ever there was one." I pushed to my feet. "Can you drive me up to the reservation's main entrance?"

She nodded. "I'll park up there and wait, just in case." A wicked smile touched her lips. "It wouldn't be the first time I've stormed a secure castle in order to save my witch."

"This time that castle contains tons of werewolves."

"If they try to attack, well, they'll discover just how dangerous a telepath on a rescue mission can be." She drained her coffee and rose. "Are you going dressed like that?"

I hesitated and then nodded. "What I wear isn't important."

"At least put some decent shoes on. Those Uggs aren't conducive to quick movements."

And I would need to be quick when she attacked.... I shoved the thought aside and raced upstairs to slip on my runners, then headed back down and followed Belle out the back door.

It didn't take us all that long to reach the main gate into the compound. As a guard appeared, Belle pulled off to one side and stopped. "Be careful."

I squeezed her hand, then climbed out and called to the wild magic. The main wellspring wasn't all that far away, so the threads answered quickly. I wrapped two around my wrists, then spun the others into a protective net around my body. While I doubted any of the wolves within the compound would actually attack me, they'd definitely try to stop me. But with the net in place, they wouldn't even get close enough to grab an arm.

The guard, who appeared fairly young, stepped in front of me. "You can't enter the compound, Ms. Grace. Not without special permission, and that hasn't been granted."

"I need to talk to the council."

"They're holding a special meeting—"

"Yeah, I know, that's why I need to be there."

I kept on walking. He shifted to stand in front of me again. "Ms. Grace, you need to stop, or I'll be forced to make you."

I smiled grimly. "You're welcome to try, but you won't succeed. Just ring the council and tell them I'm on the way."

He bared his teeth and didn't move. I raised a hand and pushed my thread barrier toward him. It pushed him back, ever so gently, and his eyes widened in surprise.

"Contact the council and tell them I'm on my way," I said, and walked on.

Though I'd only been up here once, I remembered the path well enough. As I jogged up the road, the trees closed in and cast the area in shadows, but they receded as I got further up the mountain and entered the canyon. Its sheer walls were thick with reefs of quartz and, with the late afternoon sun shining so brightly on them, they looked jewel-like and precious. Given much of the gold found in the area surrounding the compound had been found in quartz reefs, that might not be all that far from the truth.

The closer I got to the main compound, the more aware I became of being watched. Some did so openly, some remained hidden, but their tension and anger rolled around me. None of them tried to stop me, which was a small sign of hope.

Buildings appeared as the canyon began to widen out. There were varying sizes, but all of them resembled long-houses of old—and, thanks to the fact that much of the stone used in their construction was quartz, and all of them had earthen rooftops filled with masses of different grasses and wildflowers, they were absolutely beautiful. There was a proliferation of green technologies here as well, with every house having a combination of solar panels, wind turbines, and battery storage.

As I moved deeper into the canyon, the longhouses became larger and grander, until I entered the remnants of the old crater that held not only the residences of the main alphas but was also the compound's civic and industrial center.

Straight ahead of me was the grand hall. It was circular in design with an angular earthen roof that pitched up to the chimney in the center of the structure.

In front of the massive wooden doors were a dozen large werewolves, their arms crossed and expressions determined.

I slowed to a walk and continued on, a repelling spell spinning lazily around my right hand. Whether it would work against so many, I had no idea, but it didn't matter anyway, as they wouldn't get past my luminous net. If it could protect me against gunshots, it could certainly ward off this many werewolves.

Tension nevertheless ratcheted up. Doing this might well end any hope I had of living harmoniously with the packs in this reservation, but Karleen had left me with no other choice now. They needed to know where her anger was coming from and why evicting me would only make things worse overall.

"Ms. Grace," the burly wolf closest to the door said in a calm and authoritative tone. "You need to stop. You do not have permission to enter the hall, and I have been authorized to stop you."

I swept my gaze across the line of them, seeing their determination and their belief in their own superiority against a mere witch. Jaz was right. The "common wolf" really had no understanding of magic or spellcasters thanks to the fact reservation witches had never had reason to exert their presence or their power before now.

As my gaze returned to the wolf at the door, I spotted the camera and the small bulge underneath it. The councilors could see and hear everything.

Good.

"You can't stop me. None of you can," I replied calmly. "Move out of my way, or I'll make you."

The burly wolf smiled. "You really think your magic is faster and stronger than the reactions of a wolf?"

"Oh, I don't think, I know." My smile was benign and would have been warning enough to those who really knew me. "But in this case, I don't have to use my magic, because the magic of this land, the wild magic itself, protects me."

He snorted. "The wellspring's magic is called wild for a reason—it cannot be used. It can only ever be contained and protected."

"Except the councilors inside left it unprotected for a year, and that fact has forever changed the rules. Now get out of my way."

He uncrossed his arms and flexed his fingers. "No."

I blew out a breath, glanced up at the camera, and said, "The hard way it is, then."

I flicked out the repelling spell, leashed the burly wolf, and wrenched him away from the door. As he went flying across the clearing, the rest attacked, some in human form, some in wolf, surrounding me in a mass of flying fists and tearing teeth. I threw three more, then let the rest attack, just to show our watchers how little effect it had.

The net rippled and pulsed under each blow, and the force of it echoed through me. But they didn't get through, and I didn't falter. I calmly walked up to the door, pressed my fingers against the old lock, and, with the strongest unlock spell I knew, literally blasted the doors open.

As entrances went, it was pretty damn cool, even if I had to say so myself.

The doors crashed back against the stone walls hard enough to send chips of bright quartz flying through the air. The sound echoed but didn't conceal the murmur of disbelief.

I strode in, well aware that everyone watched me. My fingers twitched as I silently wrapped a repelling spell around them. The wolves in this room wouldn't see the spell, of course; they'd just see the movement, smell my tension, and undoubtedly believe it was nothing more than bravado seeing me through.

And in part, they'd be right.

The hall was set out in a fashion similar to the assembly halls of old. There were three separate tiered seating sections that hugged the external walls—all of them currently occupied—while the center of the room was dominated by a circular fireplace. It was currently covered and no doubt provided a platform from which various wolves could plead their case or petition for action.

My footsteps echoed as I strode toward the platform. No one spoke. No one moved to stop me.

Not even Karleen.

It wasn't until I stepped onto the platform that she thrust to her feet. "You have no right to enter this reservation or this hall uninvited, Liz. Not only does it show your disdain for our rules and our way of life, but it also does nothing to strengthen your cause."

"Only my friends get to call me, Liz. You may call me Elizabeth. Or better yet, Ms. Grace." I crossed my arms and regarded her steadily. "And I suggest you make no claims to know anything about me or my cause, because we both know you've made little effort in either regard."

"I know you want to marry my son, and that will never—"

"Karleen, restrain your anger and *sit* down," a deep but familiar voice said. It was Rocco Marin, one of the Marin pack's alphas and a wolf I'd dealt with before. He was the reason I was allowed access to Katie's wellspring, even though it was deep in the grounds of their compound.

"But she—"

"Sit," he growled. He was average in height and looks, but he packed a lot of punch and authority into that one word. "I am the chair for this meeting, and Ms. Grace is here under my invitation. It seems only fair that, given you wish the council to vote on her eviction, she be given a chance to defend herself."

"We should have been informed of the invitation," another voice said.

"And you would have been," he replied calmly, "were it not for the fact there are some in this room who'd have taken action to ensure she couldn't appear."

He didn't look at Karleen when he said that, but it was pretty evident that's who he meant.

I looked his way and smiled. "I do thank you for the chance."

He nodded, and though his expression was friendly, his brown eyes filled with warning. He might be inclined to believe and trust me, but there were plenty here who did not.

"Present your case, Ms. Grace. We've already heard Karleen's account on the matter."

"Exactly which matter would that be? Because there's a whole lot more going on here than just my eviction."

Karleen thrust to her feet again, her aura a mess of anger and grief, new and old. She needed retribution, she needed to attack, and she needed someone to blame, for not only recent events but also the past. To her, I was the embodiment of everything that had gone wrong in her life, and no matter what I did or said here today, that was unlikely to change.

But I might be able to change the opinions of the remaining alphas here, including the others from the O'Connor pack.

I just had to remain calm and not do anything daft.

"Ever since your arrival, this reservation has been struck

down by darkness and death," she growled, "the culmination of which was the deaths of both my mate and my brother. You are akin to the plagues of old, and it cannot be allowed to continue. You must be evicted for the safety of all of us."

There was a smattering of agreement from those seated around her, but thankfully it didn't spread across the entire council.

"The plagues of old are apparently the reason the wellsprings lost their true defenders in the first place," I replied evenly. "And while the reason for evil's incursions into the reservation lies with this council's decision to leave the wellspring without magical protection for entirely too long, it is *not* the reason the rusalka is here. *You* are."

For a second, she didn't move. She didn't even blink. Then she laughed. Not only was it a very bitter sound but also a false one. She knew well enough our theories on all this.

She waved a hand dramatically toward me. "This is a perfect example of why witches can't be trusted. They will never accept responsibility for their actions. They will always seek to blame others or simply run from their guilt."

"If I'd wanted to exact revenge for your bloody-mindedness and inability to see past your own prejudices," I said, anger getting the better of me despite my determination to remain calm, "I would have gone after *you*, not your brother or your husband. He, at least, treated me with respect."

The energy buzzing around my fingers grew more heated, and I drew in a deeper breath. I really needed to keep my cool, if only to avoid the whole "her attempting to rip my throat out" ordeal.

"Except that you can't outright attack through magic,

can you?" she returned. "Because any spell you cast to hurt me would only snap back on you three-fold."

"That's true but—"

"And conjuring a demon to take out the people *I* love means there is no price for you to pay."

I laughed. I couldn't help it. "That statement shows your utter ignorance when it comes to magic. Conjuring a demon is a risky business, and one that more often than not results in the conjurer being consumed by said demon. Aside from the fact I don't have the knowledge or the training, that's not something I would ever risk."

"Other witches in this reservation do have that knowledge though, don't they?"

"Yeah, they do, which is why we attempted to summon and banish the demon. And again, since you don't appear to be listening, it didn't answer, which means I am *not* the reason it's here."

"We only have your word for that," a woman said from the Sinclair section. She didn't stand up, so I wasn't sure who.

"I have no reason to lie." I smiled, though it was a cold thing that held little humor. "But someone in this room does."

"What is that supposed to mean?" a voice to the right growled. Not Rocco, though it had come from his section.

"I mean that Karleen has been attempting to get rid of me from almost the very beginning, and it has nothing to do with my relationship with Aiden."

She didn't say anything, but her eyes narrowed.

The voice behind Rocco said, "And given Gabe's involvement in Katie's death, that is very understandable."

"Gabe's actions were not only at Katie's insistence, but also saved this reservation from many more problems.

Thanks to Gabe's spell—a spell that took *both* their lives—her soul now protects the second wellspring that lies within the Marin compound."

Another murmur rose. Many here were obviously unaware that a second spring had developed within the reservation.

"If there is another wellspring here, the High Witch Council would have informed us of it," a new voice said.

I glanced across at him. Though I'd never met him, I nevertheless recognized him thanks to the similarities in his features to our chef. This was Carter Sinclair, Mike's uncle, and an alpha from one of the four lines inhabiting their compound. "Except the high council doesn't know about it and, if we witches have any say in it, never will."

He frowned. "Why? Isn't it customary for them to certify and protect the wellsprings?"

"Yes, but we're dealing with a wellspring that has the soul of a werewolf fused with it. It no longer needs their protections, as she can now use and direct the wild magic." I raised an eyebrow. "Do you really think that the High Witch Council would not descend on this place once the discovery of what Gabe has achieved becomes known?"

Another murmur ran through the room; they certainly weren't liking the sound of that, even if some didn't actually believe it would happen.

"Why has none of this been mentioned to this council?" he asked, then looked rather pointedly at Rocco. "Were you aware of this wellspring's presence?"

"Yes, but we were advised to keep its presence secret in an effort to stop the knowledge reaching Canberra."

"That should not have been your decision alone, Rocco."

His shrug was unrepentant. "It lies on Marin home

ground. Unless its presence endangers the reservation as a whole, there is no requirement for advisement."

"And that wellspring is not what we are gathered here to discuss," Karleen snapped. "She has very cleverly diverted proceedings."

"And you," Rocco said coldly, "have not yet answered the question on the floor—why do you hate Ms. Grace so vehemently?"

I had a feeling he didn't like Karleen, though there was little evidence in either his voice or his expression.

"I have every reason and every right not to want another child of mine to be involved with a witch."

"That doesn't explain the hatred, Karleen," he replied.

"I don't hate her," she said, even as her body language and expression gave away the lie.

There was something in the way she looked at me that had all sorts of inner alarms going off. I shifted my stance a little, and the magic spinning around me grew stronger. I couldn't unleash it, not until she attacked me, and maybe not even then. While they did need to understand the sheer force of power I could bring against them, the comments Jaz had made suggested that perhaps it was *physical* might that would bring greater respect.

The wild magic leashed around my wrists and the changes in my DNA might never give me the speed and strength of a true werewolf, but I was more than just a mere "human" now when it came to either.

Of course, every sane part of me was hoping that it never came to that. That the dreams were wrong and she didn't attack.

Hell, even the insane parts were on board with that particular wish.

"If you don't tell them the truth," I said calmly. "I will."

"You don't know the truth."

I gave her another insincere smile. "Google is an amazing tool, Karleen, and it has a long memory."

She didn't reply, not for what seemed like forever. But I could see the rage in her, see the echoes of her pain and smell the desire to destroy the woman who was a living reminder of all that had gone wrong for her family. All those emotions were at war with the alpha need for control and the knowledge that in attacking me she'd force her fellow councilors to seek answers for her actions.

I hoped it would be enough to stop her.

It wasn't.

She shifted shape and attacked.

Chapter Thirteen

All I could see was a blur of teeth, fur, and fury as she came at me.

I threw myself sideways, totally forgetting I was on a platform, and hit the ground hard. Pain rippled through my body, and a hiss escaped, but I scrambled to my feet and swung around.

She was already coming at me again.

I clenched my fingers around the repelling spell but didn't unleash it. I stood, waiting, as her leap brought her closer. Then, a heartbeat before she hit the protective net, I sidestepped and punched her with every goddamn ounce of strength I had, hitting the side of her mouth and snapping her head away from me. The force of the blow had pain rippling across my burned hand, but I ignored it, watching warily as she hit the ground several meters away.

"Enough," Rocco shouted. "Karleen, stop this insanity *now*. This is not how we deal with things."

"Let her attack," I said quietly. "I have no fear of her."

"Ms. Grace, she's a wolf," Rocco replied. "You cannot match her for speed or power, no matter how great your magical prowess. It'll will only end badly for you, and we cannot allow it."

"You cannot stop it. None of you can."

I flung out a hand and widened my protective net, letting Karleen in while preventing anyone else entering. It was dangerous and it could indeed end very badly for me, but everyone here—and more particularly, every alpha in the O'Connor section—needed to see that while I might not be her match physically, I could defend myself no matter what she threw at me.

I needed them to see that I was worthy of being an alpha's mate.

After that, it was up to Aiden to prove *he* was worthy of me.

Rocco's weight pressed briefly against the filaments of wild magic but did no more than send a slight ripple across them.

"What have you done, Ms. Grace?"

"It's just a net to prevent any of you entering." I kept my gaze on Karleen as I spoke, hoping against hope that she'd take this brief respite to calm down and regain her senses.

"How is that possible when spells are not instant, and you have not cast one?"

"It's not a spell. It's the wild magic. It's with me, in this room, protecting me."

"The wild magic cannot be used like that."

"In general, that's true, but here's the thing," I said, my gaze still on Karleen. She was back in human form but remained a coiled spring, ready to explode into action. "I'm not just a witch. My DNA was enhanced with wild magic when I was little more than a bean in my mother's belly, and it caused a link to form between me and the wellspring in this reservation. It's also giving me some of the attributes of a wolf."

Karleen snorted. "Is there no end to your lies?"

"Again, I'm not the one lying here today, Karleen, and if wolves were capable of seeing or sensing wild magic, you would be aware of its presence. Its power soaks this room."

"How very convenient for you that we can't."

I blew out a breath and said, "Fine. Let me cast an unmasking spell, so you can briefly see what I see on a daily basis."

I quickly created and cast the spell; it acted like invisible paint, spraying across the filaments of power, revealing them in all their glory.

The resulting glow was brief but moon bright.

The murmur that ran through the room was a mix of disbelief and fear.

Not the result I'd wanted, but fuck them. I was past playing their games of superiority.

"Those threads are wild magic?" Rocco asked.

"Yes." I raised my good hand and made a come-at-me motion to Karleen, inviting the very thing I'd been trying to avoid. "If you want me, come and get me. I promise I won't use any magic."

She shifted and launched at me so fast her body was little more than a blur, and what followed was brutal and bloody. She alternated between her two forms, tearing at me with her teeth before switching over to punch and kick. I danced away from some blows, stopped or knocked others away, but it was impossible to avoid them all. Enhanced DNA or not, she was too fast, too strong, and by far the superior fighter.

That didn't mean she escaped unharmed. More than a

few of my blows landed hard enough to cause grunts of pain, even if a quick shapeshift fixed it.

But as the ring on her right hand scraped across my cheek, drawing blood, I knew it was time to end it. My breath was short, sharp pants, and weariness was now slowing my reactions. The wild magic might be providing an energy boost, but the wider net remained connected, and it was drawing on my strength. I could have—should have—detached it, but it was too late now.

As she launched at me again, I ran backward, as fast as I could, keeping the distance between us as I raised a fist and created a leash spell. It buzzed angrily around my fingers, but I didn't immediately release it.

"Karleen, I think this little demonstration has gone far enough. You need to stop, or I *will* unleash magic and make you."

She didn't reply, didn't switch form, didn't alter her trajectory.

I cast the spell, wrapped it around her tightly, and threw her down on the ground. Hard. She fought the leash, her movements fierce and angry, causing pain to ripple through my brain.

I sucked in a breath that didn't in any way ease the deep pounding in my brain, then walked over and knelt beside her. Her eyes gleamed with a mix of madness and anger, and her expression was fierce. It was then I realized she *couldn't* stop fighting; that she was so mired in the pain of the past *and* the present that she couldn't find her way out of it.

I raised a hand and slapped her hard across the cheek.

As the sound echoed across the silence, she blinked, and the fog of madness cleared. The anger remained, but at least the past no longer held her captive.

"If I release you, will you stop?" I asked.

She hesitated and then nodded. I rose, stepped back, and released the net of protective wild magic but not the two threads around my wrists. Given the weariness that continued to pulse through me, I might yet need the strength they could offer. It was a better—and safer—option than calling on Belle's strength.

As the luminous threads floated away, I recalled my leash. But I let it wind around my fingers rather than dismiss it; she might have agreed to stop, but that didn't mean she would.

She slowly rose to her feet. The glance she cast me was as far from friendly as you could ever get, but that was to be expected. And, in the end, didn't matter. I'd proven to everyone in this hall that I *could* physically defend myself, even if in the end I'd resorted to magic to stop her.

What happened next was up to Aiden.

She drew in a deep breath and then turned away from me and bowed deeply. "I ask the chair and the assembly to forgive my actions here today. It was unbecoming and unacceptable, and I unreservedly apologize."

The fact she didn't blame her actions on the grief of losing her mate was a little surprising, and a spark of respect stirred. No matter what I thought of her personally, she was at least accepting responsibility for her actions.

"I would think the apology needs to be directed toward Ms. Grace rather than the council, given she's the one who has borne the brunt of your momentary lapse in judgement," Rocco said. "And why is that, Karleen? What are you so desperate to hide from us?"

She drew in another deep breath and cast me a glance that simmered with anger and frustration. It basically

305

confirmed my earlier thought that she and I would never get along, no matter what happened in the future.

"As many of you know, my family immigrated here from the Axton compound in North East Wales," she said, a slight tremor in her voice. "When I was fourteen, my sister was amongst a number of wolves who were magically restrained and raped by a passing witch. She became pregnant, but both she and the babe died at the birth."

"That witch," I added, when it became obvious she had no intention of saying anything more, "had crimson hair and green eyes—the same as me when I first came into this reservation, before the wild magic altered them."

"It would seem Ms. Grace has paid a heavy price for a minor resemblance to the witch who caused your family harm."

Karleen glanced at me as Rocco said that, and I realized then she was waiting for me to drop the hammer and expose her father's crime. But I had nothing to gain by doing so.

"I know, and I unreservedly apologize for allowing the past to color my opinions," she said eventually. "But that does not alter the fact that since she came into this reservation, we have seen a sharp influx of demons and other creatures of the night. I do not think it's a coincidence, and I fear that unless we act now, this reservation will be overrun."

"If not for Liz and the other witches," a wonderfully familiar voice said, "this reservation would already be overrun and in deep strife."

I swung around in surprise. Aiden, with Monty, Ashworth, and Eli at his back, strode into the hall, his expression as angry as I'd ever seen it.

Sorry, Belle said, *he ordered me not to warn you. He said it would be better if you were as surprised as everyone else.*

I take it, given Monty and the gang are here, that there has been a development regarding the rusalka?

Yeah, the bitch is on the move.

She's not yet singing.

No, but she's moved into the compound's boundary, and Ashworth fears she's planning something big.

"What is the meaning of this, Aiden?" Karleen growled. "You have no right and no reason to be—"

"And *you* have no right and no reason to attack the daughter of one of the most powerful witches in Canberra," he returned furiously. "A witch who is now well aware his daughter is able to manipulate wild magic and is just itching for a reason to descend on this place. If you had maimed her —or, god forbid, killed her—do you realize the danger you could have put us in? We could have lost every fucking thing, and all because you can't see past hatred long enough to understand the greater implications of your damn actions."

I wanted to cheer. Wanted to run up to him and kiss him senseless. Neither were practical or wise, of course,

Karleen sucked in a breath. She hadn't expected him to answer so fiercely or bluntly, and it made me wonder again just how well she actually understood her eldest son. "I would not have killed her. Credit me with some sense."

"To date, I've seen very little evidence of said sense," he retorted.

"The possible consequences of your mother's actions are not reason enough for you to barge in on this meeting," Rocco said, before Karleen could jump back into the fray. "You are not yet confirmed as pack alpha, and while your desire to protect Ms. Grace is commendable—"

"That has nothing to do with the reason I'm here," he

cut in. Though the gaze he cast me said that was a lie, and I think everyone there knew it.

He stopped on the opposite side of the platform to me and faced Rocco. Ashworth and Eli stopped behind him.

Monty, however, moved around the back of the platform and handed me my backpack. "Hope you haven't used all your strength proving a point, because you're going to need it for what's coming."

Though he kept his voice low, most of the wolves in this room would have heard it. And Monty was well aware of that.

Aiden cast him a warning glance, then said, "The rusalka has moved into the compound's grounds and is headed this way. It's very possible that she intends to call the entire pack and cause us untold damage."

"A siren cannot call more than one," a voice behind Rocco said. "That is common knowledge."

"Except a rusalka is not a siren, it's a demon," Ashworth said. "And yesterday, she not only called we three male witches, but also attempted to snare Liz when she—successfully—stopped us from answering. The only reason Liz stands here this morning is because she grabbed a silver blade and used the pain of it burning her skin to counter the rusalka's call."

"And that," Aiden growled, "is not an option we were-wolves have."

"Why would silver burn you?" Carter asked. "You're not a wolf."

I wearily rubbed my eyes. Would these people never listen? "As I said—and, I believe, demonstrated—I've gained some wolf characteristics thanks to my connection with the wellspring in this compound."

I didn't bother mentioning the possibility that there was

Fenna blood in my background; it would take entirely too long to explain all that, and it wasn't as if we had any evidence to back the theory.

"If Liz had summoned the rusalka into the reservation," Ashworth said, "she would have been protected from her song. A demon cannot attack its summoner until the task it was set has been fully completed."

"Well, *I* certainly didn't summon her, so why would she be attacking my family?" Karleen said. "That makes no sense."

"Demons of her ilk aren't exactly hanging around in some darkside antechamber waiting for a witch to call them into action," Monty said. "They're quite capable of causing utter chaos all on their own, and darker emotions are like honey to them."

"That still doesn't explain—"

"He means your hatred of witches and my growing frustration and anger over your actions have drawn this thing into the reservation," Aiden said bluntly. "It's now feeding on those emotions, savoring the increasing sweetness of them as it picks off our family and consumes their souls. That means the two of us bear the responsibility of putting things right, before anyone else is killed."

"And it needs to be done here and now," Ashworth said. "Because she could start her call at any moment, and no one in this room will be immune."

"No one but myself and my mother," Aiden said. "Thanks to the charms Liz created for us."

Rocco rose. "Then we should leave—"

"No," I cut in. "If she does start calling, I can probably prevent anyone in this room from answering via the net spell you saw before."

"And," Aiden growled, "it's way past time everyone in

this rooms sees and understands exactly what magic can do, and the effort and risk involved."

"Great idea, my dear ranger," Monty drawled. "Because I'm certainly a little tired of risking my life on an almost weekly basis for people who oh-so-casually dismiss my efforts."

Aiden gave him another of those warning looks, then said, "With the council's permission, we will proceed."

Rocco hesitated, glanced around the room, and then nodded. "What needs to be done?"

"Monty?" Aiden said. "Do you wish to take the lead?"

The question surprised me a little, if only because Monty was about as green as me when it came to summoning demons. But he was also reservation witch, and therefore had to appear to be in control, even if he wasn't.

He nodded and motioned toward Ashworth. "You take the lead, the rest of us will weave our magic through yours, as we did before."

Ashworth didn't bat an eyelid or make a smart remark, which suggested they'd planned this beforehand.

We created the pentagram, then wove our protection circles through and around that. It took time, but there was no conversation or restless movement in the hall. Everyone, it seemed, was engrossed in what we were doing.

Even Karleen.

Once the candles had been placed and lit, Eli handed Aiden, Karleen, and me two sheets of paper, the top one the summoning spell, the second a banishment spell.

Ashworth then motioned them toward the west point of the pentagram. "You two stand there. It's the representation of water and should strengthen your call. Liz, you'll have to stand at spirit this time."

I nodded, moved across, and placed the open backpack

at my feet, just in case things went ass up and I needed to reach for the silver knife.

Once everyone was in position, Ashworth added, "Liz will lead the incantation. When she finishes the first line of the summoning, you two begin."

"But we're not witches," Karleen said, the faintest trace of uncertainty in her voice even though her expression was determined.

"It won't matter," Ashworth said. "Just say the words, and do not stop or falter until you reach the end. And for the love of mercy, do not move from the cardinal point or disturb any of the stones at your feet."

"What happens if I do?"

"Everyone in this room will get a living example of just how nasty and dangerous a demon can be," Eli said grimly.

Karleen's eyes briefly widened, then she nodded and looked down at the paper in her hand. My gaze met Aiden's and, just for a moment, I allowed myself to drown in those glorious depths, to let the wash of his emotions flow over me, warm and deep, and so real. So *right*.

Was it enough? Would the events in this hall change anything? I didn't know and didn't dare hope. Not yet.

I tore my gaze away, took a deep calming breath, and began.

Aiden and Karleen echoed my words, and a shimmering wall of energy speared upward from the pentagram's points, forming a cage-like structure. As the spell deepened and the force of its demand grew stronger, the center of the pentagram began to shimmer—shift—in violent agitation.

A murmur rolled through the hall, but thankfully, neither Karleen nor Aiden faltered. The weight of the spell grew heavier, and the thick scent of evil and darkness stained the air.

Then the tumultuous writing in the center of the pentagram sharpened, forming a shape that was tall and voluptuous, with bluish-green skin and eyes that gleamed as brightly as fresh blood.

The murmuring increased. Footsteps echoed. People were leaving, and there was a part of me that couldn't really blame them. Hell, given any choice in the matter, I'd be joining them.

I finished the final line of the summoning spell and waited, my heart pounding so fiercely it felt ready to tear out of my chest.

Aiden and Karleen finished their part of the spell and for several seconds, no one moved. I wasn't sure anyone dared breathe.

Then the rusalka screeched, a high, ungodly sound of fury, and began tearing at the pentagram's shimmering walls with claws that were razor sharp and gleamed like midnight.

"Liz, time to start the banishment spell," Monty said, voice calm despite the tension I could smell.

I drew in a breath and began. But before I even finished the first line, the rusalka screeched again and launched straight at Karleen.

She screamed and instinctively jerked back. As she did, her foot slipped, dislodging several of our spell stones. The protective wall fell, and the pentagram's net fractured.

It was only a small tear, but that's all our demon needed. She tore open the gap with her obsidian claws and launched straight at Karleen.

I grabbed the knife and lunged forward, stabbing the rusalka's tail and pinning it to the floor. For a second, she didn't react, too intent on reaching her victim.

But as she was pulled to a sudden halt and the silver began to react against her flesh, she twisted around and lunged at me and, before I could react, clamped her claws around either side of my face and held me tight and still as she opened her mouth and drew in a deep breath.

Not to screech.

To consume.

My strength. My soul.

The air became a maelstrom that was sucked into her mouth; its force tore at me, externally *and* internally. I couldn't move, I couldn't fight it, and my soul was being inexorably dragged into the slipstream of it.

Terror shot through me. I didn't want to die like this. Didn't want all my futures erased.

A repelling spell formed unbidden around my fingers. I unleashed it, trying to force her away from me, trying to stop her.

She shifted but only fractionally. Her claws tore through my hair, then clamped down deeper, drawing blood.

The knife, I realized. It pinned her in place, even against my magic. But if I released it, she'd attack everyone else.

Then, without warning, Belle was with me, her magic fusing with mine and forming a tight ball around the inner essence of my being.

The inexorable slide toward the maelstrom stopped with a suddenness that had me physically lurching back. The rusalka screamed again, and her claws clamped even tighter against my skull, until it felt like she was about to break it.

I screamed. Screamed so hard and loud, something in my throat tore.

Then a storm of magic rose, and the rusalka's form

began to shift and shiver. The banishing spell; they were performing the banishing spell—all five of them.

She screeched again, this time in fear, and released me. Her claws tore at the knife holding her in place, but it was blessed silver, and she couldn't grasp it.

The spell's force grew stronger, the demon's twisting fiercer. She screamed again, but this time it was a smaller, weaker sound. Her body vibrated, the particles of her flesh moving, separating, becoming smoke that was swiftly sucked into the void the banishing spell was creating behind her.

Then she was gone, from this hall, from this world, back to whatever hell she had risen from.

All that was left were the shattered remnants of the pentagram, our protective circles, and the silver knife buried to the hilt in the floor.

I collapsed in on myself, rocking back and forth as I sucked in air and fought the gathering pain and the mist of unconsciousness.

Belle? I somehow said. *You okay?*

After several terrifying seconds, she said, *Yeah. But fuck, let's not ever do something like that again.*

Hands touched me, cradled me against a body that was warm and hard and familiar.

"Will someone get the goddamn medics here stat," Aiden yelled.

"I'm okay—"

"No, you're fucking not, so just shut up and save your strength for a change."

"Can't," I said. "Not in my nature."

He made a sound that was a weird mix of amusement and desperation. "Yeah, I've learned that."

"Belle," I said. "Someone needs to check on her."

"Monty's already halfway there, and we've sent a doctor after him."

"No one else was hurt?"

"No."

"Not even your mother?"

"No."

"Good," I said, but as the call of unconsciousness began to claim me, my gaze met Rocco's. He—and the rest of the council—now knew just how much power a witch could bring to the table. For good or for bad, our relationship with them was never going to be the same.

I glanced up at the board as our flight was called, then sucked in a breath and pushed to my feet. Three days had passed since the battle in the O'Connors' great hall, and while the wounds I'd received had healed, the hair around them had gone white. I had no idea if it would remain that way or eventually regain color. According to Belle, it looked as if someone had painted white streaks into my hair. Like warpaint, Monty had said. Which, given we were headed for Canberra for court battles with my father and my ex's family, was appropriate.

Monty picked up Belle's carryon, then offered her his other arm. "Let me escort you to the gate, my lady."

"Why thank you, kind sir." She twined one arm through his, leaning on him more than the walking stick she had in her other hand.

She'd been running toward the hall when the demon had hit me, and the shock of it had sent her tumbling. She'd ended up with a badly sprained ankle but had been damn lucky not to have broken anything.

As they made their way slowly toward the doors, I looked at Ashworth and said, my voice hoarse thanks to my still-healing throat, "Tell me again it'll be all right, because right now, I feel like I'm about to fly into the heart of a hell-fire I might never escape."

And I was scared. Absolutely, soul-screaming scared. I think I'd rather face a thousand rusalka than my father or my ex in-laws right now.

"Ah, lass," he said, his voice rough with emotion as he wrapped me in a bear hug. "I promise, no matter what happens, we'll be there for you."

"Every single step of the way," Eli said. "And if any of those bastards so much as crinkle a hair on your head, I'll magically blast them into the next state."

"He can, too," Ashworth said. "He did it to a relative who pissed him off one time."

I laughed, pulled away, and took a deep, steadying breath. "Let's get this show on the road, then."

Eli nodded and motioned for me to precede them. I slung my handbag over my shoulder and moved toward the business class lane, then turned as my name was called.

And saw Aiden running toward me.

My heart did a strange little flutter, and it was all I could do to remain calm. To act casual. I glanced at Ashworth and Eli. "I'll see you in there."

Eli gripped my arm, then he and Ashworth moved on. I walked back and met Aiden at the edge of the waiting area.

"What are you doing here?" I asked, voice collected and cool despite the erratic nature of my pulse. "I thought the two funerals were on today?"

"They are, and I'll get back in time for them, but I couldn't let you leave without seeing you."

"I saw you yesterday. We said goodbye yesterday."

And a strange, stilted, and somewhat awkward affair it had been too.

"Yes," he growled, and stepped close enough that his warm scent filled my nostrils and my breasts touched his chest with every quick breath. "But I didn't do this, and I should have."

His arms wrapped around me, then his lips claimed mine. But this *wasn't* just a kiss. It was heart and desire, soul and destiny, and it said everything and nothing all at the same time.

A final boarding call was made for my flight. He released me and stepped back, his eyes burning with so many unspoken emotions.

Damn it, why would he not say the truth we both knew?

What harm could it do here and now, when we were so far away from his pack and anyone who might wish to cause us problems?

"Come back to me, Liz. Please."

"I have no choice but to come back, Aiden. Whether I come back to *you* is another matter entirely."

He drew in a breath and then said, in a voice that was husky with emotion, "I love you, Elizabeth Grace. With all of my heart, and all of my soul."

"Oh, I know you do, but the real question is, are you willing to fight for me? For us? Are you willing to stand in front of your pack and claim me as your alpha mate?" I didn't give him time to answer. I simply pressed a finger against his lips and added, "I don't want the answer now. I don't need the distraction of good *or* bad news when I'm about to fly into a shitstorm of problems. Tell me when I get back."

He made a low sound deep in his throat, then gave me a short, sharp nod. I spun and ran for the gate.

But a heartbeat before I disappeared into the tunnel, I turned and met his gaze.

And what I saw had my heart singing.

The alpha *was* ready to fight for what he wanted.

Everything he wanted.

Also by Keri Arthur

Relic Hunters Novels
Crown of Shadows (Feb 2022)

Sword of Darkness (Oct 2022)

Ring of Ruin (June 2023)

Lizzie Grace series
Blood Kissed (May 2017)

Hell's Bell (Feb 2018)

Hunter Hunted (Aug 2018)

Demon's Dance (Feb 2019)

Wicked Wings (Oct 2019)

Deadly Vows (Jun 2020)

Magic Misled (Feb 2021)

Broken Bonds (Oct 2021)

Sorrows Song (June 2022)

Wraith's Revenge (Feb 2023)

Killer's Kiss (Oct 2023)

The Witch King's Crown
Blackbird Rising (Feb 2020)

Blackbird Broken (Oct 2020)

Blackbird Crowned (June 2021)

Kingdoms of Earth & Air

Unlit (May 2018)

Cursed (Nov 2018)

Burn (June 2019)

The Outcast series

City of Light (Jan 2016)

Winter Halo (Nov 2016)

The Black Tide (Dec 2017)

Souls of Fire series

Fireborn (July 2014)

Wicked Embers (July 2015)

Flameout (July 2016)

Ashes Reborn (Sept 2017)

Dark Angels series

Darkness Unbound (Sept 27th 2011)

Darkness Rising (Oct 26th 2011)

Darkness Devours (July 5th 2012)

Darkness Hunts (Nov 6th 2012)

Darkness Unmasked (June 4 2013)

Darkness Splintered (Nov 2013)

Darkness Falls (Dec 2014)

Riley Jenson Guardian Series

Full Moon Rising (Dec 2006)

Kissing Sin (Jan 2007)

Tempting Evil (Feb 2007)

Dangerous Games (March 2007)

Embraced by Darkness (July 2007)

The Darkest Kiss (April 2008)

Deadly Desire (March 2009)

Bound to Shadows (Oct 2009)

Moon Sworn (May 2010)

Myth and Magic series

Destiny Kills (Oct 2008)

Mercy Burns (March 2011)

Nikki & Micheal series

Dancing with the Devil (March 2001 / Aug 2013)

Hearts in Darkness Dec (2001/ Sept 2013)

Chasing the Shadows Nov (2002/Oct 2013)

Kiss the Night Goodbye (March 2004/Nov 2013)

Damask Circle series

Circle of Fire (Aug 2010 / Feb 2014)

Circle of Death (July 2002/March 2014)

Circle of Desire (July 2003/April 2014)

Ripple Creek series

Beneath a Rising Moon (June 2003/July 2012)

Beneath a Darkening Moon (Dec 2004/Oct 2012)

Spook Squad series

Memory Zero (June 2004/26 Aug 2014)

Generation 18 (Sept 2004/30 Sept 2014)

Penumbra (Nov 2005/29 Oct 2014)

Stand Alone Novels

Who Needs Enemies (E-book only, Sept 1 2013)

Novella

Lifemate Connections (March 2007)

Anthology Short Stories

The Mammoth Book of Vampire Romance (2008)

Wolfbane and Mistletoe--2008

Hotter than Hell--2008

About the Author

Keri Arthur, author of the New York Times bestselling Riley Jenson Guardian series, has now written more than fifty-five novels. She's won a Romance Writers of Australia RBY Award for Speculative Fiction, and six Australian Romance Readers Awards for Scifi, Fantasy or Futuristic Romance. The Lizzie Grace Series was also voted Favourite Continuing Series in the ARRA Awards. Keri's something of a wanna-be photographer, so when she's not at her computer writing the next book, she can be found some-where in the Australian countryside taking random photos.

for more information:
www.keriarthur.com
keriarthurauthor@gmail.com

 facebook.com/AuthorKeriArthur
 twitter.com/kezarthur
 instagram.com/kezarthur

CPSIA information can be obtained
at www.ICGtesting.com
Printed in the USA
LVHW021146200622
721637LV00001B/26